THE FOURTH LEVEL
ADVENT
BOOK ELEVEN

NICHOLAS HUNTLEY

"The emotion of being lost forever gives rise to a sensitive pain and sighs so deep that cause such violent screams and moans; sometimes it manifests itself through words and tears when the necessary power and strength is available. This relief however is seldom given to the soul."

- St. Teresia Benedicta a Cruce

Act 1, Scene 1

A pinkish hue set across the evening sky with stratus clouds stretched across. The sunset shined a last moment of light across the flat snow-topped land before it disappeared under the horizon. The tractors of local farms were buried by the snowfall, while the barns stood steady against the mild wind and provided refuge to the life inside it. The moment of twilight was clear below the clouds with no snowy mist in sight. A deserted freeway in the middle of the farmland went along, leading towards a small township in the center of what seemed to be nowhere but flat land.

The main road cut through the town, circling around a central park before coming back together to continue into the wild. The park was quiet and there was a whistling of wind that could be heard alongside the chime of a bell in the ambience. A church nearby rang its bell atop its tower seven times as a small group of men, women, and children left the Holy building.

The entirety of the town was christened in a thick foot-tall blanket of snow. The windows of every shop were encrusted in a thin layer of translucent frost. The ranch-style homes in the suburbs were basking in a peace of the light wind. At the end of a cul-de-sac of one of the neighborhoods, the one-story homes were grouped together around the end of the road, all similar in design, but separate in color. A warmness emitted from the bright lights beyond the window and the sigh of smoke bailed from the chimneys. Holiday lights lined the gutters of every home. In some, through the large windows of the living rooms, families could be seen huddled together on the couch in front of the fireplace. The neighborhoods of this small town had a distinct street lamp with ribbons tied up as the lamp heads diverged into three. The driveways of each home were salted and cleared. Likewise, the street was cleared too even as a light sprinkle of snow fell down to the earth.

The silence in the night was soon interrupted by the crunch of snow at the hands of a single footstep on a front lawn. A hand crept around a barren tree and a cloaked face peered around to look out and beyond. The mouth of this mysterious individual was covered up in a scarf and eyes in dark sunglasses. The entire body of this figure was under the guise of a black cloak that went down to even cover the stranger's feet.

The character remained hidden behind the large trunk of the tree of this house and watched as a police cruiser slowly came to the end of the cul-de-sac and parked in the driveway of a beige house. The car shut down and the driver door opened to reveal a policeman in a navy blue winter coat, armed with various items around his duty belt including a pistol, an electroshock pistol, handcuffs and other items. On the shoulder of the policeman was the insignia of the Royal Canadian Mounted Police. On the front of his coat was his rank, first initial and surname in capital letters, 'CST. Z. MERRICK.'

Mr. Merrick was a bearded man with short dark red hair between a shade of dark brown and auburn. He had tired eyes, but was youthful as any man in his mid-twenties could be. He had fair skin and a peaceful look on his face. His thin beard harbored crystalline snowflakes that slowly liquified by his warmth.

The officer locked his car before he walked forward to the front of his home. He took his keys and inserted them into the front door and then reached up to push the door handle forward and enter. Mr. Merrick brushed his boots before he entered and turned into the living room on the right-side.

The cloaked figure moved around and continued to look on, observing into the living room as the policeman entered and removed his coat to reveal the ballistic vest and bluish grey short-sleeved shirt underneath. He smiled as he looked to the woman before him, on the couch ahead wrapped in a blanket and with a warm mug at her right-hand. She had light brown hair and a thin face with fair skin. Her eyes were green whereas her husband's were blue. She wore a ruby red sweater and slim black sweatpants. Her nails were painted in a gentle pink.

Mr. Merrick sighed as he looked at her again and folded his jacket into his arms. Mrs. Merrick had a grim appearance and saddened face. Her eyes were bloodshot and mascara askew.

"Hey, sweetie," Mr. Merrick remarked, looking at his wife with pity.

Mrs. Merrick looked away from her husband and turned to the fireplace. Her eyes began to water, causing her man to immediately come over and sit down next to her. He brought a hand around her back and took the mug from her hand to set on the coffee table before them. He then wrapped his arms around and held her gently.

"Hey, it's okay," Mr. Merrick ensured her.

"No, it's not. You probably hate me."

"I don't hate you, Elisa. We'll get there eventually. It'll be our time soon enough. We're still young..."

"No, it's not possible. It simply not possible, Zach."

"Don't be like that. We can try again tonight, and if not, we'll keep trying because I know that it is possible."

"No," she replied, pushing her husband away, standing up and walking forward. "It's pointless. How can you even stand to be with me with the way I am? How have you not left me? You may as well now rather than to keep waiting, to keep hoping..."

"Babe, I'm not angry. I love you. If you don't want to try anymore, then we won't, but I won't leave you. I married you for better and for worse, remember?"

"I'm sorry," Elisa apologized, calming down and embracing her husband.

"Don't be sorry. It's not your fault. Perhaps... perhaps it's just not meant to be, you know? In the end of the day, we still have each other and I'm grateful for that. We're lucky to be where we are, with each other in this home. We live in one of the nicest communities in the country, and they've been extremely supportive and concerned for you to conceive. You don't have to worry or be afraid. I'm not going anywhere. I'm yours forever and for always."

"Oh Zach..." Elisa replied, placing a hand on his chest and looking at him. "I love you so much."

"I love you too," Zach said with a smile. "Come on now. It's Christmas Eve and it's time to be happy, not sad. Let's go eat, okay?"

The two let go of each other. Zach looked to his wife with a reassuring smile and she returned it with her own beam. The two then looked towards the door as they heard the doorbell ring. Elisa stepped towards the door.

"Oh, that's probably Anna," Elisa remarked. "I told her to return the dish tomorrow..."

Elisa walked towards the door and looked into the peephole. She then turned back and looked to her husband.

"Nobody's there," Elisa said to him.

Elisa opened the door regardless and took a step forward before taking a reflexive step back as she looked down.

"Oh my God," Elisa said, looking at the basket on the doorstep. "Zach!"

Elisa came down to the basket and got a better look at what was inside, or who was inside. A baby bundled in a deep layer of blankets was deep asleep with a peaceful, innocent face. The child had thin light strawberry blonde hair.

"What is it?" Zach questioned, arriving behind his wife and looking at the child. "What?"

"It's a baby," Elisa said in a hushed voice. "Oh, and it's the most beautiful baby I've ever seen. Look at him, Zach."

Elisa picked up the child from the basket and held him in her hands.

"Are you sure it's a dude?" Zach asked.

"Oh, just look at this face. He's a little baby boy," Elisa remarked in a playful voice as he brought him in.

Zach took a step forward and picked up the basket. He then stepped forward into the cold and looked around.

"Hello?!" Zach shouted. "Hello?!"

"Hey," Elisa scolded him, shushing him.

Zach looked at her and then stepped into the house, closing the door behind him. Elisa walked into the living room and set the child on the couch.

"Oh, where's my stethoscope? I need to make sure that this little thing is alright," Elisa said, examining the child.

"Who'd leave a child on our front door step?" Zach questioned, stunned.

"You better make some phone calls and call the detachment," Elisa replied, picking the child up again. "I'm going to take him to the bedroom."

"Okay," Zach responded, stepping back and going to the kitchen.

Zach picked up the telephone in the kitchen and dialed a number. He then brought the phone to his ear as he waited for a response.

"RCMP Saint-Nazaire Detachment. How can I assist you?" a female answered.

"Evening, Alex. It's me, Zach. I have a bit of a situation at my house. Have there been any reports of missing children, or infants, in the last hour or so throughout the province?"

"Let me see," the female replied.

Zach waited for a moment.

"No, there doesn't seem to be any amber alerts at the moment. What's going on?"

"Well, you'll never believe me, but somebody's left a baby on my doorstep and wandered off," Zach explained. "My wife is currently assessing the child to make sure he doesn't need to go to the hospital, but I'm not too sure what to do next."

"It's possible the child was abandoned."

"City hall is closed until the new year. I don't think there's anywhere to take the child for the time being. I'm going to call the afterhours number for Alberta Child Services. Can you put out a notification about the retrieved child and see if anyone claims him?"

"Sure, just give me a description and I'll get a file number started."

"I'm not sure how old the child is... possibly a couple of months to a year old. White skin. He's got blonde hair and... I'm not sure about the eye color. He's asleep right now."

"I suppose that's as much detail as we can get about a baby... What are you going to do with him?"

Zach thought for a moment. He then turned his neck and took a deep breath.

"I suppose... I suppose he can stay here with me and Elisa for the time being. If he's alright, we won't have to go to the hospital and we can support him until either someone claims him, or the ministry can take over. What safer place is there for a child than with a policeman and a nurse, right?"

"Alright, I'll put a notice out. Have a Merry Christmas, Zach."

"You too. You too…" Zach replied.

Zach hung up and put a hand to his head. He left the kitchen and came into the living room, crossing to enter the corridor that went to the master bedroom. He entered and looked over to his wife, with a light beautiful smile on her face as she held the boy. The child had awakened, but remained peaceful as he cradled him in her arms.

"How is he?" Zach questioned.

"He's healthy," Elisa quietly replied.

"I called the detachment. There are no amber alerts. I told them to keep an eye out. In the meantime, I said we'd take care of him until somebody picked him up."

"I'd like that," Elisa said, humming to the child to get him to sleep again.

Zach looked at the child and saw that he had green eyes like his wife.

"What can we do to adopt him?" Elisa asked.

"Adopt him?" Zach questioned. "We can't adopt him. He's not ours."

"Whoever left him didn't want him and it was their loss. He needs a home."

"There are hundreds of possibilities to who this child could be, or where he came from. His parents could be out there, looking for him. He could have been kidnapped and abandoned on our doorstep."

"You never know," Elisa replied.

Zach sighed and said, "We can look after him as foster parents, but only until his real parents claim him or the province does. He's not ours though. After all, there are so many more people in line to adopt."

"You're right," she replied, dropping her peaceful smile. "I just... I thought that God had answered our prayers for once. His name is Tristan..."

"Elisa..."

"It says so on this gold necklace of his. It has a charm of Saint Luke on the front, and on the back it says, 'Tristan' engraved alongside a date underneath: 'November 01, 2002.'"

Elisa looked at Tristan. He fell asleep again. Zach looked at the two of them. He gave a warm smile at the pair of them. He then walked over and sat next to her, looking at little Tristan.

"I don't want you to get too attached to him. He's not ours to claim... but in the event that this boy's parents can't be found and we can foster him, I suppose we could make an effort to make him our own."

Elisa turned and smiled at him.

"I have faith, Zach, that this boy is a gift from above. I'm sure it is our fate to have him with us and in our care. Somebody brought him to us. Somebody brought little Tristan to us."

"Tristan," Zach repeated. "It's a good name for our little Christmas miracle."

"It sure is..."

"Tristan Merrick."

The couple looked down at the child as he slept peacefully in Elisa's arms, blissfully ignorant of what was around him.

Act 1, Scene 2

Tristan dodged the incoming blow from the punching bar. He ducked and then pounced back up to hit it across on the rebound as he stood and thought on his toes, moving back and forth with a high force and energy. Tristan punched with fists together as he sidestepped from another incoming blow from the machine. His fists were covered in bright red boxing gloves. Sweat ran along Tristan' tired and tanned skin. He had a focused glance on his face as he continued to evade and punch back. He was dressed in dark blue shorts and a black tank top. Tristan's arms were thick from his developed triceps. His calf muscles and thighs were toned and sleek. Tristan's legs had thin curly blonde hairs from his ankle up. His shoulders were broad and large. On his right shoulder, he had a burn scar from when he had made his escape from Kielder Forest. A headband kept his medium-length strawberry-blonde hair at bay and took up the sweat that came out profusely. His green eyes were concentrated on what was before him. His gold necklace bounced atop of his chest as he moved cautiously and carefully within the boxing arena.

Diana watched Tristan from the sidelines. She was dressed in a grey t-shirt and black shorts. The couple was in the basement of Lord Phoenix Secondary School. Tristan ducked again from another incoming blow before coming up with an uppercut against the machine. Diana watched patiently with an arm supporting her head as it rested on the ropes.

"Come on, you're barely even trying today..." Tristan muttered under his breath.

Tristan quickly wiped the sweat from his forehead. He then dodged an oncoming blow before standing up and getting hit in the right-side of his face. Tristan quickly stood up and dodged the next blow, recovering and throwing a hit. Diana cringed as Tristan was hit by the machine, but Tristan went on. Tristan panted as he continued to fight.

"What's the matter? Surrendering already?" Tristan questioned himself under his breath.

The machine moved to punch him again. Tristan brought his fists to his face and absorbed the strike. He then dodged the next blow and threw an under punch. The machine hit him in the left-side, causing Tristan to stagger to the side. Diana cringed again.

"Tristan, maybe that's enough," Diana recommended.

Tristan ignored her as he recovered. He then continued.

"I'm fine," Tristan insisted.

"Tristan, it's going to knock you out," Diana argued.

"I'm not afraid of a little sleep," Tristan replied. "Come on, put me to rest," he taunted the machine.

Tristan blocked the incoming punch and threw one back at the machine. He fixed his posture and continued to bounce on his toes in his adrenaline-fixed excitement. Diana took the opportunity to vault over the rope.

"Come on, come get me," Tristan taunted under his breath.

Diana crossed her arms. Tristan threw another punch and then backed off as the bars stopped spinning on their own. He took a deep breath and then looked to his girlfriend.

"Are you done?"

"Yeah," Tristan replied, exhausted. "Just give me a second."

Diana walked over with a towel and gave it to Tristan to wipe his forehead with. He then moved to wipe his arms before dropping it on the floor due to his gloved hands. Diana picked it up and finished wiping him down for him. She then went over to his gym bag and fetched some water so that he could rehydrate. Diana squeezed the water into his mouth.

Tristan squirted out some water as she gave too much, causing Diana to move out of the way. Tristan quickly covered his mouth.

"Sorry," Diana apologized.

"It's fine," Tristan said. "Thanks for being so helpful."

"No need to be sarcastic."

"I'm serious," Tristan insisted. "Thanks."

Tristan gave Diana quick peck on the lips. The couple parted and looked at each other. Tristan looked at Diana through her dark blue eyes. He gave a light smile.

The couple were torn apart by the brute sound of a clock tower in the distance. It was the clocktower four blocks from the school at city hall. The bell chimed five times."

"Crap" Tristan remarked. "Five already?"

"I guess so," Diana replied.

"Damn, I wanted to save some time to hit some weights," Tristan said with eagerness.

"Seriously? You want to do some weights on top of all of this? You're really buzzing with mania all of the sudden, aren't you?"

Tristan gave a serious glare at Diana.

"I knew that as soon as I got home, I'd be too lazy to train on top of all the homework I have... Damn," Tristan cursed. "I'll have to train tomorrow..."

"Poor thing," Diana sarcastically replied. "Come on, or else we'll be late."

"I don't want to go," Tristan complained, removing his gloves as Diana went to fetch his gym bag. "Psychiatrists are a scam and it's all a bunch of nonsense anyways."

"Quit complaining. You agreed to go for Charles, not for yourself."

"I'm just saying," Tristan replied, taking his things from Diana, "the first session we had didn't accomplish anything. I don't see the next doing anything more. What does Charlemagne think he's going to achieve? If he's so adamant to forget about what happened last Halloween, why doesn't he hire a hypnotist or drug himself like everybody else was drugged at the end of the occupation."

"I don't know," Diana replied, walking over the ropes with Tristan. "Let's just go along with it. It's only an hour session once per week, and it's Charles' only idea to help cope with the quote on quote, 'hallucinations.'"

The couple walked out of the weight room and into the basement corridor of the school. The basement of the school consisted of smooth, hard concrete floor and dark grey brick walls. Diana and Tristan walked a short distance and reached a corridor with a set of stairs that went up to the gym. They stopped in front of the changing room doors and looked at each other.

"Psychiatrists are a scam," Tristan repeated to her. "When my parents died and child services took me in, they made me talk to one and it didn't do me any good."

"Yes, it's not like you were the epitome of repressed anger and grief when I found you," Diana muttered.

Tristan ignored her.

"I don't see what a shrink can do for us except reinforce this big lie spread around, but that won't help him. It'll make it worse – denying the truth will make it all worse. Charles' problem is that he's scared he was manipulated because we've been betrayed so many times, but we weren't. Bauer wasn't a bad man. He helped save this town – he sacrificed himself so that we could live."

"Who are you trying to convince? I believe you. You know that I believe you because I trust you, and I love you. I just don't see the big deal in whether Charlemagne believes or not – it's his loss and not a large one at that."

"What about the others? What about Moira? Or Aaron? Moira's dad died fighting against the Huntsman and Aaron's dad was paralyzed from the waist down. Do you think it's sitting well on them that they were injured in a serious of 'riots' that Charlemagne supposedly caused? Has Moira spoken to you yet?"

Diana looked to the side.

"I've been giving her space…"

"She hasn't, has she? She's mad at you – how are you not upset over that?" Tristan asked.

"Fine, Tristan, you've made your point, but that's Aaron and Moira we're talking about, not Charles. Look, we're going to be late if we keep arguing about what we've been arguing about every night for the past week. Go take a shower and get changed – I'll meet you out here when you're done."

Tristan looked at her. The couple quickly kissed before parting. Tristan left to quickly shower and change out of his gym strip. Diana entered the change room and changed out of her own gym strip and into the clothes she came to school with. Once Tristan had changed into his blue winter coat, he grabbed his backpack from his gym locker and his gym bag. He put his backpack around his back and brought the strap of his gym bag up so that it could rest on his shoulder. He then left and met with Diana outside in the hallway.

Diana had changed into a pair of jeans and her black leather jacket. Tristan's hair was still wet from when he had showered.

Diana took a comb from his bag and quickly combed it before looking at him.

"There, that should do," Diana stated.

"Again, very unnecessary," Tristan stated to her with a frown.

"You think I'm going to let you go to our appointment amess?" Diana questioned.

Tristan gave a shrewd smile. The couple proceeded to walk up the steps and come into the gym, hands held together. They then walked down to the rear exit and proceeded to walk down to leave.

The couple quickly parted as they saw the sudden appearance of Principal Phillips from around the corner. They each took a small side step and looked on with slight horror at her.

"Hello, Diana. Hello, Tristan," Principal Phillips greeted. "What are you two still doing around on a Friday?"

"We... we were just in the weight room," Tristan replied. "We're on our way out now."

"Sounds nice," Mrs. Phillips replied, checking the exit doors to make sure it was locked. "Have a pleasant weekend. I'm just checking on doors to make sure they're locked. You can exit from the front door to leave."

"No problem," Tristan replied, looking at Diana. "Have a good weekend."

The two walked off and went around the corner. Tristan gave a quick sigh of relief and looked to Diana who was neither too impressed nor pleased. She held an uncomfortable look on her face.

"Well, that was close," Tristan remarked.

"Yeah," Diana replied, walking onwards without Tristan.

"Almost too close," Tristan added with a smile.

Diana didn't reply. Tristan caught up with her for them to walk out together. He tried to take her hand, but she moved it so that she could hold on to her backpack strap.

"You're not mad at me, are you?" Tristan questioned as they walked outside.

"No," Diana replied, "I just don't like that we hide our relationship anymore."

"We don't hide it," Tristan replied. "The whole school knows we're tighter than a nut and bolt. What do you want? For people to know more? What business is it of theirs?"

"Please, just stop, Tristan."

Tristan caught up with Diana and took her hand behind the garden behind the main pathway to the main doors of the school.

"Then at least let me say this. I have a bond for you that nobody else has. No woman will ever make me feel the way that I feel about you, and that is something that might not be available because of the bond we have formed at our ripe age. You're an important part of me. Yes, it sucks that we're legally siblings and that makes our relationship a tad bit scandalous to the outsiders among us, but that doesn't change the fact that we love each other and there is nothing wrong with it. And because there is nothing wrong with it, it is of no business to others to make a sly judgement against us, because we haven't done any wrong."

Diana nodded to him. Tristan touched her cold cheek with his hand and tried to lift a smile as he gave his own.

"What about Charles?" Diana remarked. "Should we at least tell him?"

Tristan looked at Diana for a moment. He took a deep breath.

"What if I told you, I had already told him and thus knew what he would think, hypothetically?" Tristan questioned.

"What?"

"When we were in England, camping, do you remember we had this same debate? Well, I felt bad about it and went ahead to try and see how Charles would react or think of us if we were in some sort of romantic relationship. I told him that I had a crush on you…"

"And?"

"He thanked me for confiding in him, but… he didn't think it was good," Tristan answered, "mostly because of the fact that we live together."

"What?" Diana questioned. "Are you sure?"

"Yes."

Diana frowned and turned to the side. She gave a sigh.

"What if we'll never be able to tell him?" Diana questioned. "Charles has a special place in my heart for what he's done for us – he's family. It slightly breaks my heart to know that he'd react negatively to us being in a relationship."

Tristan shrugged.

"We should get on going," Tristan suggested. "We're going to be late."

"Yeah," Diana agreed. "We are."

Diana moved out of the way so that they could continue walking towards the parking lot. Tristan grabbed her hand.

"Hey, just because this is how he'd react doesn't mean that we won't tell him eventually, okay? I promise you that one day, we will tell him. Just not now, alright?"

Diana nodded to him.

Act 1, Scene 3

Tristan and Diana parked in the main parking lot of Allabrese General after a short, but silent car ride from the school. They left their backpacks and gym bags behind, and then got out of the grey pickup truck that Charlemagne had given to Tristan for his birthday last week. From the parking lot, the couple walked towards the main entrance that led into the atrium of Allabrese General.

The automatic sliding doors of the hospital entrance opened on their approach, allowing them to walk in and look around them. The atrium of the hospital was quiet and there weren't a lot of people around. Tristan walked ahead of Diana and took a deep breath.

"God, I love hospitals," Tristan said, smiling as he looked around.

"Yeah, I know," Diana replied. "You said that last time."

"Isn't it a nice atmosphere? It really just makes me want to be a doctor and spend the rest of my life coming here every morning."

"Alright, are you done?" Diana questioned. "We've got to get going or else Charlemagne will scold us for being 'irresponsible' with our time."

"Fine," Tristan sighed, following behind Diana as she led the way.

The couple walked across the atrium and down a corridor that took them to the other side of the main floor. There, they reached a set of elevators that took them to the second floor. Once at the second floor, they turned right and were met at an intersection. To the left was Cardiac Care, and to the right was the Inpatient Psychiatric Unit, but immediately before them was a set of glass doors that took them into a small office belonging to the Community Psychiatric Services ward.

The entrance of the ward consisted of a small receptionist desk and then a waiting area on the right with chairs for them to sit down. Charlemagne was already there, sitting down with his left leg over his knee as he waited patiently for the kids. Between the reception desk and the waiting area was a door that could only be passed through with a proxy card. Behind the door was a short corridor that led into four different offices. A window at the end of the corridor looked out to the south of the town. The ward had a different atmosphere to the rest of the hospital as it had more of an office atmosphere with its light coffee brown colored walls and dark brown carpet.

"Ah, you made it," Charlemagne remarked, standing up and looking to the kids. "I was growing to be afraid that you might have forgotten or you were going to be late."

Charlemagne was noticeably dressed in his three-piece plaid grey suit, but wore a black overcoat overtop the jacket and vest. He also wore a flat cap. Charlemagne had tired eyes and his light skin and steel-grey hair were much the same.

"We're not happy, but we're here," Tristan stated.

"We remembered," Diana said.

"I know you both hated the last session, but even if we don't come to terms about what happened last month, I'm sure these sessions will be beneficial for us all."

"Charles..." Tristan groaned.

"Tristan," Diana said in a stern voice, looking at him with a strict glare. "I'm sure you know what you're doing, Charles."

"Of course," Charlemagne replied, "because the sooner we know for sure what happened to us, the better."

"Oh boy..." Tristan muttered under his breath.

The door towards the offices opened and a woman in elegant clothes came out with a clipboard. She had fair skin, but a long nose and dark brown hair. She wore glasses.

"Mr. Cabernet?"

"Here," Charlemagne confirmed.

"Come on in, Mr. Cabernet," the woman said, holding the door for him and the kids to follow through. "How's your day been?"

"It's been busy, but we're here..."

"Good," the woman replied.

Tristan looked at the name tag on the woman's right breast. Her name was Dr. Steiner. Once the three of them had passed, she moved ahead of them to bring them into her office where she waited at the doorway so they could walk in before she could close it behind her.

The doctor walked over to her desk chair and sat down. She span around to face the family as they sat down at the couch on the opposite-side of the small office space.

"Well, Cabernet family. How have you been this week?" Dr. Steiner asked.

"Quite well," Charlemagne answered.

"And how about the kids? Have you been well too?"

"Yeah," Diana replied.

"Sure," Tristan said.

Tristan looked at the doctor with displeasure.

"Good," Dr. Steiner replied in a calm voice. "How have the three of you gotten along in the last week since our last session. I seem to recall there being tension two weeks ago when the quarantine had ended."

"Tension?" Charlemagne questioned. "I'm afraid I don't understand, doctor. None of us are at odds with each other."

"Well, let me ask the kids," Dr. Steiner responded. "Remember, children, you are free to speak your heart in this room. What is said here, stays here. So let me ask you, Diana. How do you feel about Charlemagne?"

"I'm alright with him," Diana shrugged. "I mean, I have no problem with him and get along fine with him ever since our last disagreement over a year and a half ago."

"Please elaborate, Diana," Dr. Steiner requested.

"Oh my God..." Tristan whispered under his breath, slipping his phone from out of his pocket to check the time.

"Well, I didn't like Charles when we first met. I think that as much was obvious to the two of us..."

"And why didn't you like him?" Dr. Steiner asked.

"Because I didn't ask or want to be adopted. I had a mentality that I had been kidnapped from my home by the Harlech Police Department, and for reasons that aren't really clear to either of us, I was put in his permanent care, which was undesired by the both of us. He didn't like me because I was an obstacle in his plans. I didn't like him because he was an obstacle in my plan.

"What plan?"

"My plan was to be free as I was... I didn't like being restrained and imprisoned in this town... but that's all in the past."

"What changed?"

"A lot," Diana confessed. "It was mostly my friendship with Tristan, but also my friendship with another boy, Arturo, who doesn't live in Allabrese anymore where I began to feel different to this town. I became a part of the town – their best horse racer in a long time, and during this period, Charles and I conflicted a lot. He was too authoritarian with me, which I detested, but in his fairness, he was learning how to be a parent. In the end, we both came to a mutual understanding, and our relationship has never diminished since."

"Very good," Dr. Steiner replied. "And Charles, how do you feel about Diana?"

"Uh, Dr. Steiner, I don't believe this has much to do with the main issue, which is coming to terms with what had occurred last month in Allabrese," Charlemagne pointed out.

"Nonsense, Charles. You'll be surprised by just how much this has to do with your case. Now then, please answer the question. How do you feel about Diana?"

"Well," Charlemagne sighed, "but it was never all well. She was right in the regard that neither of us seemed to appreciate each other when we first met. I was depressed, in a midlife crisis, and planning to sell off my company. Diana was a blockade to my desire."

"What changed?"

"Well, in the end, the kids helped me overcome my depression and over time, they've helped me see the world in a different light. Previously, I held no serious worldview. I saw meaning in only myself, my actions, my achievements and my pursuit to situate myself as a great man. Over time, I realized that I was nobody, and through the children, I saw purpose in them. I developed a worldview in which life comes and goes, but what remains the same is the cycle. By helping these children, I was securing the cycle and sending into the world children who were prepared, ready, and who had what was foremost important and rare in this day and age: human experience and knowledge."

"Did your opinion of Diana change after this revelation?"

"Well, it wasn't as much of a revelation as it was a gradual realization over the months that came. However, after our first adventure, I respected Diana and saw a bit of myself in her, mostly in the anger she held against her father, which allowed me to sort of empathize with her."

Diana looked to Charlemagne. She then looked to the ground. Dr. Steiner took notes.

"And what about after that? I understand that there was a bit of trouble towards the end of your first year, where according to Diana, you were still learning to be a parent and were 'authoritarian' with her. What was your take on this?"

"Well, the trouble there was that although I had some sort of understanding, my understanding was not complete because Diana and I are separate beings with separate experiences. She grew up in one of the poorest neighborhoods in the county, and I grew up in one of the richest households. Nonetheless, we did come to our mutual understandings of one another where we admitted our wrongs and made up. We haven't had issue since then."

"Very interesting..." Dr. Steiner replied. "Okay, now let's look at you, Diana, and Tristan. Diana, how do you feel about Tristan?"

"Good," Diana confessed.

"And you, Tristan?"

"Good," Tristan said.

"Has it always been good, Diana?"

"Well... no," Diana replied. "Tristan and I have had our conflict, especially at the beginning of getting to know each other. What I found, though, at the beginning, was that I was drawn to Tristan by our shared recent experiences – of us losing our parents and virtually being orphans. I was in a constant state of anger and sadness because of the ordeal. I loved my mother like nobody else because she was all that I had, and when she died, life had never been the same until I met Tristan who became the only person I had left. We tried to be friends, it was difficult and we came towards it, but during our trip to Russia, I began to express my own personal history to him, and to no avail did Tristan seem to reciprocate the emotion I had. He was stone cold, and that bothered me. And then, during our trip in Russia, we were separated from Charlemagne and alone. We were hiking along the Ural Mountains when Tristan fell into some ice and nearly died of hypothermia had I not saved him. I nearly lost him, and the experience reminded me of when my mother nearly died, but the most troubling part was that Tristan held no gratitude, or so it seemed…"

Tristan looked uncomfortable as Diana explained this personal history of theirs.

"Sorry, what?" Charlemagne questioned. "Why is this the first time I am hearing about this? You nearly died on that trip?"

"Charles, please," Dr. Steiner interrupted. "It is Diana's time to talk. Diana, please continue… What do you mean by, 'Tristan held no gratitude?'"

"We were both in the wrong," Diana confessed. "I was overtly modest towards him, told him not to say anything, and he allowed me to shut him up over something so serious and huge. I allowed him to bottle his emotions, and it bothered me because what I am most peeved about in regard to Tristan is how he bottles his emotions and doesn't open up to anyone, including me."

"Thank you, Diana," Dr. Steiner replied. "Tristan."

"Yes," Tristan responded, jerking his head up.

"What were your thoughts on Diana when you first met her and the conflict you had in the beginning of your relationship as brother and sister?"

"Yikes," Tristan replied, "well, I really liked her. I thought she was an interesting character, but she was also annoying sometimes. She would always assume that I know what she's thinking or that I know what she wants me to do, but I don't half the time – still don't. For example, when the first time we really got mad at each other, it was because I wasn't treating her the same at school as I was at home. I had no idea! Only after she talked to me did I understand. And then with what happened in Russia – she told me to shut up about being thankful, and then she got mad at me for not knowing that she wanted me to show my gratitude. I don't bottle up my emotions – I reserve myself. If she wanted me to talk about what happened in Russia, or about my parents, or anything else, I would have been fine talking to her about them. Granted, this was in the past, and now Diana and I have better communication with each other when it comes to discussing our issues."

"And let me now ask, Tristan. How do you feel about Charlemagne?"

"I feel fine about him," Tristan lied in a brash tone.

"How did you feel about him when you first met him?"

"I thought he was an extraordinary man," Tristan answered.

"Did this ever change?" Dr. Steiner questioned.

"Not really."

"And Charlemagne, what was your impression of Tristan?" Dr. Steiner asked.

"He was the adopted-son of my brother," Charlemagne said. "I'm not going to lie, but it was Tristan's genuine interest in some of my work that helped me the most, but that isn't to say that Diana's never helped me or wasn't a part of my awakening. I hold a lot of cherished memories between the two of us."

"Diana, how does this make you feel?" Dr. Steiner asked.

Diana shrugged and replied, "I always had a sort of impression that Charlemagne liked Tristan more than he liked me, but hearing this reverses that thought of mine. I'm happy to know of the role I played in Charles' life."

"I'll admit that Tristan and I have always had the better social relationship, but you do hold a special role in my life. I respected our boundaries, and the relationship we do have is one of respect. I'm sorry you had an impression that I thought less of you, but am glad you know the truth now."

"Excellent," Dr. Steiner said. "We are all getting to understand each other a bit more and through that, we can tackle the more serious problems that you have asked me to help you with."

Tristan gave a long sigh. He brought his arm to rest on the armrest and sunk his head and back into the cushion of the couch. He rolled his eyes as the doctor continued to blab, but paid no more attention and instead held total indifference.

Act 1, Scene 4

"Thank you for your visit," Dr. Steiner said at the end of the hour. "I look forward to our next session next week."

"Of course," Charlemagne replied, standing up and shaking her hand. "Farewell."

The three of them left the office and went down the hall to exit into the waiting room. From there, they walked back into the hospital and walked towards the lift. Diana called an elevator to take them back down to the main floor.

"So," Tristan said, looking to Charlemagne, "did you find any of that helpful?"

"With time," Charlemagne simply responded. "It's going to be a while before any of us can think clearly of what happened."

Tristan groaned and shook his head. He walked into the elevator with Charlemagne and Diana as the doors opened. The doors then closed and took them back to the main level.

"Mavis has taken this Friday night off, as usual, so that leaves us to dine out on our own," Charlemagne said. "Do you two have plans of your own, or would you care to dine with me tonight?"

"We can eat with you," Tristan responded without hesitation.

"Diana?" Charlemagne questioned.

"I have nowhere else to be," Diana answered.

"Wonderful," Charlemagne said with a smile.

The elevator brought them down to the main floor. Its doors opened.

"I'm sure you're both hungry by now, so let's go straight to the Great Range Bistro, shall we?"

"Sounds good," Tristan replied, putting a hand in his pocket.

"Good," Charlemagne said to him. "I left my car on the pavement. What about you?"

"I'm in the parking lot," Tristan responded. "I'll see you at the restaurant."

"Good, good. Please drive safely, Tristan."

"Yup."

Charlemagne left out of the south exit next to the elevators. Tristan watched him leave before looking at Diana.

"Aren't you going to go with him?" Tristan asked.

"Are you kicking me out of the truck?" Diana questioned.

"I thought you'd be a little mad at me after what happened up there."

"I'd let you know if I was mad or not," Diana replied. "I don't repress myself. Why'd you think I'd be angry?"

"It's hard to know anymore," Tristan responded with irritability as he started to walk back to the atrium. "I'm sick of guessing."

Diana looked at Tristan as he started to walk off.

"Stop," Diana said to him. "Tristan, let's please stop fighting."

Tristan stopped and turned around to her. He gave a look of pity.

"Okay," Tristan replied. "I'm sorry."

"I'm sorry too," Diana said, walking to him and letting out a sigh.

"Come on, let's go meet up with Charles and get some food. I'm sure we're just hangry – We haven't eaten since lunchtime."

"Yeah," Diana agreed. "You're right."

The couple walked together back to the atrium and out the main entrance of the hospital. From there, they returned to the grey pickup truck. Tristan unlocked the car and the two split up to go to either side and sit in.

Tristan gave a cold exhale, letting out the visible vapor of his breath before inhaling deeply as he started the car engine. Diana brought her head to rest on the passenger door window while Tristan raised the heater. He then changed gears, reversed out of their parking stall, and made his way out of the parking lot to drive the short distance to Cabernet Head Office.

Once there, he parked in the deserted back parking lot of the office space, and the couple walked over to meet with Charlemagne under the alleyway beneath the offices where Charlemagne waited for them.

"Ah, there you are," Charlemagne remarked. "Come on it's too bloody cold to be waiting out here. Let's go find us a seat inside."

Charlemagne opened the door for them to walk upstairs to the restaurant on the second floor. Diana and Tristan led the way up to the front of the restaurant where they were greeted and seated at a table within seconds. All three of them removed their coats as they sat down. From there, they ordered some refreshments and then their meals before sitting together in the warmth of the restaurant. There were not many people about, and thus a light chatter around them.

"So, what did you get up to today?" Tristan asked Charlemagne.

"I stayed home to do some work in the study, and then after lunch I went for a walk to think how it would be physically possible to telepathically communicate, influence, or even control another's mind. I thought and thought, but it was all just philosophical pondering and hypothesizing… What about you? What did you get up to today?"

"Not much," Tristan replied with a depressed tone. "Tell me more about your ideas, because I want to know how you think it could be possible…"

"Well, my ideas really surround the idea of the soul that we've talked about previously, and insisted upon an ability by which one would have to have the possibility to transmit or transceiver. Perhaps this is me thinking of the mind like a computer as many have done after the 1950s, but if it were true, why not have such abilities as that of an antenna within our minds that could project and receive like a radio?"

Charlemagne took out a pen from his jacket. He began to draw on a napkin of stick figures, one he labeled as a 'receiver.'

"Most of these ideas I've formed come from the ideas I've developed almost two years ago after our encounter with the ghosts," Charlemagne said. "You see, there is something, something – and the confirmation that there is something draws me to ponder and think of what is possible. It is my belief that all creatures possess enough of a soul to receive. We shall call those that possess only this spiritual ability, 'receivers.' And then, possibly, there are those that transmit – these would be those with the gift of psychic powers."

"Like Bauer?" Tristan questioned.

"Yes, like him, but because, in my theory, just about all advanced life forms possess the ability to receive, those that are gifted with these powers would be 'transceivers,' because they are able to both transmit and receive."

Charlemagne drew two stick figures, one with a squiggly line originating from its head and going to the mind of another.

"Now, if we were to think of the mind as a computer, why not a computer with such capabilities? It is also my belief, therefore, that the more advanced the computer, the more powerful the powers. Thus, the gift to transceive is limited to the most advanced human beings, or those that have developed in the most ingenious manner."

Charlemagne put his napkin away.

"It's been my interest to also understand how it is that our souls could be manipulated, or how it is possible that we could come to believe, see, or think of something that we do not believe, see, or think, but are made to think. Nonetheless, I'm certain that when a human dies, this component of us releases – it is that which I saw in others two years ago. The projection of Curtia and Nero... it boggles my mind to this day even though I have not stopped thinking of it since. And then there's the whole dynamic of these orbs too... I'm just one man to be able to think of this on my own. Mind you, I've talked to Barry, but we're equally stumped."

Charlemagne sighed. He looked past the kids with a humble look on his face. Tristan looked at him and then looked aside with a displeased look on his face.

• • •

Tristan drove Diana home and through the automatic gates of Cabernet Manor once they had finished dining with Charlemagne. He brought the truck up the driveway and then down towards the garage annex. Charlemagne had parked atop of the hill, in front of the front doors, allowing Tristan to back in to the immediate space before the shutter doors. Once he had parked the car, he shut the engine down and gave off a yawn. Diana opened her door and got out of the truck. She then fetched her things from the canopy in the back. Tristan joined her and then looked to her as he closed the back door.

"I've got to feed Zephyr," Diana remarked, turning from him.

"What do you want to do for the rest of the evening? I'm game for anything, unless you want to be alone."

"No, I'd rather do something with you," Diana replied, giving a light smile to him as she turned around. "Why don't we watch a movie?"

"Sure," Tristan said, nodding. "Let me take your things with me. I'm going upstairs."

Diana looked at Tristan and gave him her bags. He took them in addition to his own.

"Are you okay?" Diana questioned, looking at Tristan.

Tristan looked up to her as he juggled with the four bags.

"Yeah," Tristan replied, looking at her with surprise. "I'll manage."

"No, I mean emotionally," Diana responded, "because that's what matters right now. Are you emotionally okay?"

"You're sounding like the shrink, Diana," Tristan responded with a nervous laugh.

"Tristan," Diana responded in a strict tone. "Answer the question."

Tristan lowered his smile and gave a serious face.

"What's wrong?" Diana questioned, bringing a hand to his cheek. "Is *it* bothering you again? Is it the fight we had?"

"I haven't thought about it up to now, but no. It's not because of the 'fight' we had either. I'm more or less upset at Charles than anything else."

"Charles means well," Diana assured him. "He'll come around eventually. Hell, maybe this psychotherapy will work in our favor, and Charlemagne will realize that you were right."

Tristan let out a sigh and replied, "Yeah…"

"Are we good?" Diana asked.

"We're good," Tristan replied. "I'll see you upstairs."

Diana kissed Tristan on the cheek before they split up. Tristan went and took the freight elevator upstairs, while Diana walked over to greet her horse.

"What are you looking at?" Diana questioned, looking at Zephyr who was sticking his head out of his pen, watching the couple as they talked.

Zephyr snorted at her before stepping back into his pen. Diana walked over and opened the stall door. She then stepped in and went to pet Zephyr.

"He's lying to me, isn't he? He's deflecting – there's no way he's overly upset about Charlemagne. He's upset about the fight we had, and possibly the things I said during the therapy session. I'm the one thing keeping him sane, and I'm tearing our relationship apart. I don't want to lose him, Zeph. I don't. I should never have brought up the fact that I don't want to hide every time someone's about to see us holding hands, or about to kiss. Not now. Not in the state he's in."

Diana gently stroked Zephyr's nose.

"I don't like the way he lies to me," Diana confessed. "I don't like the way he's trying to manipulate me so that he can keep me in the dark about what's going on in his head. What is going on in his head? He hasn't said anything about it since I brought it up at the start of the month. He's such an idiot. He needs to vent himself, but he has no one he's willing to vent to. Not even Charles."

Diana took a deep sigh and slid down against the wall to take a seat in the pen. Zephyr walked around and positioned himself to sit down next to her. Diana continued to pet him as she looked blankly across the enclosure.

"He's mad at him, isn't he? He's mad at Charlemagne for some reason. I remember, when we ran from the manor on Halloween night, he blamed Charles for the death of Charles' son. Why? What happened in that forest?"

Tristan entered the store room behind the kitchen and walked out. He opened the door into the kitchen, crossed it, and then made his way towards the main entrance. Tristan then went upstairs, passing the foyer in the north wing of the house, but stopping as he was about to enter his room as the door to the makeshift lab, or guest bedroom as it now was, opened. Charlemagne stepped out.

"Tristan," Charlemagne said to him.

"Hm? Yes?" Tristan replied, looking over to him with regret.

"Where's Diana?" Charlemagne asked.

"Downstairs," Tristan responded. "She's feeding her horse. Why?"

"No matter, I'll speak with her later," Charlemagne replied. "Is everything alright?"

Tristan let out of a sigh.

"Can I talk to about something?" Tristan questioned. "It's about something we talked about back in the summer, before the forest fire and before Finn. Do you remember when I said that I liked Diana, romantically?"

"Of course," Charlemagne responded. "What of it?"

"What if she liked me? What if we could be together?" Tristan asked him.

"Tristan…" Charlemagne said with a sigh. "You're doing yourself no such favor in thinking of these ideals. The last thing you need in your life is to become infatuated with a woman. If you are certain of the way that you feel about her, then talk to her – ask her, because the last thing I want you to do is to torment yourself over such emotions. Emotions... are deadly things, and in us men, nay in both men and women, emotional control is important. I'm sure if she didn't feel the same way, it would do less harm than good for the two of you set the truths before you. I'm sure that's what must be aching at you the most – the possibility that you may be wrong, and that she does not feel for you as you feel for her. But it is important that you ask her, and do not allow this crush of yours to turn into a limerence."

Tristan let out another sigh.

"What if it's not that what I'm worried about? What if it's what others would think of us that I'm worried. You said in the forest that it would be peculiar and scandalous – that's what I'm worried about."

"You are not related by blood to her. The legality of your siblinghood to her is mere legality, and if there's one thing in this household we don't give a damn about, it is man-made laws," Charlemagne assured Tristan. "If you love her, you would not care what others would think of you two. There is no moral harm done, but only moral good. The love of a man and a woman is good, but alas, this is if you are right."

"Right. Thank you."

Tristan nodded to Charlemagne and then went into his room, closing the door behind him. Tristan's room was dark. He pressed a light switch on his right to turn on the main light. He then went across to close the blinds of the window and door to his balcony. He set his things down at the foot of his bed and then turned, crossing the home gym and the bathroom to enter Diana's room. Diana's room was dark too. Tristan went over and turned on a lamp on Diana's desk. He then picked up a picture frame of Diana's mother. He looked at it for a short second and then set it down again, gently, next to Diana's latest read, *White Fang* by Jack London. Tristan left Diana's things at the foot of her bed and then turned around to look at the mementos she had collected. She had nothing from last month.

After Tristan had finished looking through Diana's room, he returned to his and went to his desk. He opened the hatch in the middle and Tristan looked at his own items inside. Most of the pictures saved were of the two of them. However, there included pictures of Tristan and a happy couple. He took it out and closed the hatch, looking at the picture.

One of the figures in the picture was a man in a police uniform. He had three chevrons on the collar of his jacket with the insignia of the RCMP on the shoulders. The man was in his early thirties and was balding. He was with a woman in scrubs. They were in a hospital and before them was a young boy, Tristan, when he was six-years old. At that age, Tristan looked significantly different. His skin was fairer, but slightly with a tanned sheen. His hair was also lighter, more blonde while retaining its expressiveness of orange – it was truly strawberry-blonde, while his hair now had grown darker while retaining its peculiar qualities, but not become auburn and instead a dark orange.

Diana opened Tristan's door and snuck up behind him.

"What are you looking at?" Diana asked.

Tristan jerked his head around and looked at her. He handed the picture to her.

"Where did you find this?" Diana questioned.

"I didn't find it anywhere. I've kept it hidden," Tristan said to her. "I don't like looking at it too much, but today, I wanted to look at it just for a few seconds. I can't help but think of returning to such a time with you, with our own kids."

Diana blushed as she looked at Tristan.

"That's the first time I've heard that from you," Diana said. "About us having kids together."

"It's a fantasy of mine," Tristan admitted. "A motivation to return to what I used to have, but was taken from me. I love you, Diana. I want to spend the rest of my life with you and have as many children as possible. Nothing would please me more than to have our genetics fuse in representations of little versions of us."

"We'll have one, maybe two," Diana admitted, "or as many as we can tolerate."

"So, maybe one or two?" Tristan questioned with a light laugh. "I was thinking in the range of up to five or six."

Tristan smiled at Diana. She returned the photo. He set it on his desk and stood up.

"You should hang that, or at least get a frame and set it somewhere," Diana suggested. "It's not good looking at it all day, but it isn't good hiding it."

"Right," Tristan responded. "I'm happy to know that you want to have kids one day."

"Of course I want to have kids," Diana said to him. "Do you think that because I had a miserable life, that I'd be repulsed to have kids of my own? If anything, I'm incentivized the way you are. One day, when we're ready, I'll give birth to our children and they'll be the gosh darn best kids you've ever seen."

Tristan gave a warm smile and kissed Diana more passionately. Later that night, the two lay together in bed. Tristan held Diana in one arm and held on to his phone with the other, scrolling through various selections of movies.

"How am I supposed to pick a movie when Moira's not talking to you?" Tristan questioned. "She's our de facto movie expert."

"Give her a break," Diana replied. "Her dad died. She might be leaving Allabrese before graduation… and I can only imagine the emotions running through her. I'm worried about her."

"Sorry…"

"Did you remember to lock the bedroom door?" Diana asked.

"Yes," Tristan replied, finding a movie and bringing his phone onto its side for them to watch.

"I'm just checking."

Tristan brought himself closer into Diana as the movie started to play. The room was still slightly cold even though the two of them were still flushed, radiating more heat between each other than the radiator in the room. The covers went up and over Diana's shoulders, but only up to Tristan's bare chest. Tristan breathed into Diana's hair, looking down towards his phone as she was lower to him with the back of her head in his chest.

The room was dark and only the light from Tristan's phone screen lit the room. The screen faded into blackness before smoke lifted up. Tristan started to zone out as his eyes grew dry and tired, but his attention returned as a gunshot fired onto the screen and penetrated a man in a suit, standing in an alleyway. The gunman fired again, hitting the man's wife next to him. She was dressed in a white dress.

"Jeez, right into the action," Tristan remarked, not blinking.

"It's a good writing technique," Diana replied. "It draws the attention of the audience by getting them to asking a lot of questions."

Tristan flinched as he continued to watch the movie. Another gunshot had fired. He hugged Diana more tightly. She held a pleasant smile as she watched the movie. Tristan took a deep breath and relaxed as the movie went on, relaxing with his favorite person in the world.

Act 2, Scene 1

Next week, Tristan looked at himself in the mirror of his and Diana's bathroom. He fixed his hair before picking up his cologne. He then took his antiperspirant and brought it underneath his black shirt to rub it on his armpits. He suddenly cringed as he tilted his neck to the left and right, bringing his hands to feel the tightness within his neck muscles. Tristan stepped away from the mirror and returned to his room. He grabbed his jacket from his desk chair and put it on.

Diana entered Tristan's bedroom dressed in her leather jacket. Tristan grabbed his backpack and brought it around himself. He cringed again as he tilted his neck. Diana noticed. Tristan walked over to his dresser and looked at himself in the mirror again, examining his neck.

"What's wrong?" Diana questioned, walking over to him.

"My neck," Tristan complained.

"What are you looking for?" Diana asked, looking. "I didn't leave a mark last night, did I?"

"I'm not looking for a hickey," Tristan responded. "My neck is sore. I don't know why. I haven't done anything intensive to those muscles lately."

"You probably had a bad night's sleep," Diana suggested. "Honestly, you should see yourself asleep. You sleep in the most awkward positions."

Tristan shrugged and said, "Come on, let's go. We're going to be late and I'm not comfortable driving with all the snow that's out there."

"Hey, be grateful it's Friday," Diana replied, following Tristan out of his room.

"I would be grateful, but Friday means we have to go to that stupid therapy session after school. I *still* can't believe we're going to that hack after three weeks."

"Yeah, I know you are," Diana sighed, "but remember..."

"It's for Charlemagne – I know," Tristan responded, walking into the foyer with her. "Let's just go."

The couple made their way downstairs, to the kitchen, and into the garage where they put their stuff in the back of the pickup truck before entering the front cabin. Tristan put his keys in the ignition, turned the engine on, and then changed gears to drive forward. He hit the switch above him clipped into the sun visor to open the garage shutters. Tristan squinted as the brightness of the snowy outdoors hit him. A gentle vein on the side of his head throbbed. He brought a hand to it and grunted.

Tristan shut his eyes and stopped before he went anymore forward. He looked at the light again and shook his head. He continued to drive forward, along the driveway and then down the hill to reach the automatic gates. Tristan turned left onto the coastal road and then made his way forward towards the freeway to come into town, and drive himself and Diana to school.

· · ·

At the end of the school day, Diana and Tristan spent an hour in the cafeteria, doing homework, before they had to attend their weekly appointment at Allabrese General. Tristan drove them from the school to the hospital. He parked his car in the same parking lot as the week before, and once the car was shut down, they got out and walked to the main entrance, along the main corridor, and upstairs to reach the Community

Psychiatric Services office. They were the first ones there as Charlemagne had yet to arrive.

"Hm, we're early," Diana noticed, looking at a clock on the wall. "I'll sign us in. Go and take a seat, okay?"

"Thanks," Tristan replied, walking over to sit down.

Tristan sat down. He watched as Diana talked to the receptionist and then came over to join him. The couple sat together for a couple of minutes until the door opened and Charlemagne entered.

"Oh, hello children," Charlemagne greeted, waving to them. "Sorry I'm late. Have you signed us in?"

"Yes," Diana answered.

"Good," Charlemagne replied, walking over to sit next to them. "How have you two been doing today?"

"Tristan's not feeling well," Diana pointed out. "I think he might be getting sick."

"I don't get sick," Tristan responded. "I'm just tired and have had a stiff neck. It's nothing. I just want to go home."

"Oh dear, well, it's a good thing that it's Friday then. You can spend the rest of the day resting, *after* we've seen Dr. Steiner."

Tristan rolled his eyes and leaned back in his chair as they waited for Dr. Steiner to see them. Within a couple of minutes, the door opened and she allowed them to see her in her office. The three of them sat in the usual couch and looked to the doctor in her office chair.

"Last week," Dr. Steiner said to them, "we looked at the interpersonal relationships all three of you have together. Tristan, I want to revisit your relationship with Charlemagne. You said that you felt 'alright' about him. Has there ever been anytime that this hasn't been the case?"

Tristan let out a sigh.

"Why does it matter?" Tristan questioned.

"It's important to look at these moments so that we can understand each other, Tristan," Dr. Steiner responded. "Please answer the question."

Tristan sighed again and said, "Fine, a couple of times."

"What was the most recent moment?"

"Years ago, in Egypt, when he vandalized a tomb," Tristan stated. "It made me mad."

Diana looked at Tristan with doubt.

"Is that the most recent?" Dr. Steiner questioned.

"Yes."

"Charles," Dr. Steiner said, "would you say that this is an accurate statement?"

"Well," Charlemagne stuttered, "I wouldn't say it's the most recent, but certainly an important moment."

"Tristan, you can be open in this room. Please tell us what the most recent thing, even if it were so small, that Charles said or did and it upset you. What is the most recent moment of conflict between you two?"

Tristan looked to the side.

"We had a fight," Charlemagne stated, "although I'm not clear of whether this was a part of the hallucinations, but I'm sure Tristan will agree that this happened. He blamed me for the death of my biological son who perished in a forest fire last year."

"Oh boy..." Tristan muttered under his breath.

"Tristan, would you say that this is an accurate statement?" Dr. Steiner questioned.

"It's not the most recent..." Tristan said with bitterness. "We've been fighting about coming to these stupid sessions, the fact that Maxim Bauer was a good person, and that our experiences on Halloween weren't a 'hallucination,' but sure, let's talk about this instead. I'm sorry I blamed you for the death of Finn, Charles. It was crappy of me to suggest that, because you had nothing to do with what happened to him – you weren't there. You were never there for him. If there's anyone that should feel guilty about Finn's death, it's me. I was the one that wasn't strong enough to pull him up. I was the one that allowed him to let go of my hand and fall to his death. And the fact that I allowed Finn to give in to his fate like that bothers me every night and I'm consumed by the guilt that I allowed your son to die. And then there's the fact that you took apart your lab, turned it into a bedroom as if you were making it out to be Finn's room, and now every moment that I walk into that room, all I can see is what could have been – Finn living with us, safe and sound. He was my only friend. He was my best friend. And he's dead. How can you not blame me, or hold some sort of regret towards me? I openly defied you when you came to our camp to retrieve me. I returned to him, warned him that we weren't alone, and then ran off with him to go to Kielder Lake. I should have put in more of an effort to stop him even before then..."

By the end of his outburst, Tristan's face was red and his eyes wet from tears that had formed fast and spread about.

"Are you having night terrors?" Dr. Steiner questioned with intrigue.

"Yes, I'm terrorized at night," Tristan confessed. "Almost every night, I see him again, and although it's such a blessing to see him, especially since in my dreams he is so lifelike, when I wake up, I'm thrusted back into the cold, grey world to confront the truth that I'll never see him again."

"Did you dream of him last night?" Dr. Steiner asked.

"No," Tristan answered. "I dreamt of... Bauer last night."

"Please explain your dream," Dr. Steiner requested.

Tristan let out a sigh and said, "It was simple. He talked to me, and that's it."

"What of?" Dr. Steiner asked.

"I can't remember," Tristan replied.

"Interesting…" Dr. Steiner said, taking notes. "Charlemagne, how did your son's death affect you?"

Charlemagne was still in shock by the outburst that Tristan just had. He looked away from him and towards the doctor.

"Disappointed," Charlemagne answered. "I never had the opportunity to meet the lad, so I can't say I held deep emotional connection towards him. Although, I like to believe that the bond of a father and a son to exist even in absence of physical connection."

Tristan looked to the side.

"I'll admit, in response to what Tristan said, that I had taken apart my lab with the idea running in my subconscious that the room would have been perfect for Finn, but there was more towards it, Tristan, that you know of. I had to move all that equipment downstairs into the basement. I'm also sorry that this is how you have felt and would have encouraged that you opened up towards me about this. I could have done more to help Finn, but that's in the past and there's no use dreading on what could have been, but only on focusing on what one should have done and learning from our mistakes. You're not to blame for Finn's death, however. He died of his own accord – his own malice and hatred. Tristan, ask yourself this, would Finn blame you for his death?"

Tristan looked to Charlemagne. He held a saddened look.

"No," Tristan answered in a sad voice.

"Last week, we talked about Diana's parents and their deaths, so let me ask you now, Tristan, about your parents. What was your relationship with them?"

"Good," Tristan answered in a low voice.

Diana looked at Tristan with pity and then to the doctor with discomfort.

"Maybe we should talk about something else," Diana interrupted. "I think Tristan's had enough – he's tired, and…"

"Let Tristan speak for himself," Dr. Steiner objected. "Tristan, is it okay if we talk about your parents?"

"I don't like to talk about them," Tristan replied. "They died. It sucked, but I got over it – it's what they would have wanted me to do – to live on."

"The same could be said for Finn then," Dr. Steiner insisted, "but for the sake of not allowing emotions to be bottled up, let's continue to speak if you don't mind… It's healthy to revisit these topics, and it's easier to forget the past and let this dread within us linger. Our emotions don't move on so easily. Please, if you don't mind, tell us what happened."

Diana looked at the two with unease. Tristan looked to the side as he went silent for a moment. The doctor looked at him with intent.

"They died," Tristan said quietly.

"How did they die?" Dr. Steiner questioned.

Tristan went silent again and didn't immediately respond.

"Tristan?" Dr. Steiner asked again.

"My mother was shot!" Tristan shouted at her. "It happens, and I've already cried about it enough, alone, with her," he said, pointing to Diana, "and I don't see any point tapping into that emotional well again because that's what you're trying to do instead of achieving what Charlemagne is paying you to supposedly achieve!"

"Tristan," Charlemagne scolded.

"I'm serious! What the hell are we even doing here, Charles?! How is any of this supposed to help come to terms with what happened when we know what happened, but the G.D.P. lied to you, manipulated the townspeople, and covered it all up to protect Zimmerman. Bauer was a good man. He gave his life to save us all – Mr. Macmillan gave his life to save us all. Countless others gave their lives to free us from that occupation! How about instead of wasting your time and money with this scammer, you perform some actual scientific experiments to cope with this doubt in your mind."

"I'm sorry I don't have the certainty that you do," Charlemagne replied in a defensive tone, "but you have to understand that you cannot be one-hundred percent certain with what occurred."

"I am certain – you're the one that has doubts! Do you think just because your brother betrayed you, Dmitri, or Sergei, or whatever his real name was, Johnny, and Judith betrayed you, it likely means that Bauer betrayed us too? He didn't!"

"Please, do not drag Judith, or even my brother, into this conversation," Charlemagne demanded. "Lower your tone and stand down before you say something you might regret!"

"Okay," Dr. Steiner interrupted, uncrossing her legs, "I think we've deviated from our discussion. Let's all take a deep breath and refocus…"

"What discussion?" Tristan questioned, looking to the doctor. "We're not discussing anything but our personal lives, something of which the likes of you has no business in whatsoever. Seriously, what does Diana's parents' deaths, our relationship to each other, or Finn's, or my parents' deaths have to do with anything? All I see is our money being thrown at this charlatan who's stretching the meaning of our livelihoods. She probably has as much doubt, or perhaps even certainty, that we're insane. That's all she cares about."

The room fell silent as Tristan finished his rant. He fell back into his seat as he looked across from himself. Diana took a deep breath and looked to Tristan. She then looked to the ground before picking her eyes up again to look at Tristan once more.

"Wait, what did you mean by your mother getting shot?" Diana asked.

"Huh?" Tristan replied.

"You said your mother was shot," Diana repeated. "Was that a lie? You told me your parents died in a car crash."

"I didn't lie," Tristan said to her. "I- I didn't say that though, did I?"

"You said that your mother was shot," Charlemagne confirmed, "despite the fact that both your parents had died in a car crash. A fact that I confirmed with the St. Nazaire RCMP when I adopted Tristan."

Tristan flinched as he heard Charlemagne finish his words, feeling a headache come over him as he looked to the side.

"My parents died in a car crash," Tristan confirmed. "What did I say?"

"You said your mother was shot," Dr. Steiner repeated. "Why do you think you said that when you knew something else had happened?"

"I- I don't know," Tristan confessed. "I- They both died in a car crash. I remember it, because I was waiting for them to return home on Christmas Eve, but they never showed up. Instead, the RCMP came to the house at around midnight with the bad news. I stayed with my neighbor afterwards until the ministry took me. Why did I say my mom was shot...?"

Tristan leaned forward and looked to Diana. He then stood up and left the room.

"Tristan," Diana said, standing up and going after him. "Where are you going?"

Diana left. Charlemagne looked to Dr. Steiner.

"I apologize for the behavior of the children," Charlemagne said, standing up. "I suppose we should end our session today early."

"No, it's quite alright, Mr. Cabernet. I think we are finally getting somewhere. I'll see you again next week."

"I'm afraid not," Charlemagne responded. "I believe this will be our last session. I- I need to re-evaluate my decisions and perspective."

"Yes, take a moment to think and then get back to my secretary then," Dr. Steiner replied.

"No, doctor. I will take a moment to think, but regardless, we will not be returning."

Charlemagne left the room. Diana and Tristan had exited the office space and came to the elevator lobby.

"What's going on with you?" Diana questioned.

"I wasn't lying, Diana," Tristan insisted. "I swear, I thought I told the truth. I remember now what I dreamt of. Bauer didn't tell me anything – I dreamt this and he was there. It was like a flashback – I dreamt of a woman being shot, and she looked like my mother, but she wasn't my mother. She looked nothing like her, but at the same time, looked just like her."

"What? What are you talking about?" Diana asked with confusion.

"I don't know, but for some reason, I remember it so vividly. It was a busy area, there were lots of people around and she was in a black gown, or cloak. She was shaking people's hands and then a stranger came by. There was a gunshot, people panicked and the man ran off. I remember the shrieks of the people that were around us, the blood too. I remember the blood."

"Who though? When did this happen?"

"I can't remember, but I know it was real. I was there – it was like a long lost memory and in the back of the crowd, I saw Bauer. He said something. He said… What did he say?"

Charlemagne exited the psychiatric office and joined the kids.

"Are you alright?" Charlemagne asked Tristan with concern.

"I'm fine," Tristan replied, looking to him and taking a deep breath.

"Tell him about the dream," Diana insisted.

"It's fine."

"What dream?"

Diana looked at Tristan, annoyed, and went ahead to repeat what Tristan had just said to her.

"It felt real," Tristan remarked.

"You could be mistaken," Charlemagne suggested. "You're taking this idealization of Bauer too far. For all we know, you could be still being manipulated by him."

"I'm not! He spoke to me – he wanted me to see this, but I don't know why? He said something to me – it was important to the dream, but I don't remember what it was because I didn't think it was important at the time."

"You're having delusions. It's all bollocks, Tristan," Charlemagne stated.

"I'm not deluded!"

"Look, Tristan's probably tired," Diana said to Charlemagne. "He's not feeling well, and it's been a long day. How about we go home and if he wants, we can talk some more there."

"Very well," Charlemagne replied.

"I'm fine," Tristan insisted. "I'm not dying. I swear – stop being so condescending towards me!"

"We're concerned," Diana replied.

"Concerned about what? You're acting worse than that quack! What, do you two think I'm crazy now too?!"

"No, Tristan, we do not," Charlemagne responded in a calm tone. "Diana, take him home, will you? I need to go finish speaking with the receptionist to cancel our appointment next week."

"Okay," Diana replied.

"Go home, drink some water, and rest easy. It's very possible you're coming down with an illness of some sort. Take it easy and let Diana drive you home."

"Yeah…" Tristan said in response. "Okay."

Charlemagne left the couple on their own. Diana called an elevator to retrieve them. Tristan didn't say another word for the entire trip back home.

Act 2, Scene 2

Tristan sat at his bed, quiet as he stared blankly to the wall ahead of him. His eyes shifted to the door as he heard a knock. He didn't say anything and instead watched as the door opened with Charlemagne on the other side. He walked into the room. Diana was behind him with her arms crossed. She stayed in the hallway.

"How's your neck?" Charlemagne asked.

"Still stiff," Tristan replied as Charlemagne brought a hand to his forehead.

"Do you have a fever? Sore throat?"

"No," Tristan answered as Charlemagne let go. "Just fatigued."

"In that case, take some ibuprofen and rest up. We'll see if it passes in the morning. If not, it could be either a common cold, or worse, the flu."

"I don't get sick," Tristan stated. "I've never been sick before in my life. Even with Diana coughing and sneezing around me."

"Well, that record might just come to an end," Charlemagne replied, standing up to leave.

"I wasn't lying to the psychiatrist," Tristan said before he left.

"About what? About her practice?"

"All of it. I remember someone being shot, and I don't know why I mistook her for my mother, but in the dream, I associated her to be my mother, so maybe she is someone close in that sphere, or not. I don't know. Someone was shot though. It happened."

"How old do you reckon you were in this dream, or memory? Before you came to Allabrese, I assume?" Charlemagne asked.

"In the flashback I had, I didn't say anything. It was because I couldn't. All I did was watch – like a movie."

Charlemagne nodded and looked to Diana.

"We watched a movie together last week where a woman was shot," Diana stated. "Not that I'm suggesting that you're lying or confused, Tristan, but it is a similarity."

"When we were in the warehouse, right after we had arrived, Bauer talked to me. He asked me who my parents were because I looked like someone he used to know," Tristan explained. "He never said who – what if this is who this person is? Maybe I'm related to them?"

Charlemagne brought a hand to his chin and cleared his throat.

"I'm hesitant to make such an association, especially given my views on the entire incident on Halloween. I'm one to ascertain that the most likely explanation is probably the simplest one."

"Don't give me that Occam B.S., Charles," Tristan responded. "Do you really think it's a more likely and simpler explanation that we were hypnotized?"

"Calm your tone," Charlemagne warned. "I do."

"I can't believe you of all people are one to believe in that fallacy," Tristan then said. "I don't even believe in that."

"There's a reasonable explanation for everything, Tristan."

"Including the Halloween incident, and the simplest and most reasonable one is that we were right, and the lying, thieving G.D.P. lied to us."

Charlemagne let out a sigh.

"Tristan, I had a thought about all that is going on right now when I was driving home. I started to remember some details – details and memories of which occurred before Halloween. I do wish to get to the bottom of this mystery before I conclude indefinitely or make any objective statements about what had happened on Halloween. Given what you've just told me, and the sheer certainty within you, I'm of no use being your adversary or going against you. If I do, then you'll only defy me and possibly put yourself at harm's risk. Therefore, I'm going to help you and do whatever I can in my power to ease your mind about this 'awakened' memory of yours. Whatever you'd like, I will make it happen."

"Why am I just remembering this now?" Tristan asked. "Did Bauer set this upon me?"

"My guess is that, if this is a repressed memory, it was repressed due to the traumatic nature as is common in infants and children to do so. If it is a delusion, Bauer set it upon you."

Tristan scoffed and replied, "That's not what I meant when I asked if Bauer was to blame?" He then let out a sigh and said. "I meant – no, that's it! Bauer told me that God had something to tell me and that I needed to pray about it. That's what he said to me in the warehouse, and that's what he said to me again in the dream! I remember!"

"Why would Bauer cause you to have doubts about the death of your mother?"

"I don't know, but she was a motherly figure for sure. I'm not sure if she was my mom or not, because I do doubt it. My mother died in a car crash…"

"Perhaps this memory isn't as clear as you claim it to be."

"It was pretty damn clear," Tristan assured him. "I even remember the building behind the crowds of people – it was a movie theater, 'Midas Cinema.'"

Charlemagne did not immediately respond.

"I've never heard of such a brand name in either Alberta or B.C., but I'll take a look and see if I can find any such theaters elsewhere in the country."

Charlemagne let out a sigh.

"Is there anything else you want from me? To help ease this obsession?"

"I want to talk to Salmar," Tristan requested.

"Salmar?" Charlemagne questioned, turning his head. "What does my brother have to do with any of this?"

"He was supposedly friends with my parents. He's the only person I know that could possibly know of something like this. I want to talk to him."

Charlemagne looked at Tristan and held in a sigh.

"Very well," Charlemagne conceded. "We'll visit him. I'll make arrangements and we can drive to see him as soon as possible."

"Thank you," Tristan replied, looking to him. "I appreciate your help."

Charlemagne nodded to him and then left. Diana stepped forward and stood under the door frame.

"If you're coming down with something, maybe you should rest in your bed for the time being," Diana suggested. "I don't want to catch whatever you have."

"If I have something, you've probably either caught it already or gave it to me," Tristan replied with bitterness. "Sorry. I just didn't like the idea of being separate from you."

Diana sighed and replied, "I'm going to go downstairs to see if Mavis is around to make some soup. If not, I'm going to make some tea. I'll be right back."

"Thanks," Tristan responded as she left.

Tristan stood up from his bed and went to close his door, but stopped as he watched Diana leave. He followed her and caught the door behind her as she exited to the foyer. He held the door and saw Charlemagne ahead. She met with Charlemagne who was in the center of the lobby.

"You don't believe him, do you?" Diana questioned.

"Of course not," Charlemagne responded. "You know where I am right now. I'm highly skeptical and not sure what I can know or believe in. Tristan needs to re-evaluate himself. His delusion in the Halloween incident is going too far. I'm concerned about him, especially since at his age now, people with hereditary schizophrenia begin to present symptoms."

"Do you think he's a schizo?" Diana questioned with fear.

"I'm not certain," Charlemagne affirmed in a strict tone. "We only need to keep an eye on him for the time being. Understood? For all we know, his guilt in Finn's death may be escalating or taking a toll on him harder than one could anticipate. His onset of a viral infection isn't helping either."

"He said he didn't have a fever. I thought if you didn't have a fever, it wasn't likely to be an infection," Diana responded.

"He has a fever. I felt his forehead and he's burning a temperature over the mean. The best case is that he's experiencing nothing more than feverish delusions – but I doubt that."

Diana sighed.

"Tristan isn't one to believe in something unless he's certain," Diana pointed out. "I'm not even sure if he believes in God sometimes…"

"Tristan's probable atheism aside, let's focus on the more urgent issue," Charlemagne said. "I'm going to make some phone calls to the penitentiary where my brother is and see about their visiting hours. If we're lucky, we can see him this weekend as long as Tristan isn't doing too poorly."

"Okay," Diana replied. "I'm going to go see about some soup or tea."

"Thank you."

Tristan closed the door as the two parted ways. He returned to his room and gently closed the door. He then sat down and held a worried expression.

Charlemagne entered the library and went to his study, closing the door behind him and taking a deep sigh. He walked over to the chalkboard across the room and began to erase the various ideas he had on psionics, the soul, and mind control. He then went over to his desk and sat down. He looked up to the ceiling and closed his eyes. He then stood up and walked over to the fireplace, setting a fire for himself before resting hand over the fireplace mantle.

"What are we?" Charlemagne questioned. "DNA changes with every offspring and the genotype shifts. Godwilling, and the specimen breeds with its own, you have a likewise specimen that continues the legacy – that is what is right and what God intended: a continuation of asexual reproduction with moderate differentiation to combat harmful mutations – a continuation of the bloodline without extreme differentiation. What is it that drives us to reproduce? Is it an old instinct or something more? What is the purpose of all this?"

Charlemagne pushed himself off the fireplace and turned around. He put his hands behind his back and paced around the room. He then went to his chalkboard and drew a circle with an arrow pointing to a stick figure.

"DNA changes... the secret cannot be something within the code, but perhaps something within our code? Something that we code... something that remains the same... Am I being too literal? Am I obsessively looking for something physical, but is not physical?"

Charlemagne flipped the board and began to write. When he ran out of room, he flipped to the other side, erased what he had drawn, and continued to brainstorm. Once he was done, he set the chalk down and took a step back. He wiped the residue of chalk from his hands and then crossed his arms to look at what he had written.

The study was quiet. A howl of wind could be heard from outside in addition to the crackle of fire. He frowned and moved to his desk. He sat down and began to type. He looked at his computer screen for a short moment until he heard a knock on the door.

"Come in," Charlemagne encouraged.

The door opened and Diana entered. She held a tray with some tea.

"I forgot how you take your tea, so I left some sugar and cream on the side," Diana said, walking over. "I'm going to see Tristan and then call it a night."

"Right," Charlemagne responded. "Thank you. I just finished searching this 'Midas Cinema,' and it appears that it's a chain of cinemas in the United States. Specifically, within the Midwest and South."

"Tristan's never been to the United States, from what I recall at least... I'm going to ask him," Diana said. "Chances are, he's probably already searched the theater brand to try and pin the location..."

"Try not to be so blunt when asking him," Charlemagne suggested.

"Sure thing," Diana responded.

"It's possible that he was once in the United States at an early period in his life," Charlemagne said.

"Right."

"Let me know what he says," Charlemagne then said. "I'm going to phone North Alberta Penitentiary, and then I'm going to phone Miklos to have his team make sure that Tristan doesn't run off tonight."

"You don't think he'd do that, do you?" Diana asked.

"I cannot be too sure," Charlemagne repeated to her once more.

"Right," Diana replied. "How long of a drive is it from here to the prison?"

"About four to five hours," Charlemagne answered, picking up the phone at his desk "Give or take. I'll see you tomorrow. Goodnight."

"Goodnight."

Diana left and closed the door behind her. She then let out a sigh. She could hear Charlemagne speaking on the phone behind her. She felt a chill down as she heard Salmar's name in full, 'Salmar Clovis Cabernet.' Diana left the library and went back to the kitchen. She moved a pot of tea onto a tray, put a coat on it, and then carried the tray with a tea cup upstairs.

With one hand, Diana opened the door to Tristan's bedroom and saw him inside, lying on his side, above the covers of his bed.

"Still feel like crap?" Diana asked, walking over and setting the tray on Tristan's desk. "It'll help if you actually lie in bed with the covers over you."

"I'm fine," Tristan responded.

"Okay..." Diana replied, sighing. "Well, you might feel like crap, but know you're at least cherished crap."

Tristan didn't respond. Diana looked around the room and then back to Tristan.

"I finally talked to Moira while I was in the kitchen – that's why I took so long. Well, I didn't really talk to her, but Jock. He says that Moira might be leaving to go to the United States instead of returning to live with her mother."

"Good for her."

"I've never been across the border," Diana pointed out. "Have you?"

"Nope," Tristan replied. "Never."

"Huh."

Act 2, Scene 3

The next day, Diana, Tristan, and Charlemagne set off in the late morning to drive from Nattau County to North Alberta Penitentiary. Diana and Tristan sat in the back of Charlemagne's black sedan. Tristan continued to suffer from a stiff neck, but his body felt less fatigued than it was yesterday. The trip took about four hours and a half, but once they were there, they were able to park in the visitor parking lot and walk towards the visitor center.

The prison wasn't as daunting as any of them thought it would look like. It was less of a fortress, and no different than most government-owned properties. Prison-like qualities did exist from the exterior, including barred windows, a barbed-wired perimeter fence, and such. Charlemagne got out of his car and looked around the cold outdoors. The snow was much worse up north than it was in Nattau. The kids got out of the back of the car and walked with Charlemagne to the visitor center.

The entrance was warm and less formal than they had anticipated. Before them was a security desk with a corrections officer, armed with a firearm and electroshock pistol. The correction officer was dressed in black cargo pants and a black dress shirt. Overtop his shirt, he wore a ballistic vest similar to any police officer. There were multiple officers around as behind the reception desk, past a narrow aisle on the side, was a metal detector similar to the ones found in airports.

On the reception desk was a sign-in book and a sign that stated that visitors must present government identification. The corrections officer behind the desk stopped them a meter from the reception desk.

"Please state your business and present two pieces of government identification," the corrections officer stated.

"I'm here to see my brother, Salmar Cabernet," Charlemagne replied, taking out his passport and wallet from his jacket.

Charlemagne took his driver's license from his wallet, and laid it down on the table together with the passport. He then pushed them forward.

"I need two pieces of ID from each child as well," the corrections officer stated, looking at the pieces of Charlemagne's ID before returning them.

"Of course," Charlemagne replied.

The kids handed Charlemagne their driver's licenses and passports. Charlemagne gave them to the correction's officer who looked up and back at each piece of ID. He then returned them and turned around the sign-in book on the desk. He also picked up a grey bin and sat it down on the table.

"Please sign-in. If you have any metal objects, please remove them and place them in this bin, including any bags or purses."

Charlemagne picked up a pen on the table and wrote his name in the guestbook. He then handed it to the kids to do the same. Charlemagne then went forward and towards the metal detector. He stepped underneath and went through. Tristan then went next, and then Diana followed before they reunited in a waiting room that was painted in a single color of grey. The walls were grey, the concrete floor was grey, and even the chairs for them to wait on were grey. On the other side of the room was a mirror. Tristan looked at it as if someone was on the other side.

The three of them waited almost fifteen minutes until they heard a loud buzz of an alarm. A door at the opposite-side from where they had come through opened.

"Three for Mr. Salmar Cabernet, please step forward," a voice on a P.A. said.

The family stood up and walked over to enter a corridor that led to another door. A corrections officer led them through and they entered a larger and wider room with tables and chairs around. At the center of each table was a small device.

The visiting room had vending machines and a small play area for children. There were flat screen televisions on the wall and in the corner of the room was a diagonal wall with another mirror. The TVs were turned off. There were no guards in the room except the one that escorted them from the waiting room to the visitor room, but he soon left and the door behind them closed.

The three of them walked over and sat down at a table close to the next. There, they waited in the chilliness of the room for almost five minutes. Tristan looked around, eyeing the mirror. Diana also looked around, but looked at the toys in the play area and the vending machines. She frowned at the area.

"So, this is what a prison is like, huh?" Diana remarked.

"An appropriate place," Charlemagne remarked. "I hold no resentment against Salmar for what he did to me. I don't feel guilty either. He is here by his own actions."

Another buzz could be heard from a door across the room where a man behind the window of a door, dressed in blue prison garb, could be seen. Salmar's appearance was significantly different from when the children had seen him two years ago. He had a thick blonde beard and short hair. His face appeared as though he had aged ten years instead of two.

The crow's feet at the sides of his eyes were significantly more decrepit. His eyes were tired.

The door opened and he stepped into the room. Salmar was forward cuffed at the wrists and walked towards the family with shackles at his ankles. All three of them looked at him as he approached them. He then sat down at the other side of the table with a displeasing look on his face.

"I was expecting Allodia," Salmar remarked. "What are you doing here?"

"Tristan has some questions for you, Sal," Charlemagne replied. "He needs answers about his parents."

"What about them?" Salmar replied.

"You were close friends with them, according to him. He needs to know more details. Tristan, feel free to ask away."

Tristan didn't say anything and instead kept looking at his former guardian.

"Tristan?" Charlemagne questioned.

"You've grown a lot in the last two years, haven't you, Tristan?" Salmar questioned. "How has life faired you with this lunatic."

"As a matter of fact, it's been more than fine," Diana interrupted. "Charlemagne's taken better care of us than you could ever have hoped to achieve."

Salmar looked at Diana.

"Diana, you've grown too," Salmar noted. "You're more sensual to the eyes – beautiful."

"Shut up about Diana," Tristan replied. "We're here because we need to talk, not bicker or put up with you. I need to know more about my parents since you were friends with them."

"Why should I have to say anything to you, especially when you come here and talk to me like this?" Salmar questioned. "Did you think I'd so easily talk to the three of you after what I've been through because of you?"

"Because of us?" Charlemagne asked. "Have the two years not been enough for you to come to terms and realize that by your own hand and actions, you ruined your life, your practice, and your livelihood?"

"My life was ruined the moment that my wife died," Salmar simply said. "I have nothing more to live for."

"And from what I recall and believe, you adopted Tristan, accepted him to be your responsibility to honor her," Charlemagne stated, "but then in your own greed and lust for power, you abandoned him and left him to me. The least you can do is answer the little questions he has."

Salmar gave his brother a cold stare and then brought his cuffs to his lap. He had a hunch as he sat and looked away from his brother to Tristan with slight guilt as if he was a punished dog.

"Fine," Salmar said. "What do you want to know about your parents?"

"How did you meet them?" Tristan asked. "I never knew for certain what your relationship with them was like."

Salmar let out a sigh and answered, "I met your father when I came to St. Nazaire County as a mediator on behalf of the Albertan government to resolve a land dispute. In my time in St. Nazaire, your parents were hospitable towards me, invited me for dinner, and your father and I spoke frequently. I spent almost two years there, and in that time, I slowly became a family friend – your father was thankful for my assistance and we worked well together."

"Do you know if my dad ever brought me to a crime scene as a kid, perhaps on a ride along? If he did, did he ever take me to a shooting?" Tristan asked before explaining. "I keep having these bizarre flashbacks to a memory of a woman in a black cloak getting shot outside of a movie theater. I can't get it out of my head, especially since it was so vivid. I don't know why I'm remembering it now of all times to be remembering it."

"I cannot recall your father ever telling me something like that."

"Do you remember when they died?" Tristan asked.

"Of course," Salmar responded. "Do you not? After you stayed with your neighbors, I took you in as a foster parent before adopting you. The decision was difficult, especially since it required taking you with me back to Allabrese, but after the tragedy, I stepped down from my role in the negotiations and decided it to be best for you if I took you to a new environment."

Tristan looked down and then back to Salmar.

"For some reason, I keep seeing or believing the woman in black to be my mother – and that my mother was shot, but I can't remember by parents ever mentioning something like that happening. Then again, it's possible that I was very young and don't remember, but at the same time, I need to know from you – did my mom or dad ever mention to you about a time where she was shot at by a gun?"

"Never," Salmar stated.

"Why then? Why am I having these thoughts?" Tristan questioned.

Salmar shrugged. Tristan went quiet and looked to the side. After a brief moment, Salmar readjusted himself in his chair and brought his hands onto the table.

"I will say this about your parents," Salmar remarked. "Their death was not an accident."

"What?" Tristan replied. "What are you talking about? I thought the car reared off because of the blizzard that night...

Isn't that right, Charles? That's what the police report said, right?"

Charlemagne didn't respond. Tristan looked away from him and back to Salmar. Salmar began to laugh, looking around as if there were others in the room, laughing with him.

"Like Charlemagne said, it's only fair that I share the truth, so why not the whole truth? Your parents didn't die in an accident, they were assassinated, by a man on a motorcycle who shot their tires out while they were travelling along the highway."

Salmar continued to laugh to himself and then wiped some drool from the corner of his mouth. His handcuffs jingled and the others were speechless.

"Oh, come on," Salmar said. "You seriously didn't know? Even with my brother, for the past two years, keeping an eye on you – even in his own curiosity, he never looked deeper into the details of this supposed tragedy? He didn't look at the damage done to the tires, or the bullet holes on the rims?"

Tristan looked at him and began to grow pale. He started to lightly pant.

"Y-you're lying," Tristan accused him. "You're just messing with me!"

"Ask Charles then," Salmar replied.

Tristan looked to Charlemagne.

"I read the police report, and the RCMP concluded poor driving conditions to be the cause of the car accident," Charlemagne said. "He's lost it."

"How would you know if it was an accident or not?!" Tristan barked.

Salmar continued to laugh.

"Who killed them?!" Tristan shouted.

Tristan stood up, and as he stood up, Salmar raised himself and brought the chain of his handcuff around Tristan's neck.

"My master!" Salmar yelled as he attempted to strangle Tristan. "My master was the one to kill your parents!"

Charlemagne and Diana intervened. Charlemagne looked towards the mirror.

"We need help here!" Charlemagne yelled out.

"He will redeem me with this sacrifice!" Salmar chanted. "He will deliver me from this prison and punish the decadence of society! Hail Satan!"

Immediately, several corrections officers stormed the room and tackled Salmar onto the ground while another small team escorted the family out. The echoes of laughter could be heard as they were brought back into the waiting room. The corrections officers checked up on them to make sure they were okay.

"What a psycho!" Diana remarked, shocked.

Tristan sat on a chair and rubbed his neck. The chains in the attempted strangulation had left a red mark on the skin of his neck.

"Sorry about that," a corrections officer remarked. "Were any of you injured?"

Charlemagne finished examining Tristan and then turned around.

"He'll be fine," Charlemagne concluded. "Don't be sorry about him, though. He's a lost cause."

The corrections officer nodded and the family was escorted out of the prison through the way they came. They signed out on the guestbook and then stepped outside to return to the car.

"I hope you're okay," Diana said as they walked together to the car.

Tristan had his eyes focused ahead of him.

"They were murdered…" Tristan simply replied.

"Don't listen to that crackpot," Charlemagne pleaded. "He's lost it. For all we know, not a single word from his mouth was the truth. He was stalling to attempt to get at you."

"Why me?" Tristan questioned. "I didn't do anything against him? If anything, it'd make more sense to go after you."

"You did swing at him with a pipe…" Diana replied.

The trio returned to the car. Tristan stopped at the passenger seat door and looked to Charlemagne.

"How can we know for sure if he was lying or not?" Tristan asked. "You had access to the police report. Could we look at it again and see if there's any way that he could have been telling us the truth?"

Charlemagne sighed and looked at Tristan.

"The police take investigations seriously, and their conclusion was the most obvious sort. Your parents were driving on a poor night – a night in which it was recommended to drivers to not drive, but to stay indoors. The simplest explanation, as the police concluded, was for the weather to have been the cause of the crash, but in their urgency to return as it was Christmas Eve, they didn't listen."

"Are you saying that their urgency to see me, and make sure I didn't spend Christmas alone, was the reason they died?" Tristan questioned. "That's certainly cheerful."

Tristan opened the passenger seat door and sat inside.

"No, it's not…" Charlemagne responded, rolling his eyes.

Charlemagne and Diana looked at each other. Tristan sat in the car and looked annoyed. Diana entered and sat next to him. She held a worried look.

"Who could have killed my parents?" Tristan muttered under his breath before looking out the window.

Charlemagne entered and sat in the front. He ignited the engine and looked at Tristan through the rear-view mirror.

"I'm sorry my brother didn't give you anything helpful," Charlemagne said. "I knew it would have been a bad idea, but I'm supportive with whatever it may take to help you remember, or come to terms with what it is you're dealing with. I hope you know that."

Tristan didn't respond.

"Are you going to be alright?" Diana questioned.

"If my parents were murdered, it means they could have been spared. It means I could have still had them in my life…"

Diana looked at Tristan and then away from him. For the rest of the car trip home, the car was silent.

Act 2, Scene 4

Diana woke up on the following Monday in bed, stretching her arms and legs across to her right-side, feeling around at the emptiness beside her. She turned her neck and looked at the space where Tristan would typically sleep with her. She then sat up and looked around her room. There was a coldness in the room. She looked around, at the repaired glass from the fight that occurred in October when armed mercenaries attempted to storm the manor, and then atop of her desk before looking across the closed bathroom door.

The covers were pulled forward, and Diana got out of bed and grabbed a sweater from her desk chair. She pulled it over herself and walked towards Tristan's room. She passed the bathroom, which looked as though there had been steam from a shower as it was fairly wet inside, and then passed the gym to reach Tristan's room. Tristan wasn't in his room. The bed was made. His backpack was atop of his bed alongside his gym bag. Diana went around the bed and exited from Tristan's room. She went into Charlemagne's old lab and looked around. The room was empty. Diana continued her search downstairs, through the kitchen, and then came to the library before going to Charlemagne's study.

Diana knocked on the door and waited for a response. She then knocked again.

"Charles, it's Diana," Diana shouted in a calm tone. "I need to talk to you."

The door opened, but not by Charlemagne. Tristan, dressed and with a mess of dark orange hair, looked at her with grim eyes. The outlines of Tristan's eyes, which were usually dark, were darker than usual. He also looked tired.

"What's up?" Tristan asked.

"Tristan," Diana said, "what are you doing here? Are you with Charles?"

"No," Tristan responded, widening the door, "I'm just... doing a little research is all."

"On Charles' computer?" Diana questioned. "What's wrong with your computer?"

"Nothing," Tristan replied, walking back over to the desk and sitting down. "What's up?"

Diana walked and looked over to him.

"Did you sleep last night?" Diana asked, looking at Tristan's tired eyes.

"Yeah," Tristan replied.

"How are you feeling?" Diana then asked, walking over and bringing a hand to his cold forehead. "Your fever is gone."

After Diana had touched Tristan's forehead, she ran her hand through his hair and then rested it on his cheek for a moment.

"Hm?"

"I'm the same," Tristan said. "I had a hard time sleeping last night, so I woke up a little early to get ready for school and have been here to not disturb you."

"Right..." Diana replied with slight doubt. "Have you eaten?"

"Not yet," Tristan answered.

"Well, get something to eat then. Come on, you need to take care of yourself," Diana stated. "How else are you going to take care of patients in the future if you can't care for yourself?"

"Sure thing," Tristan replied. "Let me finish up here and then I'll have some cereal or something."

Diana nodded and then left. Tristan watched as she walked out and closed the door behind her. He then looked back to the computer screen. Diana went back upstairs to get ready for school, showered, and changed before going downstairs to have breakfast. Diana entered kitchen with disappointment as she noticed that Tristan was not here. She proceeded to make breakfast for the two of them only to be joined by him moments later.

The two sat together in the darkness of the dinette as the sun had just started to rise. The two talked minimally and ate awkwardly alone together. Once they were finished, Diana returned upstairs to round up her things into her backpack while Tristan went to his room. He then went to her room to meet with her. Diana brought her backpack around and looked at him. She was dressed in a white winter coat this time, while Tristan was dressed in his blue winter coat. He had both his backpack and gym bag with him. She walked over to him and gently fixed his hair. Tristan passively allowed her to touch his hair.

"Are you going to be okay going to school? Going to gym?" Diana asked, resting her hands on his side and looking at him.

"I might struggle a little, but I think I'll be fine," Tristan replied. "I don't think I was ever sick to begin with. I'm just under the weather is all, but saying what I said during the therapy session did do me a little good and I feel like I got a lot off my chest."

"Good..." Diana replied, letting go.

The couple walked out of Diana's room and then walked side-by-side downstairs and towards the garage. The truck waited for them, parked so that they could drive off immediately. Diana and Tristan brought their backpacks into the back canopy of the truck. Diana then went over to quickly feed Zephyr his morning meal while Tristan started the truck.

Tristan waited for Diana to finish, tapping the fingers of his right hand on the steering wheel and holding his head up with his other arm that had rested against the door. He looked out the windshield and directly ahead, looking at his cold breath in the cabin while the heaters continued to heat the cabin up. Diana returned after less than two minutes and sat down next to him.

Once she was inside, buckled up and ready, Tristan opened the garage door shutters and changed into drive to drive forward. He went up and over the hill to reach the automatic gates, and then pulled left onto the road to make his way towards the freeway.

"Hey, since you don't think you're sick," Diana said, "it'll be nice to have you back in bed since it's been awfully cold and lonely without you."

"Yeah, I know what you mean. Of course," Tristan replied as he reached the bridge. "I've missed you too."

"But I think you should see a doctor first," Diana remarked as they got to the end of the bridge. "I mean, you've felt terrible all weekend and it's not going to get any better. I don't want to catch anything as tempting as it'd be just to sleep with you again."

"I'm not sick," Tristan stated. "I don't see any signs of me being sick. I don't even know what it feels like to be sick, but from what I've heard from you and others: unpleasant. I haven't had a sore throat. I haven't had a runny nose or cough. My neck used to be stiff, but now my entire body is sore and that's why I'm a little grumpier than usual. I'm getting tired easily. I get the occasional headache, especially from looking at all this damn, bright snow."

"Maybe you're just weary from all the work you do at school and the gym. We're almost at the end of the year and winter break is just around the corner... hold out."

Tristan looked to Diana and then back to the front of the road as they approached the hill to town. He let out a sigh, but didn't immediately respond. He waited until he turned around the corner and made his approach towards the school.

"Okay," Tristan said after long hesitation, "I'll go to the walk-in clinic at the hospital after school and get a second opinion."

"Thank you," Diana replied with genuine gratitude. "I mean, what's the worst thing the doctor can say? That you're sick? We'll simply sleep in our own beds for another couple days and that's it. I mean, in reality, the worst thing that could happen is that they try to draw some blood. I know how much you hate needles, and..."

"Yeah," Tristan interrupted, reaching the school and looking forward with focused eyes. "Needles..."

"Hey! Watch out!" Diana shouted.

Tristan refocused and looked ahead. A cyclist crossed in front of the pickup truck. Tristan quickly hit the brakes, causing them to lurch forward and the vehicle to shake as the anti-lock braking system kicked in. The pickup truck stopped a foot from where the cyclist had been, but the cyclist had disappeared from their sight.

"Did I hit him?" Tristan questioned, shifting gears and looking around.

"No, don't think you did," Diana replied.

Diana looked around at all the people in front of the school who stopped and looked. Tristan saw the cyclist who had fallen over before them stand up, pick his bicycle up and look over to him with a red angry face.

"Pay attention, you maniac!" the cyclist shouted, walking across the crosswalk and onto the sidewalk. "You could have killed me!"

Tristan looked away from him and began to notice all the people around. He was breathing heavily. A car honked at them from behind, causing Tristan to look in the rear-view mirror and then to Diana.

"What are you doing? Let's go!" Diana remarked with a slight scold.

Tristan didn't reply. His heart continued to patter and he continued to breathe heavily. Diana observed that his right hand was trembling as he changed gears and switched into reverse. The car went backwards and nearly hit the car directly behind them. Tristan quickly braked as it honked.

"Christ!" Diana yelled out, holding on. "Tristan!"

Tristan frowned and changed back into drive, pressing his foot down to accelerate and go towards the school parking lot.

"Nice driving! You could've killed that man!" Diana nagged.

Tristan continued to pant lightly and turned into the parking lot. He looked around and over to the school and then made a loop around before reaching the exit from the parking lot. Without stopping, he turned left and began to drive past the school again. Diana looked at the school as they made their pass and started to make their way back to the freeway.

"Uh, where are you going?" Diana questioned. "You just left the school."

Tristan didn't respond and looked ahead at the green light at the intersection with the freeway with no oncoming traffic from the opposite way. He accelerated and sped forward, embracing the adrenaline within him as he went over the speed limit and turned left back onto the freeway. Diana held on.

"What are you doing?!" Diana complained, looking at her mute boyfriend. "Tristan! Say something! Where are we going?!"

Tristan sped along the freeway, left town, and went down the hill and back towards the bridge. Instead of turning left to return to the manor, he went right and in the direction of going towards the airfield. Diana noted the change in direction and later noted that they passed the exit for the freeway. She had given up in attempting to communicate with Tristan, but her concern remained as she too began to pant lightly and grow pale. She took a deep breath and looked at Tristan.

"I swear to God, Tristan," Diana said. "First, this obsession over Halloween, and then, this obsession over this... this 'memory,' and now...? What now?" she asked. "Please, Tristan, please talk to me and tell me what it is you're doing?"

Diana expressed herself with genuine fear and concern. Tristan eased his fingers from around the steering wheel and slowed down as they rolled along the highway, going north, and exiting the county. He glanced over to Diana and saw the fear within her.

"You think I'm a schizo, don't you?" Tristan asked with disappointment. "You and Charles think I'm losing it... but I'm not, Diana! I'm not..."

"Tristan, we're just concerned because we don't know what's going on in your head. I of all people in your life want to know what it is that's going through your head, but in order to do that, you need to communicate with me. So please, please tell me where we're going."

"I'm sorry," Tristan responded with remorse. "I didn't mean to scare you..."

"I love you like no other," Diana said. "Sometimes I feel like you don't understand that, so when you do stuff like this, and you act like this, it makes me fearful because it is the man that I love who is doing this, and it's like he's not mindful of me."

Tristan let out a sigh.

"I'm sorry..." Tristan apologized. "I just... I just need honest answers, Diana. You need to understand that as much. I need to know who that woman who was shot was, who my parents were and how they died, and I need to know why... why this is all happening to me now."

Diana let out a sigh of her own and replied, "Okay, Tristan."

"Are you okay then?" Tristan asked.

"I mean, it's not like I have any say in the matter since you've practically kidnapped me..." Diana replied. "You could have just asked... but then again, I can understand your reluctance to."

"I'm sorry," Tristan repeated, "it was more of a heat of the moment sort of thing. I won't ever do something like this again. I promise."

Diana sighed again and then asked, "Where are we going?"

"We're going to my hometown," Tristan answered. "St. Nazaire. I need to learn more from the people there about all these questions I have. Hopefully, I can get some answers."

Diana nodded and rested her head against the passenger seat window. She looked out and down towards the canyon where the Nattau River was. By the time that the couple had settled, it had started to snow as they began their journey northwards to the little town of St. Nazaire.

• • •

Charlemagne stood at his chalkboard in his study, staring at an equation on the board and tapping his lower lip with the piece of chalk as he thought. He soon gave up and returned to his desk, sitting down and signing into his computer. He then looked to the side of his desk where there was a picture of him, Judith, and Barry, which had previously been in Judith's office.

A knock on the door caught Charlemagne by surprise, causing him to pivot his chair back and look ahead.

"Come in," Charlemagne remarked, tidying his desk and looking over as the door opened.

Mavis walked in with a tray of tea and a plate of cookies.

"Time for you tea and snack, Mr. Cabernet," Mavis remarked, walking over and setting the tray down on his desk.

"Thank you, my dear," Charlemagne replied, looking at the empty cup with sugar cubes at the bottom and the white pot of steaming hot tea.

Mavis picked up the pot and began to pour some tea into the cup as he phone rang. Charlemagne looked over and saw that the machine listed the number as 'Lord Phoenix Secondary School,' forcing him to roll his eyes as he checked the time.

"It's not even ten minutes past ten," Charlemagne said with a sigh. "What has Diana done this time?"

"Let me answer it," Mavis offered, setting the pot down and wiping her hands with the cloth around her waist.

"No, no," Charlemagne replied, putting his hand around the phone. "I'm responsible for her. I'll answer."

Charlemagne picked up the phone and brought it to his ears.

"Cabernet Residence, Charlemagne speaking," he said, leaning back in his chair and expecting to hear Sabrina on the other line.

"Hello, Mr. Cabernet, this is Meredith. I'm calling in regard to the unexcused absence of Diana and Tristan from homeroom this morning as well as first period. I am unsure of whether this absence is to your attention, and would like to clarify with you the means by which you can call in sick for either or both students."

"Oh?" Charlemagne questioned, scratching his head. "They were absent from class this morning? I... I believe Tristan was feeling unwell, but I'm not sure about Diana. You'll have to accept my apologies, love, but I've had a busy morning. I must've... forgotten to call, but nonetheless, please excuse them from their classes today as I come to recall, they are both ill as Diana just today, began to come down with a terrible fever. I'll ensure they rest well and are able to make up for the lost time as soon as possible."

"Thank you, and no worries, Mr. Cabernet," Meredith replied. "I'm just calling to ensure that they're not being truant is all. Have a good day, and if they won't be attending tomorrow, please just call before the school day has begun. Have a good day!"

"Yes... have a good day yourself," Charlemagne replied, bringing the phone down.

Charlemagne looked over to Mavis.

"Did Diana or Tristan go to school today?" Charlemagne asked. "I was out at the time."

"I believe so," Mavis responded. "I saw them off when I was in the kitchen."

"Well, the school just called and said that they were absent," Charlemagne replied, slightly frustrated. "What are they up to?"

Charlemagne opened a software on his computer, which displayed a global map. He clicked around and presented

Tristan's name on the map, hovering and moving along the northern highway.

"Where is he going?" Charlemagne questioned, zooming out to view the entire province and neighboring provinces and states.

Act 3, Scene 1

Diana and Tristan were silent for the majority of the five-hour road trip from Allabrese to St. Nazaire. They had left the Nattau Valley hours ago, leaving behind the Rocky Mountains and Nattau River and exchanging them for the smooth plains and farmland of the province's interior. The skies were grey and a bright silhouette of the sun could be seen poking through the clouds. The sun continued to shine down, but was headed towards the western horizon with minimal daylight remaining.

Tristan focused on the road, driving with both hands at the steering wheel and maintaining a serious expression. Diana continued to lean her head against the window and mindlessly thought to herself. The radio was turned off, the heater kept the cabin warm, but the silence divided them. Diana's eyes watched the passing scenery, which was all engulfed in a thick blanket of snow. It continued to snow, but lightly as they drove. The roads were clear.

Diana straightened her posture as she moved her head away from the window and brought it back against the headrest of her chair. She could see glimpses of civilization on the horizon ahead of them. She read a passing traffic sign, instructing them that they were less than five kilometers from St. Nazaire. Diana gave off a sigh and crossed her arms.

Tristan continued to drive with the lack of traffic going into town, going along the straight road with an incredible attention to his surrounding and a fixation to not make Diana regret helping him.

The pickup truck passed a colorful sign welcoming them to St. Nazaire, which made Tristan's stomach flip and palms sweat as he returned home. He continued to drive, reaching the town and causing Diana to look around. She eyed the various structures and observed the quiet nature of the hamlet that made Allabrese look like a bustling metropolis.

"So, this is where you grew up then…" Diana commented in a quiet voice. "It's… certainly a contrast to where I grew up."

"Yeah," Tristan replied, "this is where I grew up."

Diana looked ahead at an old building with a domed roof, and then back to a church with a bell tower much like St. Allan's in Allabrese. They drove down a single road that brought them past many shops and got closer to a large roundabout with a park in the middle. Diana began to see more people walking about in the quiet snowfall.

"Alright, so where to now?" Diana asked with a coarse voice, keeping an eye out.

"I'm trying to remember the directions to my neighborhood," Tristan replied, going around the roundabout and then turning left. "I still remember. It's coming back to me. I used to walk home on my own."

Diana observed the RCMP detachment with various white police cars parked on the curb, a fire hall with a fire engine parked out, and other sights. Tristan drove them away from the town and back into some suburbs where the homes were a single-story tall in contrast to homes in Allabrese which were typically two-stories in height.

"Oh look," Diana remarked. "Cute little rancher homes…"

Diana looked at the homes, seeing some to be quite patriotic with the red ensign Canadian flag waving on poles from the roofs of homes. Tristan turned left down a road, reached a street called 'Gardner Avenue' and then continued along as they started to reach a dead-end. Diana noticed a cul-de-sac at the end of the road.

Tristan slowed down. The appearance of the neighborhoods, other than the size and style of the homes, was distinct to the town. The street lamps were traditional-looking three-headed lamps on black poles. The sidewalks were thinner than the ones in Allabrese and the roads were thicker. Tristan stopped the car ten meters from the start of the cul-de-sac, pulling over and shifting gears as he looked ahead nostalgically.

"Are we here?" Diana queried. "Which house was yours?"

"The beige one," Tristan answered. "The one on the right from the middle."

Diana looked over at the five rancher homes and saw the one that Tristan had described. A jeep was parked in the driveway of the home, and lights could be seen lit up inside. Diana looked over to Tristan who wasn't looking at the home, but digging his nails into the steering wheel as he simply looked forward.

"Thank you for bringing me to your home," Diana remarked, taking Tristan's right hand and looking at him. "I'm glad I was here with you for this. What now though?"

"I don't know," Tristan replied. "Do you want to go look at the house?"

Diana gave a warm smile to Tristan and nodded. He opened the door and got out of the car, walking around to rejoin Tristan as he got out from the driver's seat. Tristan locked the car and looked at Diana who walked with him.

"Thanks for coming, Diana."

"Of course," she replied.

The couple walked along the sidewalk together. Diana paid attention to the howl of the wintery wind in the background as well as the whistle of birds nearby. They reached the cul-de-sac and Tristan led Diana over so that they could stand in front of Tristan's old home.

"It's smaller than I imagined," Diana remarked. "I always thought you came from a larger home. Like Salmar's house."

"Yeah, it's smaller than I remember to be honest," Tristan replied. "I remember when my dad taught me how to ride a bike on this very driveway, or when I fell out from that tree over there and my mom had to bring me in for stitches."

"What about friends? Did you have any that you had to leave behind when you moved?"

"Everybody was friends with everybody in this town. It's such a small town that you can't really forget or not know somebody. We had a strong community – the church helped with that, and it really played a large role in the cohesion of the townspeople. I remember all my friends from before…"

"That sounds nice," Diana replied. "It sounds like the polar opposite from the big city. I barely knew anyone, and those people that I do know, I have some sort of negative connotation with them."

Tristan gave a light laugh and turned around.

"I remember playing on these streets with the neighborhood kids. We used to play all sorts of games no matter the season," Tristan recalled. "And with the boys, we'd used to turn the street into a hockey rink, or sometimes a soccer pitch. It was great…"

Diana turned around as she heard a door slam behind them. She saw a lady with blonde hair walk out from her home with a beagle on a leash, coming to a sidewalk and begging to take a stroll. Directionally, she was making her way towards them. The woman was dressed elegantly, in black clothes with a brown cloak over her torso. Diana ignored her and looked back at the former Merrick Residence.

"If we don't build our own home in the countryside like we said we would when we're older, then I want to move into a rancher like this," Tristan said.

"Okay," Diana replied, listening to the jingle of the dog's collar and steps of the woman headed towards them.

Tristan took notice of the lady, turning his neck to her and the dog as they got closer. The lady smiled at him, which as when Tristan recognized her. The woman recognized him too and dropped an expression of shock.

"Tristan? Tristan Merrick is that you?!" the woman questioned. "What are you doing here? I thought you moved away?!"

Tristan smiled. The woman looked at Diana with an equally large smile.

"It is me," Tristan said with a warm smile. "I did move away though…"

"And who is this young lass with you?" the woman asked, smiling to Diana.

"This is my adoptive-sister, Diana," Tristan replied. "Diana, this is Mrs. Templeton. She was my godmother at my baptism, and she also took me in after my parents died."

"Pleasure to meet you, Diana," Mrs. Templeton said, shaking Diana's hand before looking to Tristan. "My, you've grown so much! What brings you back here? Just a visit?"

"No," Tristan responded, "actually, I'm here because I've been curious about my parents lately. I wanted to know some answers about their death…"

"Oh, what about their death?" Mrs. Templeton asked with a saddened face. "Their death was such a tragedy. You don't understand how heavily it impacted our town. We all miss them very much."

Mrs. Templeton said, looking at both of them. She then looked to the dog.

"Sorry, I was just going to walk the dog, but why don't you come back with me for some tea? Do you remember Gamaliel? Oh, of course you do – I'm sure he'd be pleased to see you again when he gets back from school. What grade are you in? Weren't you in the same grade? I suppose you'll be graduating soon and going on to university. Oh, come and follow me back to the house. He'll love to see you again, and perhaps we can help with some of these curiosities of yours."

Diana looked to Tristan as he started to follow her. She looked uncomfortable, but followed Tristan as they went to this woman's home. Mrs. Templeton unlocked the front door and then entered with the dog. She let the dog off the leash and removed her shoes as she went forward. Tristan followed with Diana and proceeded to take off his own shoes.

"Shoes, Diana," Tristan warned in a whisper before taking off his jacket.

"Come and make yourself at home in the living room," Mrs. Templeton remarked. "I'll put the kettle on and be back in a bit."

Mrs. Templeton left the kids in the foyer of the house. Diana removed her shoes and jacket, and then walked with Tristan into the living room where they sat down on a couch. The dog had followed the woman into the kitchen. She later returned with a plate of cookies and sat them down on the coffee table in the middle of the room. Mrs. Templeton then sat down on another couch at the other side of the room.

"So, what is it about your parents that made you come all the way back here?" Mrs. Templeton asked. "Where did you move to – with Salmar, right?"

"I moved to Allabrese," Tristan answered. "It's a small town south from here. Salmar took me in, but I didn't stay with him for long. I'm now with his brother, Charlemagne, which is why I'm with Diana."

"Oh, and what happened to Salmar?" Mrs. Templeton asked.

Tristan told her about what had happened that summer between Salmar and Charlemagne. He explained the plot to attempt to force Charlemagne's fortune into his hands, the endangerment that Salmar had placed him through, and his incarceration. He also told her that Charlemagne had adopted him afterwards with Diana as his adoptive-sister.

"My goodness, I would never have imagined that Salmar to be such a fiendish character," Mrs. Templeton remarked, standing up. "Excuse me while I fetch the tea."

Mrs. Templeton left and then returned with a pot and four cups on a tray.

"How has life been with Salmar's brother? You must be living well if he's such a rich man," Mrs. Templeton remarked.

"Charles has been a good parent. He's an interesting person and he's taken care of the both of us as if we were his own," Tristan explained. "As a matter of fact, I talked to Salmar last weekend, and when we talked, he told me something that made me uncomfortable… He told me that my parents' death wasn't an accident, but that they were assassinated – killed."

"Killed?! Oh my…" Mrs. Templeton replied, bringing a hand to her chest. "An assassination in our little town?! Who – why?!"

"Salmar knew about it, he was a part of it, but he didn't do it. I believe him because he was fiendish enough, as you say, to attempt to kill his own brother, but I'm stumped as to why this was dismissed by the police and who it was that killed them.

Why?" Tristan said. "Do you know about anybody that could have hated my parents? Did they ever upset anybody in town? Perhaps something gang-related?"

"My, oh no," Mrs. Templeton responded. "Your father, of course, was in charge of the detachment here, but there has never been any gangs in this town, ever. I couldn't think of anyone that would hold such a vendetta against your parents. After all, they were model citizens – well respected and loved. We were always by their side, even during the worst of it. Oh, we prayed and prayed for them during the hard times they experienced, what with your mother's infertility and all."

"Infertility? What infertility?" Tristan questioned.

Mrs. Templeton looked back at Tristan. She held an embarrassed look and picked up the pot. She avoided eye contact with Tristan and became shy.

"Tristan..." Mrs. Templeton expressed, pouring tea. "I suppose you had never heard from them, nor were they given the chance to ever tell you about this, but... You deserve the truth. Tristan, you were adopted. Elisabeth and Zachariah Merrick aren't your biological parents."

"W-what?" Tristan questioned. "How? I don't understand..." he responded, panting lightly and growing pale again. "No, this can't be true. They were my parents. I... I can't be adopted. I look just like them – I look just like my mother. Our phenotypes... are a match! I have his chin... I have her eyes... I..."

"I'm sorry I have to be the one that tells you this, especially since it was no right of mine, but it wouldn't be right if you left here without knowing. You deserved the truth so that you can make peace with it," Mrs. Templeton stated before sighing. "Let me explain. Your mother was heavily infertile. She and your father had trouble conceiving, but then, on one Christmas

Eve, you were left on their doorstep. Your mother described it to me at church as it being a Christmas miracle, because it truly was. From nowhere, you appeared in their lives as the most beautiful littlest boy… and they instantly fell in love with you and adopted you. Finding a child on your doorstep is something out of fiction – something you'd expect to read, or see in a movie, but not in real life…"

"How old was I?" Tristan questioned, growing more depressed.

"Two months old," Mrs. Templeton stated. "You were two months old. You were just a little infant at the time. Your father sent a province-wide notice about your appearance so that your true parents could retrieve you, but that never happened. When nobody claimed you, they fostered you and then adopted you."

"I can't believe this…" Tristan responded. "What the heck? Who are my real parents then? Who left me here?"

"That is something that I do not know, Tristan," Mrs. Templeton remarked. "Not even your own parents knew who you were, or where you had come from? All they knew was that you were theirs and God had delivered you to them."

Tristan took a deep breath and leaned forward, clasping his hands together and resting his elbows on his knees. He looked to the side, towards the fireplace. Diana watched him as she drank her tea, showing pity as Tristan endured the truth.

"Don't be down from this," Mrs. Templeton requested. "You were brought to two wonderful people – a couple that loved you very much as if you were their own flesh. They did all they could to raise you as well as they could before they had passed away. For all they cared, you were theirs and they were your parents. Even if they didn't get to see you born, name you, or understand where you had come from?"

"Name me…?" Tristan questioned.

"That's right," Mrs. Templeton responded. "On the night that they had found you, they chose to respect the name that had been given to you already. Your mother said that you were found with a necklace around your neck. The necklace had a charm on it of Saint Luke, and behind it was your birthday and name, 'Tristan.'"

Tristan reached into his shirt and dug out the necklace with the charm.

"Yes, that's it!" Mrs. Templeton cheered. "I'm so happy you have it still. It's all that was left with you by whoever your true parents were."

Tristan looked at the icon of the saintly figure and then turned around to read his name. Diana looked at Tristan before looking over to Mrs. Templeton. The three of them then looked over to the foyer as they heard the front door unlocking and then opening. A young teenager, the same age as Diana and Tristan, entered and looked over to them. Tristan and the boy instantly recognized each other.

"Tristan?" the boy questioned.

"Gam," Tristan greeted.

"Oh, Gam!" Mrs. Templeton said, standing up and smiling as she went over to her so. "Look who's here! It's Tristan Merrick. Come… Why don't you sit down and catch up?"

Gamaliel was brought over and forced to sit down with his backpack, shoes, and jacket still on. Mrs. Templeton looked over with a happy smile.

"Rumor around school is that you moved to a bigger town," Gamaliel remarked to him.

"Yeah, I did," Tristan replied.

"Mal, your shoes," Mrs. Templeton scolded, standing up. "Oh, Tristan, we'd be more than happy if you stayed for dinner. We're interested to learn more about your new life with Charlemagne in Allabrese."

"Diana and I would love to stay," Tristan replied, looking at Diana who gave him a look that said the opposite.

"Excellent," Mrs. Templeton cheered. "Gamaliel's father won't be much long – he'll be home soon. We won't keep you around for too long…"

Mrs. Templeton stood up and left to the kitchen. Gamaliel followed her to the foyer so that he could properly arrive, removing his jacket, shoes and backpack before disappearing for a moment.

"Tristan…" Diana said in a light whisper, "can I have your phone? It's a quarter past three and I think it'd be a good idea if I called Charles to let him know that we won't be returning home from school for a while."

"Yeah, good idea," Tristan replied, taking out his phone and looking at the lock screen.

The couple looked at the twenty or so notifications that filled the screen, which consisted of text messages from Charlemagne as well as seven missed phone calls.

"Oh jeez…" Diana muttered. "Busted."

Tristan looked at his phone with horror, but gave it to Diana to hold on to. She put it away in her pocket as Gamaliel returned. Diana observed that he had dark brown hair and was about as fit as Tristan, if not slightly larger and taller.

"So, you live with a billionaire now, huh?" Gamaliel exclaimed.

'Yeah," Tristan replied with a nervous laugh. "I do."

Diana looked away as the two old friends began to banter. She looked towards the fireplace and held a worried look on her face, thinking of the inevitable lecture that awaited them in Allabrese.

Act 3, Scene 2

Diana and Tristan stayed at the Templeton Residence for another two hours until Gamaliel's father, Simon, returned so that they could have dinner. All of them were fascinated to learn what Tristan's life had been like since he left St. Nazaire and came into the care of Charlemagne de la Cabernet. Likewise, Tristan was happy to be with them again.

At the end of the meal, Mrs. Templeton had started to stand up as she took plates to move them to the kitchen. Tristan stood up to help as the others got up, but she looked over to Tristan with a scolding look.

"Now, now," Mrs. Templeton remarked. "Your sister and you are guests. We can't let our guests doing housework."

"Sorry," Tristan replied with a shameful smile, sitting down.

The family took the plates and moved them to the kitchen, leaving Tristan and Diana alone for a moment.

"We should think about getting back on the road," Diana said, looking at the time on Tristan's phone. "We have a six hour drive ahead of us, in the darkness, and even I'm starting to get nervous about what Charles is going to say to us when we come home past our curfew."

"Not yet," Tristan said. "I still have more questions. We still don't know why my *adoptive-parents* were murdered, who killed them, or what the motive was. We don't even know who that lady in my memory was, or anything. We'd be leaving with more unanswered questions. If there was some sort of plot so that Salmar could adopt me, I want to know what that could have possibly have been. I want to know who I am, and what is so special about me to warrant all this secrecy..."

"And do you expect to get all of those answers in the next hour or so? We have to head back home now. It's getting to be late and it's a long way home. Aren't you getting tired?"

"I am tired, but I have an incentive to put all my needs aside for the day if it means getting some solid answers. I need to know who that woman was in that memory... Was she my mother? It would make sense now. It's probably why I mistook her for my mom."

"You were less than two months old," Diana rationalized. "How could you remember something that happened when you were two-months old?"

"I don't know," Tristan replied, "but I have a good feeling about it. For all we know, my real parents could be alive. I might not be an orphan! Isn't that worth the sacrifice? To find out?"

Diana looked at him and didn't share the same sentiment. Mrs. Templeton and Gamaliel returned from the kitchen and sat down at the table.

"Tristan, my wife and I were just talking in the kitchen, and she told me about what you had learned from Salmar – that your parents were supposedly murdered. I worked with your father for fifteen years, and I'd hate to think that his death could have been prevented if it were in the hands of another man, but I also worked on that investigation and didn't see how it could have been possible that they were killed..."

"Salmar described tires getting shot by a man on a motorcycle," Tristan replied. "That's all the information he shared with me."

Mr. Templeton nodded and thought to himself.

"Well then, why don't you two come with me down to the station and I'll let you review the case file yourself. I understand how much this must pain you to know that your parents were taken from you by a man and not nature, and so it's the least I can do to honor your folks."

"That would be really nice of you," Tristan replied, standing up and looking over to Diana.

Diana was not pleased. Tristan looked back at Mr. Templeton.

"Can we go now?" Tristan asked.

"Of course," Mr. Templeton replied. "Let's get over there before it gets any later. It's already dark out."

Diana and Tristan followed him to the entrance of the home where they got their boots and jackets on. Mr. Templeton put on an RCMP jacket with three chevrons and the front lapel reading his name, 'SGT. S. TEMPLETON.'

"Drive safely," Mrs. Templeton warned. "You never know what the weather out there might turn on you!"

"Of course, dear," Mr. Templeton replied. "Come on, we'll ride in my cruiser."

Mr. Templeton opened the front door after he put on his coat. He then stepped out and went to the police cruiser parked behind the jeep. He unlocked it and then opened the back door for the kids to ride in the back. Diana and Tristan sat inside and saw that it was not the most comfortable back seat as it wasn't cushioned and very tight. The plastic seats were cold too. Once the kids were settled in the back, Mr. Templeton drove the car out from the cul-de-sac and then forward down the street.

Diana looked at the pickup truck, which had been covered in a medium layer of snow since they parked it. Tristan felt nervous as they rode with Mr. Templeton like a pair of criminals behind the bars that divided the front and rear of the car. He looked outside and towards town. He then looked over to the RCMP detachment where his father used to work at. Diana looked with him.

The RCMP Detachment was not a large building. It was quiet and a few lights were turned on outside. Mr. Templeton parked on the curb with the other police cars and opened the back door for the boys to get out. They then walked up the steps and into the station were a single police officer stood behind a desk in the small office.

"What brings you back so soon?" the constable questioned, straightening up in his chair. "Is that who I think it is?"

"Yes it is," Mr. Templeton responded. "It's Merrick's kid. He's concerned about the fate of his folks, and I thought I'd do him a favor and show him the police report."

"Right," the constable replied as Mr. Templeton walked over to a series of filing cabinets in the back of the room.

Mr. Templeton took out a set of keys from his belt and unlocked the filing cabinet, taking out a thick folder and bringing it over to a desk that belonged to him. It had a picture frame with his family in it.

"I miss your father, son. He was like a brother to me – to all of us here," Mr. Templeton remarked, sitting down at his desk and bringing the folder down. "I hope you can find what you're looking for."

Mr. Templeton nudged the cover of the folder over and opened it up. He then stood up and allowed Tristan to sit.

"Take your time," Mr. Templeton encouraged. "Please."

Tristan looked at the first sheet of paper, reading its title, which read 'Autopsy Report.' He started to rummage through all the pages, assessing each one and trying to figure out where to begin.

"Can you help me?" Tristan asked Diana, dividing the stacks of paper.

"Sure," Diana replied, taking her stack and getting to work.

Tristan read the autopsy report over and over again, learning what it was in the crash that managed to take their life. Mr. Templeton left them and conversed with the constable. Tristan sighed.

"At least they died quickly..." Tristan muttered, reading that they had died of snapped necks due to the force of the crash.

Tristan continued to read and found nothing unusual about their corpses. He then went over to the assessment of the vehicle, seeing for himself that both tires on the right-side had blown out, but also the ones on the left. Tristan showed Diana the vehicle assessment.

"Are there any pictures?" Diana asked, finishing the police report.

"I think there are some of the wreckage," Tristan replied, going through the papers.

"Oh, here they are," Diana said, finding them in the stack. "Look at the tires..."

"How can we tell if they were shot out?" Tristan replied, looking at the pictures. "Something like that would be such a minor detail..."

Diana took the pictures back and they continued to go through the papers.

"They had different blood types from me," Tristan said.

"What does that mean?" Diana asked.

"It means they weren't my parents after all," Tristan replied, sighing.

The telephone rang at the front of the station, catching Diana and Tristan by surprise as they looked over. The on-duty constable picked it up and answered. Diana looked over as the phone was given to Mr. Templeton.

"Hello, RCMP St. Nazaire Detachment," Mr. Templeton greeted. "How can I help you?"

Diana watched him before going back to look at the picture before him. She looked at the tires with doubt. She couldn't tell if the damage to the right-side was deliberate or an effect of the accident. Diana began to compare the right-side with the left-side.

Tristan quietly took a picture of the autopsy report with his phone. He then sat back with a dissatisfied look on his face.

"Are you okay?" Diana asked.

"I'm sore, tired, and hopeless… There's nothing here that tells me that Salmar was telling the truth or not."

"Tristan, the bottom-line is that your parents are dead, and even if we did find something that did prove otherwise, it wouldn't do much because we'd have no idea who it could have been that murdered them."

"What Salmar told me is bothering me – his master. Who was he talking about? Who was his master?" Tristan questioned, looking over to Mr. Templeton as he looked over to them whilst talking on the phone.

"I don't know, and honestly, the way he said that makes me think that he was lying," Diana confessed. "He's a lunatic, Tristan. He's been in prison for two years – his sanity is gone."

"Maybe," Tristan replied, "and then again, it still led us here where I at least learned the truth about them not being my biological parents."

"Hey, they may not have been your biological parents, but they were still your parents. Don't forget that about them."

"Right," Tristan responded, smiling at her.

Mr. Templeton walked over.

"I just had a word with your guardian, Charlemagne," Mr. Templeton remarked, crossing his arms. "He asked about you two, said that you had gone missing, and that he thought you might turn up here because of all this business with your parents. I'm not going to scold you, but I told him that you were with me and that I'd keep an eye on you."

Tristan swallowed his breath as he looked at Mr. Templeton with shame.

"I didn't realize you two had ran off," Mr. Templeton said, "but nonetheless, I told your guardian that you were safe. He wants you to come home as soon as possible, but I said it was too late and that I'd personally drive you back tomorrow morning rather than tonight. It's a long trip from here to Allabrese, and you've learned quite a lot about your parents, Tristan. My home is open to you again, and your sister, to stay the night."

"Thank you, Mr. Templeton," Tristan replied, feeling extremely gracious for his hospitality and patience. "Really."

"Don't worry about it, Tristan," Mr. Templeton replied. "It's a good reminder for you to know that you're still a part of this community. Both of you."

Tristan nodded and looked over to Diana. Mr. Templeton looked past them as the door to the police station opened. Diana and Tristan turned their necks over to look at the two men who had arrived and stood in front of the front desk. Each figure was rugged in appearance, sporting different degrees of unshaven facial hair and buzz cut hair. They were stocky, wearing different colored winter coats, one brown with a white shirt and the other blue with a striped collar shirt.

"How can I help you?" the constable at the desk greeted.

"We are here to retrieve the children," one of the men replied in a thick Russian accent, pointing over to Diana and Tristan.

Tristan's stomach flipped as he heard that accent.

"What seems to be the problem?" Mr. Templeton responded, going over with a hand at his holster.

Tristan watched as a thug took out a handgun from his jacket and shot at Mr. Templeton.

"Christ!" Tristan remarked, ducking with Diana as the other constable opened fire.

"*Khvatay yego!*" the thug cried out, pointing over to the boys as the other shot the other officer. "*Nye day im uyti!*"

Tristan saw one of the thugs come over with a pistol pointed at him. He grabbed the chair behind him and threw it at him, while Diana seized the picture of the tires and stuffed it into her jacket.

"G-get out of here!" Mr. Templeton yelled from the floor, firing back at the man.

Diana looked over to Mr. Templeton as he had been shot in the vest. Tristan grabbed her and fled with her into the back of the police station. Gunshots could be heard.

"Holy crap, what do we do?" Diana questioned, panicking.

"Come on," Tristan encouraged, knocking a shelf over and then running to a fire escape.

Tristan and Diana left the police station and continued to hear gunfire as they looked back. The two then ran off as they escaped into town.

Act 3, Scene 3

Tristan ran down the sidewalk, running as fast as he could with Diana at his side. He looked for somewhere for them to hide.

"Over there," Diana remarked, eyeing the church ahead. "We can hide there!"

The couple passed city hall and made their way across town square to reach the front of the steps of the church. They went up the steps and opened the doors. They then quickly closed the doors behind them as soon as they went in. Afterwards, they took steps away from the door, panting deeply with fright as soon as they hoped it was over. Diana looked to the side of the door and saw a bar used to lock the front doors. She went over and picked it up, bringing it down over the handles and then taking Tristan's hand as they rushed deeper into the church to hide behind the altar.

"I can't believe that just happened," Tristan remarked, putting an arm around Diana. "What the hell... that was Gam's dad!"

"We don't know for sure if he's dead," Diana reasoned. "For all we know, those mercs ran off and came after us."

Diana turned her neck over to the left as she heard footsteps against the wooden floor of the church. There, she saw an old man dressed in a sleeping gown, holding a gas-fueled lamp and squinting at the two of them.

"What is all this commotion?" the old priest asked, walking over to them. "Who are you and what are you doing here?"

Tristan stood up and looked over at the priest, recognizing him.

"We only want refuge, Father," Tristan replied. "We're escaping two mad men with firearms that are after us."

The priest looked at Tristan.

"You," the priest said. "Why have you returned?"

"I wanted to know more about my adoptive-parents – the fact that they were murdered, and now that these mercenaries are after us. They shot Mr. Templeton and might be coming here."

"How do you know you were adopted?" the priest questioned. "Your mother told me she was only going to tell you when you were of age... which she never did though..."

"You knew?" Tristan replied. "God, did everybody in this town know except me?!"

"You should never have returned," the priest warned. "Do not pursue your true mother – it'll only put you and those around you in great danger. Look at what has happened now – leave while you are ahead and return to your safekeeper! There is nothing you need to know from here on out!"

"Why?" Tristan remarked. "Who's my mother?!"

The priest looked at Tristan, but before he could reply, a loud thud was heard at the door.

"Police! Open up!" a voice shouted from outside.

"No! Don't open it!" Tristan shouted. "It could be them!"

The priest brought a finger to his mouth, telling Tristan to be quiet as he turned around and then looked back over to the boys. He walked over to them and pointed to a door near the altar.

"Go through the cemetery while I talk to these men to buy you time. I'm giving you a final warning, Mr. Merrick. Let this be the end of your curiosity in regard to your past – it is for the best of all of us."

The banging on the door got louder as Diana grabbed Tristan's hand. She nudged Tristan away as the two watched the priest turn and go to the door.

"Let's go," Diana said, dragging him away.

"Okay," Tristan replied, letting go and leading him to the back door.

Tristan opened the door and went out, leaving Diana to catch the door and stand in the frame as he looked over to the priest.

"What's that? Police outside?" the priest shouted. "One moment while I unlock these doors…"

Diana took a deep sigh, fearing for the old man as she set the gas lamp down on a table and slowly unlocked the doors as the banging got louder and more desperate. Tristan grabbed Diana, and forced her into the cemetery with him.

The coldness outdoors was bitter and a wind picked up alongside an onslaught of snow.

"Where's the exit?" Diana questioned, looking around the mess of graves around.

"Over here," Tristan replied, trudging through the thick layer of snow and going to an iron gate to the far-right.

Diana could still hear the banging on the front door. She looked sad and worried as she looked back. Tristan continued to lead her across the cemetery, stopping to realize that she had stopped again, but not because of her pity for the old man.

"What are you doing?" Tristan remarked.

Diana had stopped at a grave. Tristan trudged over to look at what she was pointing at.

"It's you parents, Tristan," Diana stated.

Tristan looked down and saw the shared grave of his parents, Zachariah and Elisabeth Merrick, who had both died on December 25th, 2016. He concentrated on the earth before the tombstone.

"Yeah…" Tristan said in a sad tone.

Tristan continued to reflect. Diana looked at the tombstone and read the epitaph, 'Therefore, my dear brothers and sisters, stand firm. Let nothing move you. Always give yourselves fully to the work of the Lord, because you know that your labor in the Lord is not in vain.' Tristan sighed.

"*Tam!*" a voice shouted. "*Tam oni!*"

Tristan and Diana turned their heads towards the backdoor of the church where the Huntsman mercenary had shown up and begun to fire at them. The two quickly ran off, sprinting through the sea of snow and getting to the sidewalk at the end. They then turned left, running back towards city hall and the police station as they went deeper into town.

Another gun had started to fire at them, met by the ignition of a car engine as they passed the police station. Diana and Tristan continued to run for their life, heading into the neighborhood and making their way towards Gardner Avenue as the snow picked up even more.

The couple soon arrived at the pickup truck when Tristan began to rummage through his jacket for the keys. Once he had found them, he opened the driver door and rushed Diana in. Tristan saw lights coming down from the end of the street of the perpendicular road. He quickly got inside and closed the door behind him. The shock of him slamming the door shut caused some snow resting on the door window to fall over, exposing them slightly. The windshield and passenger seat door window was covered in a light blanket of snow.

"Damn," Tristan cursed, looking around the dark cabin and grabbing Diana's hand. "Get down!"

Diana and Tristan ducked down and came to the floor of the cabin. The couple laid low with their backs to the floor. Tristan was between Diana's legs with his face looking upwards to the exposed window. A shine of light passed them. The couple listened to their own breathing and heartbeats as they anxiously lay together.

The light passed again. Diana closed her eyes and muttered something. Tristan waited a few minutes until he climbed up and looked out. He then sat properly on the driver's seat and looked to Diana. She sat up and fixed her hair.

"Where's my phone?" Tristan questioned, feeling his pockets and finding it.

"What are you doing?" Diana asked.

Tristan turned on his phone, reading the notifications of the many unread text messages and missed calls from Charlemagne. He unlocked his phone and proceeded to make a phone call.

"Who are you calling?" Diana questioned.

"Emergency services," Tristan replied. "We have to let someone know of what happened at the police station."

Tristan dialed 9-1-1 and then brought his phone to his ear.

"9-1-1," the dispatcher answered. "Police, fire, or ambulance?"

"Police, and maybe ambulance too," Tristan responded. "St. Nazaire, Alberta – there's been a shooting."

"What's the emergency?" the dispatched questioned.

Tristan briefly gave a synopsis of what had occurred from the perspective of a passerby, stating shots fired in St. Nazaire and that two officers were possibly shot before they could radio for backup. Once he was done, he hung up before the dispatcher could ask him for his personal information. Tristan then looked over to Diana.

"What now?" Diana asked.

"I think we should get out of here and go as far as we can," Tristan replied, "and then, we find refuge for the night."

Act 4, Scene 1

Tristan drove the pickup truck into the parking lot of a plaza at the side of the Trans-Canada Highway where there was a truck stop, service station, and motel. He took a deep sigh and turned his glance to Diana, who looked back at him as he shut off the engine. They took a moment to relax. Two hours had passed since they were in St. Nazaire, and the gas tank of the pickup truck was running low. Tristan leaned back into his seat and looked out the window as the cabin was lit by the cheap lighting of the motel sign.

Diana looked at Tristan and took pity in his grim expressions.

"I've never rented a motel by myself," Tristan remarked. "I don't even know how this works – don't you need a credit card or something?"

"I think that's just a hotel," Diana replied. "I have my wallet in my backpack. I can pay for a room for the night."

"No, it's fine. I'll pay," Tristan responded. "I got us into this mess, so it's not fair to use your hard-earned cash. Here."

Tristan took his wallet out from his jacket. He took a twenty dollar bill and then gave the whole wallet to his girlfriend.

"Wait for me outside when you're done. I'm going to go to the gas station convenience store to get something for my aching muscles."

"I forgot you're still fatigued," Diana said. "You must feel awful after what we just went through…"

"I feel worse about other things, Diana. My body can take a bit of pain, but my mind… not so much."

"Don't be so full of self-pity," Diana warned, shaking her head. "Come on, let's go and find somewhere to rest."

"Sure," Tristan replied, opening his door and stepping outside.

Tristan looked around the quiet parking lot of the small plaza. He took notice of the salted black asphalt, which was wet and reflected the lights around the bright complex they were at. Diana retrieved her backpack from the back of the truck. The couple separated, Tristan went towards the gas station little more than fifty feet away while Diana went forward to the motel.

Diana looked at the motel office and made her approach to the glass doors. She looked through the doors and saw a lone East Indian man sat behind a counter, reading a magazine as he smoked with the other hand. She opened the door and entered the room, noticing the shanty appearance of the office as well as the out of order ice machine and empty vending machines.

The man behind the counter looked over to Diana, lowering his magazine and putting his cigarette to his lips. The man had crimson dark skin – dark. He was also perhaps in his fifties or late forties with aging features, wrinkled forehead, crow's feet, etc. He had curly black hair and a thick moustache. The room stank of tobacco and Indian spices.

"I need a room with one double-bed, please," Diana requested in a sheepish voice.

"Identification," the man replied in a thick accent to his ethnicity.

"What?" Diana questioned.

"I need to see some ID," the man said, taking his cigarette away from his mouth and blowing out some smoke towards Diana.

Diana set her backpack atop of the surface of the counter and took out her wallet. She looked around for her driver's license and then presented it to the man. He took it into his hand and then looked back at her.

"Too young," the man rejected.

"What do you mean?"

"Minimum age in the province is eighteen."

Diana frowned and looked back at him.

"I need a room," Diana insisted. "My brother and I are three hours from home and have nowhere else to stay. You've got to understand…"

"Too young," the man simply repeated.

Diana continued to frown at him, looking to the side to read a list of room prices. She looked at the money that Tristan had and saw that she had enough. She then rummaged through her backpack.

"Do you like to smoke? I used to too. Here," Diana said, taking out a box of cigarettes she had been given by Mr. Cohen. "Manson's Cigarettes – the best. They're yours if you let me rent a room."

The man blew smoke towards Diana, causing her to frown again as he didn't reply. Diana gave a deep sigh and opened her own wallet, taking out some cash and laying it on the countertop. She then took out the money Tristan had in his wallet and put it together.

"Look, I have eighty dollars for the room," Diana stated, pointing to the money Tristan had given her, "and there's another sixty if you please let us stay the night."

The man looked at her and then down at the money on the table. He then nodded and took the money.

"Room 20," the man remarked, standing up and taking a key from the cabinet behind him. "One night, and if you are not gone by noon, then I call the police to take you home."

"I'll be gone earlier than that," Diana remarked, grabbing the box of cigarettes.

"Leave those," the man said, sitting back down as he counted the money. "No smoking in the rooms."

Diana glared at him and left them for him to snatch. She brought her backpack back around, took the key and then left the office to wait outside for Tristan to return. It was cold outside – below freezing. Diana took a deep sigh, looking around the strange place in the middle of nowhere and displaying a certain glum look on her face as though she was homesick, or perhaps it was loneliness.

Tristan left the convenience store of the gas station with a small plastic bag. He walked across the parking lot and over to Diana.

"Hey, how'd it go?" Tristan questioned as they regrouped.

"Poorly – the stupid hack in there didn't want to rent me a room since I'm under-aged, so I had to bribe him," Diana replied, walking with Tristan towards the rooms. "Come on, let's go to our bedbug infested room and get some rest."

Diana led Tristan to Room 20 and unlocked it for them to step inside. The room was cold, plain and simple, and the furniture was cheap, battered, and/or dirty. It was everything they could come to expect from a motel off the highway. The bed covers looked cheap with a cheap design, and there was a small stain in the carpet ahead near the door to the bathroom. Diana turned on the lights for them to get a better look, and closed the curtains and blinds.

"Well, I've slept in worse," Diana stated with a sigh, stepping forward and taking off her backpack.

Tristan closed the door behind them.

"Here," Tristan said, handing Diana the bag of stuff he bought. "Some toothpaste and two toothbrushes for us. I also bought some ointment for my muscles."

"Why didn't you get some ibuprofen?" Diana questioned.

"It doesn't do me any good," Tristan stated, looking at Diana and focusing on her eyes. "How are you doing?"

"Well, I've been kidnapped, saw two police officers get shot, and then had to run for my life lest I be shot as well by some crooks who want to actually kidnap us," Diana replied, moving over to sit on the bed, "but all that considered, I'm doing fine. I should be asking you how you're holding up."

"I'm sad about it, but I hope Mr. Templeton and the other cop are okay. Also that priest... I don't who those people were, or how they found us – that freaks me out the most."

"Yeah, I've been thinking about that too..." Diana replied. "I'm more or less certain that they were Huntsman by their stupid Russian accents. I've just never seen them in plain clothes before, which is probably scarier than seeing them in uniform."

"I know what you mean," Tristan replied, sitting next to her, "which is why I need to ask you something important."

"What?"

"They wanted us, Diana. I don't know why, and I don't what they're capable of, but if they're easily willing to murder cops, subject our town, and do God knows what else, then maybe we should reconsider going back to Allabrese."

"What?" Diana questioned. "Are you suggesting that we run away from Charles?"

"N-not exactly, but that is the gist of it," Tristan responded. "Not permanently, because I do want to return one day, but for the sake of Charles and the rest of the town, let's not return. I mean, think about it, ever since the G.D.P. were in town covering up the occupation, the Protection Squad was forced to neuter itself. They've been effectively disarmed, and little is protecting us anymore... I don't want to bring trouble to Charles either. What if these people are the same people that killed my adoptive-parents? Or the woman from my memory? I don't want Charles to die because of me, and after all that's happened, I feel like I'm to blame in some sort of way. Don't get me wrong, the mansion is a fortress, but I would rather go into hiding until we can return. It's the smart idea."

"The G.D.P. isn't going to stop Charles from ensuring our protection," Diana stated. "If firearm legislation didn't bother him before, it won't bother him now. The Protection Squad won't be disbanded and they'll find a way to hide their arms to ensure that we are safe."

"But how long is that going to take?" Tristan wondered. "Not soon enough..."

"What then? Where do we go?" Diana asked.

"I think we should go and find my real mom," Tristan suggested. "The woman from my dream – or memory."

"What if that woman isn't alive anymore?" Diana replied. "There's no guarantee that she survived, and if she's dead it would explain why you were taken to your adoptive-parents?"

"Someone had to bring me to them – someone had to go around the conventional method of ensuring a child is adopted so that I would be placed in their care instead of anybody else. A simple will would see to that..."

"What if these people find us? We can't protect ourselves..."

"We'll just have to hide... I won't let anything happen to you because of me though. If you want, I can take you back to Allabrese so that you can be with Charles, but you won't stop me from running away because what Father Brooke said might be true, and pain might come if those grunts can't get to me. Charlemagne can't stop me either – he'd be a hypocrite to. He disappeared on us for two months, lied to us; all to look for Finn. Why can't I do the same for my own mother?"

Diana was silent. Tristan sighed. He looked at Diana and made eye contact.

"Do you want me to take you back to Allabrese?" Tristan asked.

"No," Diana rejected, shaking her head. "Stop, Tristan. You're talking nonsense. Let's just go back home and move on with our lives. Enough of this... enough of this memory, or the fact that your parents may have been murdered, or even the fact that they're not your biological parents. What is any of this going to accomplish? She left you – if she didn't want you then, what makes you think she'd want you now?"

"We don't know that," Tristan said in a quiet voice.

"Tristan, forget her. I'm with you. I want you. I love you. Why is it so hard for you to realize, or understand that?"

Tristan didn't immediately respond. He looked shy.

"Diana, I'm not asking for your permission to go out and find her. I'm going to go and look for her whether you like it or not. All I'm asking you is if you want to come with me, because the last thing I want for you, the love of my life, is to get hurt."

"You would go after her no matter what I'd say to try and stop you?" Diana questioned.

"All I care about is your safety, Diana," Tristan replied. "I'd prefer if you didn't come and instead returned to Charles, but the choice is yours. I won't force either of the two... What happened today... me bringing you with me – that was an accident. I didn't mean to travel with you – after I hit that cyclist, I panicked! You triggered me when you started talking about needles, and… I originally planned to ditch school after I dropped you off and to disappear without you noticing. The fact that you're with me right now is purely an accident…"

Diana frowned and looked aside.

"Not an accident…" Diana said, shaking her head. "There are no accidents…"

Tristan sighed and looked at her.

"Well?" Tristan questioned.

Diana sighed as well and reached out her hand.

"Give me your phone?" Diana asked.

"Why?"

"Just give me your phone," Diana said again.

Tristan took out his cell phone and handed it to her.

"What are you doing?" Tristan questioned as Diana fiddled with the side of the phone, forcing a compartment to open and a chip to pop out.

Diana took the chip, stood up, and walked over to the desk ahead of them. She picked up the desk lamp and smashed the chip.

"What the hell?!" Tristan shouted. "Why'd you do that?!"

"Back in England, Charles and Miklos talked about attempting to track you with the SIM card in your cell phone," Diana stated. "For all we know, he didn't know we'd go to St. Nazaire on a whim, but by the fact that he's been tracking us."

"Oh…" Tristan replied, looking at his phone as he read the lack of a signal without the SIM card.

"If you want my opinion, I think we were followed by the Huntsman," Diana said. "It makes sense. Charles phoned the police station, and less than five minutes later, they showed up. After what happened on Halloween, our house might have been bugged by them while we were in Allabrese."

"And?" Tristan queried. "Am I taking you home tomorrow or not?"

"Tristan, I love you, and obviously we've been together for almost two years, and in that time our love has gotten really strong, so no. I can't leave you because I won't ever leave you on your own anymore – even if it might be putting us in danger, if you're in danger, then that's my problem too now. We share our miseries... After we were separated in England, I never wanted to be separated from you for a prolonged period ever again because it hurt me, especially after the fact when I saw what had happened to you with Finn and all."

Diana sighed and wiped a tear from her eye.

"I just need you to remember one thing as we carry on, and that's that we need to trust each other and be of one mind," Diana stated.

"Of course," Tristan replied, standing up and hugging her. "I just don't want to be to blame if you get hurt because of me though."

"You won't because it won't be your fault if I get hurt or die, okay? It's mine," Diana said, parting from him. "Say that – Tell me that you won't blame yourself if something happens to me like you blamed yourself over Finn."

"Okay," Tristan replied, nodding.

The couple embraced again, but didn't part for almost a minute. When they did, they looked at each other.

"Where to next then?" Diana asked, holding Tristan's hands.

"Well, let's start by heating up this room, and then we can try and narrow down a location."

Diana let go of Tristan as he went to turn on the heater. Diana removed her coat while Tristan left to retrieve his backpack and gym bag from the car. He then returned, brought them atop of the bed, and removed his own jacket. Tristan then went to his backpack and took out his laptop, bringing it over to the desk and setting it down on the desk so that he could plug it into the Ethernet cable provided by the motel. He then raised the cover, turned on the computer, and sat on the desk chair.

"Where do you think your parents could be from?" Diana asked as she stood behind Tristan.

"Probably somewhere on this continent if not in Europe," Tristan replied. "I'm sure they'd have to access this country at some most, so the most likely is local, Canada...."

"What about the United States?" Diana questioned. "Charles did some research about that movie theater you saw, and it's a brand from within the U.S. Midwest and South. For all we know, maybe you're American."

"The Midwest is close to the Albertan border – it's probable. Why didn't you tell me this beforehand?" Tristan asked.

"I didn't want to throw this curveball into the mix," Diana replied, "but at the same time, I'm surprised you haven't searched this on you own."

"I thought it was the name of a theater in St. Nazaire," Tristan replied. "I never thought it would be across the border..."

"So, if you are American, why were you taken across from there and into Canada?" Diana queried.

"I don't know... maybe to safeguard me?" Tristan suggested. "Then again, we've seen that ultimately fail if it were true..."

"What connections do you have to the United States?" Diana asked, putting a hand on Tristan's shoulder. "Or, your adoptive-parents for that matter of fact. Isn't your adoptive-mother American?"

"Dutch," Tristan replied, "but they were immigrants to the United States in North Dakota. She met my dad in Canada when she was in nursing school and moved over before I was born, or adopted. My adoptive-father was full stock Scottish-Canadian, so I don't think it has anything to do with him."

"So, maybe whoever left you in the care of your adoptive-parents knew your mother and came from the states. What do you know about who your adoptive-mother was before meeting your dad?"

"Well, her surname was Witeveen. She was born in North Dakota, studied there, and then moved over here."

Diana paused for a moment and then looked back at Tristan, asking, "Did she have any siblings? What did her parents do?"

"Her father was a wheat farmer. I don't know anything about them other than that. They were modest people. I thought about her sister, my aunt, but according to my adoptive-mom, she was a nun. I really doubt a nun could get into trouble with such shady characters, or have even conceived me."

"Well, that's just great then," Diana replied, "the strongest connection we have to the U.S. is through your mom, and her sister was a nun."

"We should still travel south and cross the border tomorrow," Tristan said, looking to Diana. "It's the next step in all this…"

"Do you want to go to North Dakota?" Diana asked.

"If we can't find anything else," Tristan replied.

"Surely the U.S. has some sort of birth registry that we could search. We know your birth name is Tristan, and we know you were born on November 1st, so maybe would find who your mother was based on that."

"There are over three hundred million people in the United States, and I'm sure I wasn't the only one named Tristan born on that date."

"Sorry, sometimes I forget that I'm with the only Tristan that matters to me," Diana replied, looking at Tristan as he raised a smile.

"Well, what else can we do once we get over there?" Tristan asked, looking back in front of him and raising his hands over his keyboard. "It'll be a long trip from wherever we are now, all the way to the border. It'll probably take the majority of tomorrow."

"What state do we border?" Diana queried, looking over Tristan's laptop screen as it showed a map. "Montana? We can stay there for a night…"

"Well, we'll just have to bribe another motel manager," Tristan replied. "We can probably find an ATM at the border where we can exchange for some American cash."

Tristan continued to look at the brightness of his laptop screen, causing a pulsating pain to summate at his temple. He quickly closed the laptop screen and squeezed his eyes shut.

"Hey, are you okay?" Diana asked.

"No, my headache isn't going away and I've never felt this bad, physically, in my life."

"Let's go to bed then," Diana replied. "We've got to get out of here early anyways and have a long drive ahead of us."

"No," Tristan refused, "we've just started to brainstorm."

"We have a destination for tomorrow, and can draw more ideas as we go there. After that, we have an evening to decide where within the United States we're going," Diana said, rubbing Tristan's shoulder. "It's time to relax. We've had a hell of a day and need to calm down."

"Why is this fatigue happening to me now of all times?" Tristan complained as Diana walked over to turn off the heat.

The room was warm enough now.

"You're going to get better, Tristan. Don't worry," Diana said, walking back over to Tristan and taking his hand. "Stand up."

Tristan stood up and turned to Diana with his tired face. Diana gave a warm and energetic smile, bringing the other hand to Tristan's cold cheek. Tristan looked through Diana's eyes and leaned into kiss her before parting as they started to hear some loud yelling coming from the room above. The two of them looked up and then back at each other, communicating wordlessly with plain expressions before Tristan leaned forward and brought his forehead upon Diana's.

"I'm exhausted," Tristan remarked, wrapping his arms around her.

"All the more reason to rest."

Diana removed Tristan's shirt, lifting it up and throwing it to the desk. She embraced him and brought her head to rest on his shoulder while she stretched her hands over his back. Tristan looked across the room as she attempted to make him feel better. He closed his eyes and squeezed them as though he were in pain. Diana separated herself from him, but Tristan opened his eyes and continued to hold his hand around her waist. She brought a hand to his chest and then to his sides. Tristan's eyes simply looked back onto her, into her mythical blue eyes.

"Do you remember the first time we had sex?" Tristan asked. "It was slow, awkward, but ecstatic... I'll never forget that night."

"Me neither," Diana replied, looking at Tristan. "It was the same night you chased me to the airfield before I could leave to Harlech."

"The same night you won that tourney."

"The same night that everything changed for us…"

"If I wasn't in such a bad shape right now…"

"Don't worry about it, Tristan. It's the last thing on my mind right now, and I'm sure the same can be said about you."

"How about I help with the pain ointment before we get ready for bed," Diana suggested. "Afterwards, we can take a shower, brush our teeth, and then sleep."

"Sounds like a plan," Tristan replied.

The couple did just as they had planned. Diana helped Tristan undress and applied the ointment he had purchased. He then allowed it to soothe his aches while Diana showered and brushed her teeth. After the ointment had settled, she left the bathroom wearing a t-shirt from Tristan's gym bag and her underwear. Tristan showered, brushed his teeth, and then joined Diana at the bed. Diana took Tristan's cellphone and left it charging. She did the same with his laptop and then folded Tristan's clothes. Tristan was left to wear his gym shorts and went to sit down atop of the bed. Diana finished drying her hair and then put away the toothbrush and toothpaste into her backpack. She then turned off the desk lamp and then went and turned off the main light in the room, plunging them into slight darkness. A fair bit of light remained, pouring from brightness outside. She went to the opposite side of the bed from Tristan and got in. Tristan moved the cover over so that he could get in with her. The couple then moved to share heat together as he held her.

"It's nice that we have each other," Tristan quietly said, embracing Diana with his hands at her stomach.

"It's nice that you envelop me now," Diana remarked, closing her eyes. "If you were to fall into ice again, I don't think I'd be able to save you by your sheer size."

"Thanks…" Tristan responded, moving closer to Diana, "but going back to what I was saying, I think I'd be more depressed if I was on my own than with you."

"You don't have to ever worry about being alone, Tristan," Diana said, turning onto her side and looking at Tristan through the darkness in the room. "You should know that by now."

Tristan looked back at Diana. Streaks of light from outside could be seen on his face as well as Diana's side. The sound of trucks passing along the national highway could also be heard. Tristan ignored them and instead fixated on Diana's blue eyes. He leaned in and kissed her, bringing her closer to him before parting. Tristan then held her in his arms as she rested her head against his chest. He rested his chin atop of her head.

Diana felt the coldness of the gold chain necklace and brought her hand to it. She brought the charm, or amulet of the necklace into her hands and looked at the figure of Saint Luke on one side, and then Tristan's name and date of birth on the other side.

"What was St. Luke known for?" Diana asked.

"A lot of things," Tristan replied. "All I know or really cared about was that he was the patron saint of doctors."

"Wow, that really fits you, doesn't it?" Diana replied, focusing her eyes on the design of the front. "I can understand why he was your baptismal saint."

"What was St. Anne known for then?" Tristan questioned. "Rebellious attitudes?"

"You're the one with the rebellious attitude," Diana bickered, "but as a matter of fact, St. Anne is the patron saint of equestrians and poverty. Everyday I'm grateful that my mother chose her to protect me."

Tristan didn't respond.

"Whoever left you with your parents in St. Nazaire must've been religious," Diana stated, looking at the icon. "The priest in St. Nazaire sounded awfully suspicious of knowing who your parents might have been – your mother specifically."

"Right... I forgot about him. God, it was so deep into the action that I nearly forgot about what he was about to say to me," Tristan said in a low voice.

"He warned you not to go looking for your mother. He was very specific about your mother."

"The woman who was shot."

"Maybe she knew that priest."

"Maybe that priest was there."

"Maybe."

"I don't see how that could be possible... Why else would he warn me though? Was he just making a general claim? Or maybe, just maybe... he knew about the assassination."

"It begs the question, 'Why would your biological mother send you to live with your adoptive-parents of all people?'" Diana pointed out.

"Maybe Father Brooke was a medium between the two. He knew my mom was infertile and would have accepted a baby in her life. He could have made her day, or Christmas for that fact, organizing me to be placed with them. A religious connection explains the necklace for sure."

"It'd explain how he knew your mother," Diana said, noticing some marks around the figure of St. Luke. "What do these words say? I think it's in Latin – not Saint Luke's name, but the inscription above. Do you know what it says?"

"I've never translated it. I thought it was something about eternity, or whatever…"

"*Deus Aeternum*," Diana read. "What is that supposed to mean? God eternal?"

Tristan shrugged. Diana looked back at him before mentally reading the words in her head again.

"Maybe these words can help us," Diana said, looking back at him and dropping the charm.

"We'll have to find out tomorrow," Tristan replied, closing his eyes. "Goodnight."

"Goodnight," Diana responded, cozying up to her boyfriend. "Goodnight…"

Act 4, Scene 2

Charlemagne paced around in his study, nervously looking over to the phone every now and again.

"Oh, the nerve of Tristan to go behind my back like this," Charlemagne remarked, clenching a fist as he lowered his arms. "What has gotten in to him?"

Charlemagne looked at his desk, specifically the answering machine as he waited for a call from the RCMP in St. Nazaire, but no response came from either them or Tristan. The strike of twelve o'clock on the grandfather clock caught him by surprise. He then slammed a fist down atop of the table in the middle of the room.

"Damn him!" Charlemagne shouted. "I told him to text me before they left town, and I told that sergeant to call me as soon as he saw them off!" he shouted, going to his desk. "It'll be dark soon, and I don't trust Tristan enough right now to even trust him to drive in the dark – no less with Diana in the passenger seat! Oh, this is mental!"

Charlemagne went to his desk and looked around for a notepad with the phone number of the RCMP detachment. He then grabbed the phone on his desk.

"Oh, they are grounded for this defiance. No matter the excuse!" Charlemagne said, taking the sheet of paper and dialing the number. "Here and back – I'll even split them apart from the duration of it if it means teaching them a lesson. I've been too soft on them, and this is my reward: pure defiance."

The phone rang as Charlemagne waited, tapping his foot on the floorboard underneath his desk as he got a machine on the other line.

"Thank you for calling the St. Nazaire RCMP," the automatic machine said. "If you are calling about an emergency, please hang up and dial 9-1-1. If you are calling in regard to a police incident or would like to report an incident, please wait until one of our operators can get ahold of you."

Charlemagne waited for a couple of minutes. His face was red with anger and seriousness. He sat down as he waited for almost ten minutes before slamming the phone down. Charlemagne then picked it up again and dialed Tristan's number. He then waited a split second before he got the machine from Tristan's service provider.

"The number you are calling is not available. Please hang up and try again."

"Dammit!" Charlemagne snarled, slamming the phone down once more. "If this is how they'd like it, then I'll go there myself."

Charlemagne turned on his PC and then signed in. He opened the program used to track Tristan's cellphone, but when he selected him, the program simply stated, 'Unavailable.' Charlemagne clicked around and displayed location history to see Tristan's movement. He looked at Tristan's journey towards St. Nazaire from Allabrese, and then his activity within the town until approximately seven o'clock in the evening when they left and drove on the Highway 2 southwards. His last known location was on the outskirts of Edmonton at a service station and motel. Charlemagne looked worried. He picked up the phone again and dialed a number.

"Miklos," Charlemagne said, "I need you and another to come to the manor in one of the LUVs. There's a slight situation that needs to be addressed in regard to Tristan. We've lost coverage of his cellphone and he hasn't returned from St. Nazaire…"

Charlemagne put the phone down and stood up. He took out his cellphone and grabbed his coat. He put his winter coat on and then left into the library, going into the foyer. He made another phone call.

"Henry, it's Charles," Charlemagne said. "No, they haven't returned. I've requested Miklos to come to the manor at once to escort me north to St. Nazaire so that I can investigate, but the more dire issue is the loss of coverage on Tristan's cellphone. I need technicians to assess what could have possibly happened... I also want additional resources diverted to Allabrese to assist in finding them."

Charlemagne then put his phone away and turned to the living room. Mavis hurried through and met with him.

"Mr. Cabernet, oh horrible news," Mavis stated, presenting him with a national newspaper. "Take a look."

Charlemagne took the paper and looked at the headline, 'Two Dead, Two Perpetrators At Large,' with a lower heading stating, 'RCMP searching for two unknown suspects in a shooting last Monday in St. Nazaire, Alberta.' The image below the headline showed a low-resolution closed-circuit surveillance image of two figures with firearms at the front of a police station.

"Good Lord," Charlemagne remarked, opening the newspaper to read the story.

Charlemagne looked at the image in the main story and saw another low resolution image of Diana and Tristan in the back of the police station.

"How... How is this possible?" Charlemagne questioned, looking to Mavis. "Oh, what I fool I have been... They're in trouble!"

Charlemagne returned the paper to Mavis. He then went to the living room and turned on the television, switching to a news channel. Mavis followed.

"Tristan isn't answering his phone and it goes straight to the phone company," Charlemagne stated. "What if he's been killed?"

Charlemagne crossed his arms and looked at the local news network for their region. It was currently playing advertisements.

"I can't even track his location. He's gone completely dark on me again," Charlemagne said. "How could I let this happen again?"

"Please," Mavis said, "do not strain yourself."

"How can't I? I'm responsible for him?" Charlemagne said in a saddened tone. "They're my children."

"I'll go make you some tea to help you settle down," Mavis suggested, leaving.

"Yes, that's what I need..." Charlemagne replied. "Some tea..."

The news channel returned to its scheduled programing.

"Terror has struck the small town of St. Nazaire in northern Alberta last night when two unidentified gunmen entered the RCMP detachment and seemingly opened fire at two officers. Two witnesses to the attack had escaped, but have since then gone missing and not been found by local police. The first identified victim of the attack was 44-year old Sergeant Simon Templeton, who was reportedly off-duty, and the other was on-duty 33-year old Constable Kevin Jackson. Constable Jackson was pronounced dead at the scene by first responders who were phoned by an anonymous caller, while Constable Templeton is in critical condition. RCMP from other regions arrived to assist, but by the time that they had arrived, the mayhem appeared to have settled..."

Charlemagne studied the CCTV footage that played on scene of the two strangers entering the station, briefly talking, and then pulling their firearms. The footage cut to hide the gunfight, but then cut to show a different point-of-view of Diana and Tristan, fleeing the horror.

"A memorial service will be conducted in town later this week. RCMP have been inquiring into the identities of two unknown witnesses, and if they are alive, to come forward so that investigators can begin to understand what has occurred in this poor little town. As if this tragedy wasn't enough, the local town's Roman Catholic church had been found to have perished as a result of a deadly fire. First responders produced the corpse of what has it this point assumed to be Father Timothy Brooke. The Chief Medical Examiner of Alberta will be conducting an investigation into the cause of death, which at this point, is unknown. RCMP are currently investigating whether this incident was related to the shooting at the detachment on the same night..."

Charlemagne's eyes widened as he saw the remains of a church with firefighters digging through the ruins. He scratched his cheek and then turned off the TV. Charlemagne produced his phone and fast-dialed a number in his contacts. He then brought the phone to his ear.

"Hudson, it's me," Charlemagne stated. "We need to talk and I need you to get into contact with the RCMP for me. It's about my kids..."

"Charles, I know," Sergeant Hudson responded. "We heard just a few moments ago from them after they had talked to the wife of Sergeant Templeton. They've identified one of the witnesses in the shooting over in St. Nazaire as your son, Tristan, and we've put two and two together to deduce the other to be your daughter, Diana."

"What will be done?" Charlemagne asked.

"RCMP are on high-alert throughout the province looking for them, but we'll find them. I was just about to drive over and speak with you... I'm sorry you had to hear from elsewhere about this..."

"No matter, but I won't be staying in Allabrese," Charlemagne replied, looking outside as he saw an LUV drive up along the driveway. "I've got to find them myself... Give me a phone call later on if you need anything... I've got to go."

"Wait, Charles..."

Charlemagne hung up and put his phone away. He then left the manor and went towards the LUV where Miklos and Lukas were waiting.

Act 4, Scene 3

Diana and Tristan travelled down the four-lane highway headed towards the busiest border in Alberta between the United States and Canada. The car rolled over some rail tracks at a train crossing while Diana looked out the window as she struggled to stay awake. The radio was on, but projecting quiet country music into the cabin. Tristan held his own tired eyes open as he focused mindlessly on the road before him.

Around the couple were acres and acres of flatland, but they couldn't see how far it rolled due to a thick fog about half a kilometer from the highway. The highway followed a power line to their right that continued as long as the road went. They started to bend left on the road, but nothing could be seen ahead of them in the mid-afternoon.

Diana looked away from the window as she gave a long yawn before looking over to Tristan lovingly. She straightened herself out and focused her eyes on him. Tristan held a serious expression as he focused on the road. He loving expression soon opted for one of concern.

"You look really pale," Diana observed aloud, shifting her eyes to Tristan's hands.

Tristan had fair skin as opposed to the tanned sheen that Diana was so familiar with. Diana leaned forward to raise the heater as she felt the cabin become cold again. She looked back at Tristan and smiled.

"You look like you've fallen into some ice-cold water again," Diana remarked, "except without the rosy cheeks."

"Wow, too soon," Tristan replied, lifting a smile as he looked over to Diana briefly. "I'm fine, I swear. I feel fine, I mean. A little achy, but fine otherwise."

"Whatever you say," Diana replied, slouching again as they passed a small town. "You're probably right. I'm just on edge that you've caught something because I don't want to get sick."

"Have you felt like you've caught something?" Tristan questioned.

"No…" Diana replied, conceding, "and we practically share germs, so I should stop thinking as if there's something pathological here or something."

"I'm just… not getting enough protein, or something, for my muscles to heal properly. I know! I haven't taken my supplements or been eating properly. There you go – there's your cause and effect."

"Fine, smart ass."

Tristan grinned as they continued to drive, reaching the limits of seeing a blockade ahead on the road alongside several buildings on the side. Diana took notice of what they were approaching and looked worried.

"Don't forget to pullover at the duty-free store. We need to exchange what cash we have left – not that it'll be worth much in American dollars, but it'll be a little," Diana said, getting her wallet out.

Diana proceeded to put their money together as well as their licenses. She looked up and noticed a two-story building with large banners hanging from the second-story window that read 'Duty-Free' in large font. The store looked like most buildings in this part of the province: cheap paneling on the exterior walls – poorly and quickly constructed in the last several decades, similar to a portable home.

Tristan changed lanes, passing into a truck lane, and then merging onto an exit lane to go into the parking lot where two large commercial trucks were parked outside of the duty-free shop. He drove around and parked the pickup truck randomly in the center of the lot.

"How much do we have?" Tristan asked, looking over.

"About twenty-dollars," Diana said.

"Welp."

"Should I buy anything inside?" Diana questioned.

"No, don't bother, it's probably all over-priced. Do you still have my wallet? I'm going to withdraw some more money because twenty-dollars isn't enough to survive."

"Take my card," Diana insisted, opening her wallet.

"No, just give me mine. I told you that this is my mess, so it's coming out of my bank account."

"Tristan, you don't work. How much money could you possibly even have?"

Tristan didn't respond and took his wallet. He then handed his debit card to her.

"What's your pin code?" Diana asked.

Tristan paused for a moment and then said, "Your birth date and month."

"16th of August, or August 16?"

"16th of August."

"Okay."

"Are you coming with me?" Diana questioned.

"No, I'm just going to get out to stretch my legs before we drive anymore…"

"Do you want me to drive the rest of the way? You look exhausted – six hours of non-stop driving cannot be good for you."

"It's fine," Tristan responded, rubbing his eyes.

Diana sighed and continued to look at him with pity.

"Hey, you know that once I make a withdrawal, it'll leave a lead to anyone looking for us that we were here and most likely crossed in the U.S."

"Yeah... probably, but I'm willing to make that gamble," Tristan responded. "Come on."

The couple got out of the pickup truck and regrouped at the front of the vehicle. A light gust of wind started to pick up, but the weather wasn't as traumatic as it was further north, although the fog was denser, which made it harder to see ahead.

"How much money am I taking out?" Diana questioned.

"How much do you think we can take out?"

Diana shrugged.

"Aim for the maximum then," Tristan responded. "Okay?"

"Fine," Diana replied, walking off to the store.

Tristan watched her and then leaned on the front of the truck. He looked to the ground and closed his eyes. He appeared as though he was in pain. Diana reached the ATM and looked at a sign above that read that there was a withdrawal fee. She sighed and took out her wallet, inserting her own debit card and withdrawing a hefty sum of cash. She then took Tristan's debit card and inserted it, taking out almost seven-hundred dollars in total – less than she took out from her account. She collected all the money and then went inside to exchange it for American dollars. Tristan opened his eyes and saw that she had gone inside.

Diana entered the shop and looked around, seeing a lot of different items for sale and seeing them to be as Tristan said, over-priced. She went to the teller and took her money to him. The Canadian dollars were exchanged for a fraction of what they had – about four-fifths in American dollars in the form of twenty-dollar bills. Diana collected them and then left, eyeing a newspaper stand on her way out and looking at the front page. She saw the incident in St. Nazaire to have made the headlines. She also saw that they were being searched for by RCMP. Diana looked at some of the newspapers briefly before leaving.

"How much do we have?" Tristan asked as Diana joined him.

"A lot," Diana stated, showing him. "Is that enough?"

Tristan shrugged as he saw all the bills.

"I hope so," Tristan replied.

The couple went back into the cabin of the pickup truck. Tristan ignited the engine and Diana organized their wallets before taking out their driver's licenses. She handed them to Tristan. Tristan took them in hand.

"I think we'll need our passports," Tristan stated, looking at their licenses.

"We don't have our passports," Diana replied.

Tristan looked at her with a nervous expression.

"We have our passports?" Diana asked. "I thought you didn't intend to make this trip with me?"

"I- I came prepared," Tristan reasoned. "They're in my backpack. I snatched them off Charlemagne's desk yesterday morning before he had a chance to put them back in his safe."

"Of course you did," Diana replied with a sigh, taking Tristan's backpack to rummage through and find them.

Tristan changed gears, lowered the parking brake, and then took a deep breath before stepping onto the gas pedal. He drove towards the merging lane and then returned back onto the quiet road leading up to customs about a tenth of a kilometer ahead. Tristan drove them closer to the customs office where Diana observed a multi-story building with two flag poles on each side. On Diana's side, a parking lot could be seen with a blue sign that said, 'Export Parking.' Behind the lot, a fence separated one-story structures that looked similar in design to the duty-free store. A sign above the highway stated the intention of the separate lanes as each one diverged into two more for a total of four lanes leading up to the office. The two lanes on the left were reserved for regular vehicles, while commercial trucks were to onto the two on the right. An additional sign that was blue read in white font that trucks were to use the left lanes only if a yellow-light was flashing. Beneath each phrase on the signs was the translation in French. The initial two-lanes for regular barriers had split into four, and each led to their own checkpoint that was riddled with yellow barriers, gates and stop signs. The entirety of the border was beneath a skywalk that went from the customs office, all the way to a small building between the regular vehicle checkpoints and two boxes for the trucks to go through. Tristan drove on the correct lane for them.

Diana grew nervous as she examined the site carefully. She looked fearful. A low-wall of flagstone and a sidewalk started to separate them from the customs office on the left. Three cars were ahead of them, and it started to snow lightly. Tristan had a strict and focused face as he waited with anticipation. Only their lane was open. The other three lanes had yellow gates across them, marking them as closed with additional red stop signs in front of them. Tristan got behind the car in front of them, and the waiting game started. Diana read everything she could around her in the meantime.

A green sign in front of the structure at the end of the skywalk read, 'Vehicle Inspection,' while a white one said, 'Be prepared to show identification. Declare all articles acquired outside of the U.S.A.' In front of the white sign were some small, thin skeletal trees frosted in snow.

Tristan drove forward as the car ahead of the line passed into the United States, and allowed the next in line to face customs. Diana looked further ahead to the other box offices where they had a red X in the center above the windows looking out at the cars, while the one they were driving to had a green arrow pointing down, or forward. She looked over to the commercial side of the entrance, and saw the line to be longer with a lot more trucks waiting to get in than personal vehicles. Diana focused ahead as Tristan started to drive forward again with another car in front gaining entry.

Diana's heart pattered gently. She looked nervous. She looked at Tristan who seemed to be surprisingly calm. She then looked out her window to where a red stop sign in the middle of each lane said, 'Stop until lane clears.' There was a large gap between the car in front of them and the car at the box office. Diana saw a border guard walking around, crossing the lanes ahead of them and going onto the sidewalk.

"Maybe this is a bad idea," Diana gently said, seeing the series of cameras that were equipped near the box offices.

There were about three cameras in total pointing at the second car ahead of them.

"Huh?" Tristan questioned, driving forward as the latest car drove in. "Why?"

"I don't think we'll get in. I mean, for a start, we're minors. Don't we need Charles' permission to leave the country?"

"Relax. We're seventeen. We're not going to get forced to turn around, and if we do, I have an idea on how to get in illegally."

Diana looked at Tristan with even more concern.

"Don't you worry, Diana. Just let me do all the talking."

Diana looked away and looked to see what waited ahead of them in the United States. A grey structure was seen in a large, mostly empty lot that took up a large space before diverging into a single lane that went on and onwards. The car ahead of them passed on, and it was now their turn.

"Here we go," Tristan said, releasing his foot from the brake and gently accelerating to be in vision of the three cameras around them.

Tristan opened the car windows and took out the identification cars in his pocket. He looked past the window between them and saw the serious face of the guard behind. He was dressed in black, had a firearm strapped on his waist, and a thick moustache across his upper lip. He wore a cap and looked to be about the same age as Charlemagne. The intimidating expression on the office's face caused Tristan to drop his own serious glance and to frown.

"How are you two today?" the guard asked in a deep voice as Tristan handed them their passports.

"We're good," Tristan said in a nervous voice.

"Neither of you look like a Charlemagne Cabernet," the guard stated, looking at the pickup truck.

"Sorry?" Tristan asked.

"The vehicle," the guard clarified, "is registered to a Mr. Charlemagne Cabernet."

"Oh, he's our guardian," Tristan replied, "but I'm co-registered to drive the vehicle."

The customs officer looked at each of their passports and seemingly scanned them on a reader in his booth, looking at a screen of a computer inside.

"Are you by yourselves?" the border guard asked.

"Yes, sir," Tristan replied as the guard looked back at him and Diana.

The guard looked at the pickup truck and then looked at his monitor.

"What is your destination?"

"West Glacier... in the Rockies," Tristan replied.

"And what is the reason for your visit?"

"I'm visiting my aunt – she's a nun at the Convent of Our Maidens there."

The border officer typed into his computer before looking back over to Tristan.

"Where are you both from?"

"Allabrese, sir," Tristan answered

"Any alcohol?"

"No."

"Tobacco?"

"No."

"Weapons?"

"No, sir."

"Are you bringing anything into the United States at this time, such as any undeclared fruits, vegetables, and/or eggs and meats?"

"No, none of that."

"Very well," the guard replied, continuing to type.

Diana looked at the guard who seemed to have dropped his brute tone, and appeared to be not as harsh as she had suspected he'd be. He looked ahead to the large lot before them that separated them from the highway into Sweet Grass, Montana.

"Alright, you seem to check out..." the guard said, taking a deep breath, returning their passports.

Tristan observed as another, younger guard approached his colleague from the other side, opening the door and whispering into his cohort's ear. The man looked back at the kids with his partner. A red light lit around them. Tristan looked ahead as the gate closed in front as well as behind them. They were trapped. Tristan dropped a look of surprise.

"I'm sorry, but the two of you are wanted by the RCMP," the guard said, looking at them. "I'm going to have to turn you into your authorities."

"No…" Diana muttered. "Dammit…"

"I'm going to have to ask you to raise your hands over the steering wheel and exit the vehicle. Please leave the keys in the ignition, and we will escort you to the customs office for further action."

Tristan froze in shock as he looked around confusingly. Two additional guards had shown up in front of them. Diana unlatched her seatbelt. Tristan was not complying with the guard's directions.

"I am not going to ask you again. Please exit the vehicle before we force you out."

"Tristan," Diana said, "don't do anything stupid."

Tristan looked at Diana, and in a split second, he nodded and felt his focus return. He unlatched his seatbelt and peacefully got out of the car. A guard was assigned to each of them, and they were told to come into the U.S. side of the border before being led into the U.S. customs office. Tristan complied, walked forward in defeat, and walked with Diana into the double glass doors of the border office.

Diana turned around as she looked behind him while a third guard took the pickup truck and drove it out of the way, into the parking lot outside of the customs office so that vehicles could continue passing through. She took notice of where it was parked, and then continued to look forward.

Act 4, Scene 4

"Under the conditions, we are taking you to Canadian authorities to hand you over to them when your guardian arrives to retrieve you as opposed to the Royal Canadian Mounted Police. We recently got off the phone with your guardian, Mr. Cabernet, and he is on his way to retrieve you. In the meantime, you are to wait with us and not leave the room," a U.S. customs officer said from the doorway.

The door shut behind him as he left, leaving the couple in the dim and cold room that was an evidence lockup. They sat in chairs lined on one side, facing each other where their supervisor sat behind a cage with the keys to the pickup truck sitting on a counter.

Both Diana and Tristan had yet to speak to each other. Tristan was rife with a gloomy expression, while Diana appeared to be rather calm. The room they were in was deep within the customs office, on the second-floor with a view looking out into the corridor.

"Thanks for not doing anything irrational," Diana confessed as she looked at Tristan with pity. "I know you might be really pissed, but this is probably for the best... Charles can be understanding, and although he might be mad right now, he'll calm down to know we're safe. It'll be for the best if we involve him now that we know you were adopted."

"I don't agree," Tristan simply responded, "but whatever..."

Tristan fell onto his side as they sat together in discomfort of their makeshift prison. Between the U.S. border and Allabrese, Tristan calculated there to be at least eight hours for them to burn in misery until they'd see their guardian.

Tristan awoke to the nudging of Diana as he slept across three of the world's most uncomfortable chairs. He looked over to Diana with minor annoyance.

"We're being moved," Diana said as Tristan woke up. "Apparently he's here."

Tristan sat up and then stood up. He stretched his body before following Diana out and into the corridor. They were brought to the end of the hallway and to a single door that separated them from the Canada and the United States. A border guard behind them returned the set of car keys to Tristan, and then opened the door for them to step back into Canada

The couple were taken in by a Canadian customs officer and then escorted to a conference room where they were asked to take a seat.

"Is our guardian here?" Diana questioned.

"Sit down and be quiet," the customs officer replied. "RCMP will want to have a word with you about the shooting in St. Nazaire."

Diana crossed her arms and sat down at the conference table. The customs officer stood guard at the door. Diana looked around at the glass walls that looked into the rest of the customs office. Her ears then poked up as she heard a distinct, but all too familiar sound of gunfire. She looked around. The customs officer was distracted by the noise. Diana observed he had a pistol holstered.

"Was that gunfire?" Diana questioned, looking at the customs officer.

The guard didn't respond, but did listen as another round of the noise went into everybody's ears.

"I'm ninety-nine percent sure that was gunfire," Diana remarked, looking over to Tristan.

"Are you sure?" Tristan questioned.

"Be quiet," the customs officer replied, opening the door as he heard shouting from down the hall.

"Why would someone attack a border station at ten at night" Tristan whispered, looking at a clock in the conference room. "Do they have a deathwish?"

"Sit down and stay down," the customs officer instructed.

"Don't you have a gun? We're safe, right?" Diana remarked in slight panic.

The guard looked back over to the couple with slight embarrassment. Diana realized that the pistol holstered around his belt wasn't a firearm, but an electroshock weapon.

"Are you sure that's even gunfire? It could just be... fireworks?" Tristan questioned.

"Tristan, you're talking to me who grew up with this as ambience. I know an automatic rifle when I hear one."

"Stay here while I go investigate – for your own safety, do not leave this room," the guard said in a slight nervous voice, leaving them.

Tristan listened as some more shots were fired and an alarm went off.

"Okay, that's gunfire," Tristan remarked, standing up with Diana. "What do we do?"

"I don't know... I don't really want to go out there," Diana replied.

"Okay, let's stay in the transparent room in the middle of the building then, that'll be a safe option," Tristan sarcastically remarked.

Diana and Tristan both glanced over as they saw several armed U.S. customs officers, dressed in tactical gear, cross the border and enter into the Canadian offices with assault rifles in hand. Tristan could hear the sound of sirens in the distance.

"Thank God," Diana remarked as the Americans passed them.

Two officers opened the door and kept it open for them, motioning them to get out.

"You're not safe here – the border is under attack. Get out and go find cover on the other side! Move!" the American customs officer yelled.

Diana and Tristan didn't hesitate to stay in the office and ran out. They went down the hall and returned into the U.S., moving out of the way as another team of U.S. border guards rushed down the hall.

"Go find cover and keep your head down," another U.S. border guard instructed them.

Another officer came around and directed them into the U.S., yelling, "Go downstairs and stay there! Find cover and don't come out until it's clear!"

Diana nodded and took Tristan's hand for them to run down the hall and come into the stairwell. A third squad of guards came running up. The couple went into the foyer of the American office, which had been completely deserted. Diana went to run behind the counter, while Tristan broke off from her and stood in the center of the office space.

"What are you doing? We've got to hide!" Diana remarked.

"The truck is right out there," Tristan remarked, eyeing the car in the night fog of the brightly lit parking lot.

"Don't be crazy, Tristan. We're not abandoning the federal authorities in the middle of an international crisis! We'll be charged and sent to prison for sure! Imagine what this would do to Charles!"

"Charles is only responsible for losing track of us from Allabrese to St. Nazaire, and then to here. As far as I'm concerned, the Canadian authorities, or maybe even the American authorities, are to blame if we disappear."

Diana looked from behind the counter as two regular U.S. border guards entered the lobby from outside. They had their pistols drawn and looked over to the couple.

"You two stay hidden," the guards said. "Let us handle the situation!"

The guards then left and went upstairs to join the others. Tristan watched them off before looking back at Diana.

"It's now or never," Tristan said as they stood divided.

"Don't do this," Diana pleaded. "Please, Tristan."

Tristan looked at her with pity.

"I'm sorry," Tristan replied, stepping back and leaving the office.

Tristan came outside and ran for the pickup truck. Diana growled at him and vaulted over the desk. She went after him.

"You idiot!" Diana remarked under her breath. "I'm the one with the keys!"

Tristan got to the pickup truck, went around the back, and noticed it was locked.

"Dammit," Tristan said, turning around as Diana arrived.

Diana grabbed Tristan's arm and quickly forced him to hide behind the opposite-side of the truck with her. She then proceeded to hit Tristan.

"You moron! You complete idiot!" Diana shouted under the noise of the alarms. "You could have been shot! They could have mistaken you for an attacker, or anything else! What the hell is wrong with you?! You could've died! You could've been arrested, or... or worse! Why?! Why would you needlessly do that to me?!" she questioned, eyes watering as she stopped hitting him. "Why?!"

Tristan looked at his girlfriend as she cried in front of him. He looked back at her with slight shock, but little emotion.

"I'm sorry," Tristan simply admitted.

Tristan hugged her as she attempted to hand him the keys. The keys fell on the snow beneath them.

"I'm sorry…" Tristan simply said again in a cold voice.

"Don't you ever do that to me ever again – Don't you ever put yourself in the face of danger like that *ever* again."

"I won't, "Tristan replied. "I promise. No more."

"Good," Diana said, parting as they heard the sirens come closer as well as a new pair from the other side.

"Should we go back?" Tristan asked, picking up the keys and handing them to Diana.

Diana looked at Tristan who looked back at her.

"Tristan?" Diana questioned, looking at her boyfriend as he tipped forward.

Tristan caught himself and looked around.

"What the hell?" Tristan remarked, looking around.

"Are you okay?" Diana asked.

"Yeah, I'm okay," Tristan replied.

Diana looked at him. She looked around, looked at Tristan and then with the keys in hand, she unlocked the side of the pickup truck.

"What are you doing" Tristan asked.

"We're leaving," Diana simply said as she opened the door. "Get in!"

Tristan looked at her and quickly got in. Diana got in behind him and closed the door behind her. Together, they sat in the cold cabin of the pickup truck. Diana put the keys in the ignition and turned on the engine.

"Turn off the lights," Diana advised.

"Yeah," Tristan replied, putting on his seatbelt and turning the lights off.

Tristan then wiped the windows of the snow before them and looked ahead.

"Let's go! Hurry!" Diana said.

Tristan quickly switched gears and went towards the exit. They drove to the single lane exit where the entirety of the lot filtered into. They then came to a stop sign and another checkpoint, but it was abandoned. The only discomfort Diana had in her sudden change of heart was in the single security camera that was behind them, at the last checkpoint, but it was the least of her worries as they went on. Tristan sped up.

The vehicle came to an underpass with signs above that read 'Great Falls on the Fifteenth South Highway,' and 'Sweet Grass on Exit 397.' A blue sign next to these green ones read, 'Rest Area' Tristan drove under them and went along, steering straight and joining merging traffic coming from an onramp.

Diana saw many police vehicles driving towards them, on the opposite-side of the highway, and although they slowed down to let them pass, none of the police forces stopped them as they went to assist with the border crisis.

Tristan looked carefully ahead of him, focusing on the dark road ahead. He turned on the truck lights and then continued onwards. Diana remained quiet as they went on. Tristan cleared his throat.

"Why'd you change your mind?" Tristan asked, looking over to Diana who was huddled in the corner of the cabin.

"It wasn't for you," Diana simply replied. "It was for Charles."

Tristan looked at her.

"Care to elaborate?"

"Who do you think arrived at our discreet location with firearms and the gall to attack a federal office? Who has a history of attacking federal armed forces and is suspected of wiretapping the manor?"

"Oh right," Tristan responded. "When they called Charlemagne, they must have heard we were being held prisoner and dared to strike…"

Diana sighed and said, "You were right. If we go back to Charles, they'll just come for him to get to us. The Protection Squad isn't armed or in a state to deal with that right now. If we stay away from him, they'll have no reason to attack him, but if we stay near him, then…"

"Right. I understand."

"You better, because I'm genuinely not happy that you nearly got yourself killed just now," Diana argued. "You have total disregard for my emotions."

Tristan didn't respond. Diana crossed her arms.

"Just keep driving until we find the most rural town you can possibly imagine," Diana stated. "We'll hide there and rest for the night where they won't possibly dare to find us."

"Okay," Tristan quietly replied.

Act 4, Scene 5

Diana woke up suddenly as the pickup truck hit a pothole. She looked over to her side, to Tristan, and then straightened up as she had realized that she had fallen asleep. She checked the clock on the car dashboard to see that it was nearly midnight and they had been driving for close to two hours.

"I fell asleep," Diana said.

"Yeah, you did."

"How long was I out?"

"Not long," Tristan replied. "And before you ask, what happened earlier today wasn't some sort of hallucination or mind game."

"I wasn't going to ask, but thanks for reminding me that we just crossed into a foreign country illegally," Diana remarked. "We should probably pull over soon."

"We're coming into a town in another mile or so," Tristan replied. "You're right. I need some shut eye."

"I could use something to eat – hopefully someplace is still open at this hour."

"Yeah, hopefully," Tristan replied.

The darkness and breadth of the snow drifting down rapidly made it hard for Tristan to see in front of him. They were driving down a single lane highway with tall evergreen trees covered in snow on the side and the occasional rocky cliff every once in a while.

Tristan saw some lights ahead within a minute or two, and he slowed down to get a better look at what was ahead of them. He saw a diner ahead, on their right, along with a gas station and several other small shops in what was a smaller hamlet than St. Nazaire. He slowed down and turned right to enter into the parking lot of the diner.

"Nothing like a twenty-four hour diner," Diana remarked, going through her backpack for their money. "How're you holding?"

"Tired, but I'm fine otherwise," Tristan lied.

Diana gave him a look of pity. The couple then exited from the car and walked through the parking lot to reach the diner. Tristan pressed through the front doors, causing a set of bells to ring as they went in. The interior of the restaurant was quiet with a light sound of music in the background. There was a movement and shifting of glassware in the kitchen, and a CRT, long-reared, TV above them played an old Western film by the bar.

"Hello there, fellas," a waitress said from the kitchen, coming out and wiping her hands on her apron. "Feel free to sit anywhere. Can I get you anything to drink to start off?"

The waitress appeared to be in her late-forties, early fifties with golden blonde hair and wrinkled skin. She had tanned skin and her uniform was blue with a white apron. She had a notepad in her pouch and a pen behind her ear. Her hair was tied in a bun.

"Some tea would be nice," Diana requested, looking to Tristan. "What about you?"

"Tea, please," Tristan agreed, moving over to a stool to take his coat off and sit down.

"Sure thing," the waitress replied with a heartfelt smile.

Diana and Tristan sat down, and in under a minute, the waitress returned with two mugs of hot water and a packet of tea for each of them. She also brought over two menus which she set down before them. The couple looked at the menus as she returned into the kitchen again.

Tristan shivered at his stool, looking down at the menu before taking the cup of hot water into his hands to warm him up. Diana looked at the menu, thinking to herself before picking up the tea packet. Tristan did the same after setting his mug down. Diana observed a terrible tremble in Tristan's hands as he set his tea bag in his mug. Tristan pretended like nothing was wrong.

"Why don't you put your jacket back on?" Diana suggested.

"I'm fine, really," Tristan insisted. "I'm just a little chilled."

The waitress returned.

"You kids fancy anything in the menu?" the waitress remarked. "You're out rather late for a Tuesday. Where are you off to?"

"We're just doing a little late night driving," Diana remarked. "Nothing special – just got hungry and decided to come in."

"Are you from around here?" she asked in a friendly and charismatic tone. "I don't think I've seen kids like you around here before."

"Oh no, we're from West Glacier," Diana replied.

"Oh, you're awful far from home then. I suppose it's understandable to have a snack before the long drive ahead. What'll it be then?"

"I'll have a burger with fries, please," Diana asked, not having time to look at anything else.

"Good choice – our specialty is burgers. What about you, son?"

"I'll... have the same," Tristan replied, handing back his menu. "Thank you."

"Don't mention it," the waitress replied, writing down their orders. 'Fries okay?"

"Sure."

"Alright, two burgers with fries, coming up," the waitress nodded, finishing to write their order before ripping the piece of paper from her notepad. "Hey, Daryl! Two burgers with fries!"

"You got it, Sherri!" a voice from the kitchen shouted.

"It'll be a little while," Sherri said. "Give me a shout if you need anything else."

The couple settled down as Sherri left them. Tristan caught a break as they waited for their food. The two of them seldom talked. Diana was groggy from her nap, but also shaken up from the incident earlier. Within a couple of minutes, Sherri returned with their late dinner and sat it down before them. The couple then ate.

Diana finished her dinner promptly with a hefty appetite. Once she had finished, she looked over to Tristan who had barely touched his food. She had a smile on her face and shook her head at him.

"What?" Tristan questioned, looking at her.

"I was just thinking about what happened... at the border..."

"What about it?"

"God, you're such an idiot, Tristan," she said, lightly laughing. "I can't believe you ran for the car without remembering that I had the keys. What would you have done had I not followed you?"

Tristan shrugged.

"Funny of you to be thinking it was funny when I'm still feeling awful about what you said to me," Tristan replied.

"No duh," Diana said, shifting to a serious face. "Tristan, it's like you don't understand... I don't know if it's because you don't understand, but we've been a couple for almost two years, and I used to say to you that you were all I had after my mom died, and that's still true, but the thing about being a couple is that we become emotionally invested to the point where... How do I explain this?"

Diana paused for a moment.

"It's like we're a team," Diana explained. "Everything that happens to you has an effect on me. Wouldn't you agree the same to be true about everything that happens to me? If I were to... transfer to a high school in Harlech like I almost did because of Judith, or even something minor like take up a new sport, or whatever, it affects you and because of that, I'm mindful about certain decisions I make. It's why communication between us is more important than ever. It's why, when I didn't know what was wrong with you, I assumed the worst, because... when something was wrong with you, it's like something was wrong with my other half – and I was freaking out because I had no idea – my other half wasn't talking to me. Do you understand?"

Tristan stayed quiet and simply nodded. Diana sighed.

"We don't have far to go," Diana remarked. "Hopefully, we'll get some answers from your aunt."

"I don't know how we're going to return to Canada after this," Tristan remarked. "We don't have our licenses or passports – they kept them."

"We'll figure something out," Diana replied. "There's always a way."

Tristan brought up a wide smile as he looked at Diana with care. Euphoria fell over him as he looked at her, thinking of the words she had just said. He brought his hand over hers atop of the counter.

"You're really all I have," Tristan said.

"You're really all I need," Diana replied. "You have your quirks, your ups, and your downs, but in the end, I love you the same."

Tristan smiled at her. The couple dropped their smiles as they turned to the front entrance and listened to the sound of bells announce the entrance of some more customers. A small group of rugged men dressed in leather with helmets at their heads walked into the diner. They were tatted and seemed like a group of tough bikers who talked loudly at each other with aggressive and booming voices. All of them were of fair skin, some of brutish, dirty appearance with tattoos and bald heads, and others of slim, and slithery appearance like a snake. They were the lowest of lows, and led by a man who on his leather jacket, his name read 'Jack.'

"Hey, Sherri! It's your favorite boys!" Jack shouted.

"Fire up that coffee pot, Sherri!"

Diana cringed at the sound of their voices, disturbing the peace between her and Tristan. She looked at them as they sat down at the other side of the bar.

"Hey, Marley, take a look at this princess," a thug said, tapping his buddy's shoulder and looking over to Diana.

Diana frowned as she heard a wolf whistle come from these brutes.

"Hey, sweetie," Marley yelled to Diana. "How about you ditch that faggot and come ride with us?"

"I'll ride her," a third thug muttered.

The other bikers laughed. Diana gave the bikers a dirty look and forced Tristan to look away from them.

"Ignore them," Diana cautioned, sensing a discomfort from Tristan.

"It'll be hard to," Tristan replied.

The bikers continued to laugh and banter together. Diana clenched a fist over the counter and watched Tristan attempt to finish his food. Sherri soon came around with a pot of coffee. She brought up four mugs from underneath the counter and started to serve them some brew. Diana looked over and began to eavesdrop.

"Hey, Sherri-hun," Marley said. "Who's that sweetheart over there?"

"Who?" Sherri questioned as she poured coffee.

"The cute one by the jukebox. She next to that red-headed faggot."

"Marley, you really do call anything you don't like a queer, don't you?" Sherri replied, finishing to pour coffee. "Leave those two alone – they're good kids."

Sherri walked over to Diana and Tristan. She left their bill on the counter.

"Ignore them," Sherri said.

"It's fine," Diana replied. "Thank you."

"It really isn't," Tristan whispered as soon as Sherri left.

"Yeah, and what are you going to do about it?" Diana asked, looking at him.

Tristan looked back at her and picked up his napkin. He wiped his mouth and then span around, standing up from his seat and going over to Marley who sat nearest to them. Marley stood up and looked down at him. He was about three inches taller than Tristan. Tristan looked at him.

"What are you looking at, princess?" Marley questioned, glaring down at him.

"Are you talking dirty about my girlfriend?" Tristan asked.

"Girlfriend," the other thugs laughed, mocking him.

"Don't make us laugh, squirt," Marley said, laughing.

Tristan began to cough. He coughed into his arm. Diana stood up and went over to Tristan to bring him back, but before she could, she looked up at Marley and noticed that Tristan had coughed blood into his face.

"Oh my God," Diana remarked.

Marley held a look of deep anger.

"That's disgusting," a thug behind Marley remarked, seeing the blood.

"I ought to skin you alive!" Marley shouted.

Diana looked over to Marley as she attempted to get Tristan to leave. He stopped coughing.

"We're sorry," Diana replied. "We'll go…"

"Hell no," Tristan rejected, looking back at Marley. "Why don't you come at me then, big guy?"

Marley stepped forward upon wiping his face.

"Hey, take it easy, Marley," Jack warned. "They're just two stupid kids."

"Mess that faggot up!" another encouraged.

"The only faggot here are you two – the ones wearing the leather bondage gear," Tristan remarked.

"Oh my God…" Diana muttered.

Marley tightened his grip on a knife on the table and approached Tristan.

"I'll fix you up, queer!" Marley remarked.

"Hold on there. I know you like it rough with your pals, but I have a girlfriend, and we enjoy it nice and easy. Don't we, Diana?" Tristan remarked with a wide smile as the thug got closer.

"Tristan, stop," Diana warned.

Diana moved Tristan back over to their side as Marley approached them. Tristan looked at Marley with slight fear as he raised the knife towards him. In her panic, Diana grabbed the mug of tea and threw the water towards the thug. The scald caused him to shriek in pain, dropping the knife and bringing his hands to his reddened face. Tristan then broke off from Diana and punched him in the stomach, causing him to lurch down and then slamming his face into the countertop. Diana then quickly embraced Tristan to bring him down as she noticed a knife coming for them.

The knife grazed over them and pegged itself into the wall behind. Jack was left in shock of what had just happened. His expression had turned from sympathy towards the kids, to pure anger and wrath,

"Get them!" Jack shouted, pointing over to them as Marley fell over. "I want them alive so we can make it hurt!"

Diana let go of Tristan as they stood up with a thug vaulting over the counter and another going around to come the way that Marley came. A thug came for Tristan, causing him to quickly evade out of the way. The thug straightened up, cracked his neck, and raised his fists up. Tristan raised his own fists up and ducked as the biker tried to get the first strike. Tristan pounced up in return and struck the man under the chin, causing him to quickly envelop in anger.

Meanwhile, Diana grabbed her dinner knife as she faced the other biker behind the counter who laughed at her as he pulled out his own, a much longer and pointier switchblade, out. Diana stepped forward to face the biker who immediately lunged forward to try and slice her. Diana took a step back, evading the slice to her stomach and then taking a long step back as the thug tried to stab him in the abdomen instead.

Tristan continued to evade the slow strikes from the biker, punching him back again and causing him to trip and fall into a booth. The biker quickly recovered, trying to kick Tristan as he shot out and stood up. Tristan moved quickly and punched him across the face, causing some blood to shoot out from the side as he fell towards the jukebox. Tristan quickly moved over and grabbed the biker by the head, smashing it into the glass of the music player and knocking him out.

Diana evaded another attempted swipe from the thug she was dealing with, reaching the back wall under the TV, and causing her to look up. She jumped up, grabbed the TV by the sides, pulling it off the wall and hurling it towards the biker. The thug fell backwards, setting the TV monitor atop of him. Diana grabbed the switchblade and ducked down.

"You're pathetic!" Jack shouted to his friends. "Beaten up by a bunch of sissies!"

Jack placed his hand down on the counter and prepared himself to vault over. Diana crept forward and popped the knife into the man's hand while Tristan quickly went to his plate, grabbed it, and threw it towards him, hitting him in the face. Jack howled in pain and grabbed his hand. He then quickly left, tripping on one of his friends as he attempted to leave.

Tristan looked down at the thug and raised a fist. The man flinched and curled up.

"Please, just leave us alone!" Jack requested.

Diana looked at him and scoffed. She walked around to get her coat and threw Tristan his. Diana left some money for Sherri and then felt Tristan grab her hand so they could leave. The couple quickly left and then reunited outside in the parking lot where Diana hugged him. Tristan was fairly surprised to feel Diana hugging him, but embraced her. Diana soon parted and took his hand so that they could return to the pickup truck.

The couple entered the car. Tristan started the engine, pulled out, and then the two returned onto the highway to leave town.

"Well, that was fun," Diana said, looking out as they drove on.

"I think we're even now," Tristan simply replied. "You've done your dumb thing and I've done mine."

"Oh please, we're still doing your dumb thing," Diana remarked to him. "You're not seriously blaming that fight on me, are you?"

"You encouraged me to fight him," Tristan responded. "I wasn't going to let him dis' my girl like that!" he added, looking at Diana smiling.

Diana's smile grew wider. She continued to look out as they drove on.

"You know, I think I'm starting to enjoy this," Diana said, continuing to smile.

Act 5, Scene 1

Tristan woke up with Diana in his arms as they both lay down across the seats of the pickup truck cabin. The interior was dim as a fresh heap of snow covered the windshield glass, but it was still bright enough to irritate Tristan and give him a headache. He quickly closed his eyes and buried himself into Diana's hair to get a grip. He then pulled himself out and looked around with a heavy discomfort. He grabbed his phone on the dashboard and saw the time. It was nearly noon.

"Jeez..." Tristan said, nudging Diana. "Wake up..."

"Hmm..."

"Diana, wake up. It's noon and we need to keep going..."

Diana woke up and turned onto her back. She brought her hands to her eyes as Tristan sat up with their jackets over their bodies.

"It's so damn cold..." Tristan complained, putting on his coat.

Tristan turned on the car engine to bring in some heat. He then got out of the car while Diana opened her backpack to get some snacks for breakfast. Tristan got out of the car and touched down onto the snow of the causeway he parked at last night. He closed the door behind him, but froze and gritted his teeth. He grunted and fell to his knees, clenching his stomach and bending over to cough into the snow. His vision blurred and he saw before him blood touching down into the crisp, clean white snow. Tristan wiped his mouth with his hand and stood up. He took a deep breath and stood up, steadying himself as he held onto the exterior of the truck. Tristan gave himself a moment before he stood on his own. He then began to wipe the snow off the windows of the truck before returning to the driver's seat.

Diana handed him a granola bar, he ate, and the two then parted from the rear of a motel they decided to park at to sleep.

"I didn't think we'd sleep in," Diana said as they returned to the road.

"Yeah, me neither," Tristan replied, focusing on the road.

Diana looked at Tristan and saw that he was about as pale as he was yesterday. The two barely talked in the next two hours, but that didn't stop Diana from sitting right next to Tristan and resting her head on his shoulder. She looked forward through the windshield as they drove along, eyeing a sign that greeted them towards West Glacier.

"Here we are," Diana said, giving a light smile.

"Yeah, here we are," Tristan replied, looking around the small town and turning right to go along the major road to the convent.

"What are we going to do if your aunt doesn't know anything? What if she really is just a nun and not your mother?"

"The chances are too slim for that, Diana. She's a member of the same order that has their slogan engraved into my necklace – a necklace I've had since before I was adopted," Tristan stated. "The only logical conclusion is that I came from her."

The pickup truck continued to drive down the lone road bordered by a mess of tall evergreen trees. The car proceeded uphill as they drove along the cliff-side of a large gorge and then reached a bridge that crossed over the ravine. From there, they continued along the cliff-side road and then went into the forest around them to reach the isolated convent.

Within a couple of minutes, they were at the gates of the nunnery. Tristan turned off the truck engine and looked forward. The sky around them was bright, cloudless, and the trees at either side were covered in snow, and the ground covered in the bright white powder. The sun shined down in a way that reflected Tristan's happiness.

"What is it?" Diana asked, looking at him.

"I can't believe we're here," Tristan replied. "I'm actually going to get to see her... My biological mother is behind these gates... Can you believe that?"

"I'll believe it when we meet her and she confirms it," Diana replied, opening the car door and exiting. "Come on."

The couple stepped out and walked over to the iron gates that led onwards to the convent. The gates were simple, black, and round at the top. They connected to stone pillars, which connected to a tall iron fencing the stretched into the forest around them. The couple walked towards one of the pillars where there was an intercom.

Tristan looked at the intercom and saw that there was a camera in the middle, and a button below. He pressed the button. The button caused a buzz to occur. He waited for a response.

"Welcome to the Convent of Our Lady's Maidens," a voice responded. "Sister Erika speaking, how can I help you?"

"H-hi," Tristan responded. "My name is Tristan Merrick and I'm here to see Sister Witeveen? Please?"

"I'm sorry, but the convent does not accept visitors from males," Sister Erika replied.

"Please, it's important," Tristan responded. "I'm her son."

No immediate response came.

"Please hold," Sister Erika finally said.

The couple looked at each other and waited for almost five minutes.

"Hello, this is Mother Doherty. How can I help you?" a fragile old voice questioned.

"Hi, my name is Tristan Merrick. I'm here to see my mother, Sister Witeveen. I'm not sure what her first name is, but she's at this convent... and I know she's my mother."

"I'm sorry, but Sister Sophia Witeveen is not expecting any visitors... nor do we accept male visitors, even from family members."

"No, you don't understand. I *am* her son. She left me with my aunt (her sister), Elisabeth Witeveen, when I was two-months old and with a necklace of St. Luke. On the necklace is your convent's motto, *Deus Aeternum*, so I know – I know that she left me with her because of this necklace. It's important that I see her – it's an emergency!"

There was a brief pause before Tristan got a response.

"I'm sorry," the initial girl spoke, Sister Erika, "but this is a convent for virgin sisters of our Lord, Jesus Christ. I believe you may be mistaken to believe that Sister Witeveen could be your mother. She's been with us for over twenty years... and *Deus Aeternum* is a common Catholic Latin phrase. I'm going to have to ask you to leave now. Thank you and God Bless."

The intercom then went silent.

"Wait," Diana stated, interrupting and brushing to the center of the camera "I'm a girl. Can I visit Sister Witeveen? Please?"

The intercom didn't immediately respond.

"I'm sorry, but our convent does not allow visitors from non-family members. Good day."

The intercom then went silent again. Tristan looked at Diana, stunned.

"What the hell..." Tristan remarked. "I'm her son! Let me see her!"

"Tristan..." Diana muttered, pulling him away from the intercom. "Maybe... Maybe they're not lying... Maybe... this is it. Maybe this is the end."

Tristan's hand shook as he was forced away from the intercom and back to the pickup truck. Diana moved him away as he passively resisted.

"Come on, we don't need trouble from the police..." Diana warned.

Tristan looked over to the gates in defeat. Diana opened the driver's seat door for him. He looked away and stepped inside. Diana closed the door for him and then quickly went around via the front of the pickup truck, and entered on the other side.

"What now?" Tristan questioned. "We've broken so many laws... We ran away from Charles, the police, the federal authorities... We beat up a bunch of pervy bikers... What for?"

"We had an adventure, Tristan," Diana stated. "Sometimes, they don't end the way we'd hope they'd end. It's not over yet though... We can regroup and look at other places to check, perhaps think about driving over to North Dakota?"

"What'd be the point..." Tristan replied, looking forward.

Tristan looked pale. His hands continued to tremble despite the heat blaring from the heater. He sniffled as if he had a runny nose and then looked at Diana.

"Diana, there's something you should know," Tristan said, "about when I ran from the border and you brought me behind the truck to hide."

"What is it?" Diana asked, looking at him with a warm smile.

Tristan looked back at her and froze up.

"I..." Tristan said, hesitating, "want you to know that I'm sorry. I really am. I know you love me, and that what happened in Russia with me almost dying of hypothermia was traumatic for you, but despite knowing that, I still almost brought the same fear within you… The way you got mad at me then – the anger you had towards me for not considering you. You love me more than I love you… I'm questioning whether I love you at all, deeply, because…"

"Oh, Tristan…" Diana replied, wiping the tear from his eye. "It's one thing to say I love you, and it's another to say it with your actions. You've done both, but I don't expect either of us to love each other in the same intensity. If this relationship were equal-sided, it would have ended a long time ago… but it hasn't because it's not. We're still learning about each other, and this adventure has been worth it for that alone."

Diana kissed Tristan on the cheek. She then parted and looked at him with pity. Tristan looked at her for a brief moment before he turned the keys in the car and ignited the engine. Diana smiled and held on to Tristan's right arm as he changed gears.

"Let's get out of here," Diana said.

"Sure thing," Tristan replied.

Tristan made a three-point turn and started to head back down the road from where he came. He was discontent, anxious and fearful, all at the same time, but nothing could be done. He reached the single lane road on the cliff of the gorge. Below them were endless coniferous trees covered in snow for about a kilometer to the other side. The two cliff-sides came together further ahead at where there was an iron bridge at a fifty meter gap. The two sides then diverged again on the other side, but as they came to the bridge, Tristan began to notice the sound of a motorcycle. He looked and saw someone on a motorcycle, coming towards them.

The rider was riding a large motorbike that was loud and obnoxious, but he wore an interesting choice of clothes. The individual wore a gas mask over their face and a dark brown leather Sherpa jacket. He also wore brown cargo trousers, black snow boots, and a steel helmet. His trousers were equipped with various canisters. He was armed like a commando. The rider drove past the truck and over the bridge.

Tristan didn't make much of the rider until he looked in his side-view mirror and turned around. He became even more fearful as he stared at the man's gas mask and began to remember.

"Are you seeing this?" Tristan questioned as the driver got closer to them.

"Did he turn around?" Diana replied instead.

"Yeah, he did," Tristan said, watching the biker produce a pistol in their hands. "Oh no… It's him… Duck!"

Diana and Tristan ducked their heads down as shots fired through the rear of the pickup truck, piercing through the glass of the windshield.

"What the hell!" Diana shouted, looking forward. "Steer straight!"

Tristan raised his head up and controlled his steering as he swerved on the narrow bridge. The mysterious stranger drove forward so that he was next to them on the opposite direction lane. He took his pistol and pointed it at their tires. Tristan swerved the truck towards the motor bike in an instinctive manner, hitting the motorcyclist as he backed off and drove behind them. The mysterious stranger continued to fire towards them.

Diana found the sound of bullets hitting the back of the pickup truck to be unsettling. Several shots entered the cabin. The truck turned onto the opposite cliff-side road.

"What do I do?" Tristan shouted, braking to slow down as he turned.

"I... I don't know!" Diana replied. "I don't think there's anything we can except drive, or... fight?!"

Tristan pressed down on the brake harder as he noticed mysterious stranger directly behind them, but he swerved out of the way again and drove up next to them. Tristan turned the steering wheel to try and run him off the road, but he was too fast. The figure simply evaded them and continued to fire until he ran out of bullets.

Diana watched as he put his firearm away onto a holster on his leg and then brought both hands to the handle of his bike. The figure then pulled back.

"I think he's out," Diana said, looking behind and then facing forward.

Another series of bullets started to punch through the rear glass, causing it to finally shatter and hit the windshield in greater volume. The mysterious stranger drove closer and started to hip fire as reached a mild turn. A loud burst filled theirs ears followed by the truck slouching in the rear and bumping up and down. Tristan soon lost control of the vehicle, forcing him to let go of the brake with the tires blown out, but they came into a turn too fast and began to swerve uncontrollably.

Tristan let go of the wheel as the car mounted over the road-side barrier. He grabbed Diana and opened his door for them to fall out and hit the side of the cliff instead. Diana held on to Tristan as they started to slide down the steep side of the ravine, going down and seeing the truck fly through the air and go further alone than them. Diana saw the bottom of the cliff as they passed through the sharp branches and dodged the trunks of several trees before hitting the bottom and rolling at the landing.

Diana had held on to Tristan throughout, and when they reached the plush snow at the bottom, she opened her eyes to look up. A sharp explosion was heard in the distance (most likely the truck), which caused Diana to instantly get up and go over to Tristan who was breathing heavily. Diana tried to help him up, touching his right forearm, but Tristan shouted out in pain and forced her away as he struggled to move.

A barrage of bullets started to rain down on them from above. Diana looked up, struggling to see the road or the mysterious stranger. She walked around to Tristan's other side, avoiding his wounded arm, and instead helping him up from the other side so they could run deeper into the forest.

"My arm... I think my arm is broken," Tristan remarked as they ran along.

"Yeah, I know," Diana replied, struggling to hold on to him to help him run.

Bullets continued to rain down, forcing Diana to intensify her hold onto Tristan and run faster through the forest. Diana looked over to Tristan and saw a sudden appearance of blood on his face, causing her to panic and hasten.

Eventually, the barrage of gunfire settled down and stopped, but the couple continued along as Diana lost control of herself and simply continued forward. She passed underneath the bridge and went into the area beyond. She continued on and on, clueless of what to do, frozen over the fact that Tristan was heavily wounded. Soon, he started to slouch over, forcing Diana to grab him and try to pick him up.

"I... I can't go on," Tristan said, panting.

"No, get up!"

"No... I... I can't."

"God dammit, Tristan, get up!" Diana shouted, pulling at his healthy arm.

"Go… Get out of here! I'm slowing you down!" Tristan said, coughing up more blood into the snow.

Tristan then fell over, face first into the snow.

"No…!" Diana remarked, tearing up as she continued to pull him. "Get up, Tristan! Please, just get up!"

Diana looked around the forest impatiently and with desperation in her eyes. Her voice quavered. She ran her hands through her hair and thought carefully on her own as Tristan had passed out. She looked behind and imagined the mysterious stranger hot on their tail. She then looked forward and took a couple of steps towards the fog. In the distance, she saw a small wooden house.

"Look! Tristan! A cabin! Come on, you can make it! You're going to be okay!"

Diana helped Tristan back onto his feet. He had regained some slight consciousness, but was dazed. She brought his healthy arm around her neck again and helped him over where she saw not one, but several wooden structures and tens ahead in the cold, dense fog. Diana soon reached one of these structures.

"Help!" Diana shouted as loud as she could. "Help!"

Diana reached one of the doors of the cabins and began to knock as hard as she could to get the attention of the occupants. The door eventually opened to reveal a woman with extremely long hair standing under the door frame. The home smelt a little bit like skunk. The woman wore a long shirt over her torso. Her skin was dark and her hair black as coal. She wore handmade boots at her feet and black stretch pants at her legs.

"Please, you have to help us! My friend is injured and we're being chased by a maniac! Please, help him!" Diana pleaded.

"Oh my – Svante!" the woman shouted, helping Diana and Tristan into the cabin. "Svante, come quick!"

Act 5, Scene 2

Diana waited in the living room of the cabin belonging to a man and a woman who went by the simple names of Svante and Nirvana. The building was warmed by a fire at a fireplace and the couple had brought Diana an extra blanket sown locally for her to rest on their couch. The local physician was currently examining Tristan, who was in a guest bedroom. Twilight had struck and it was nearly dark outside.

Nirvana had brought Diana some special herbal tea to share and Diana drank a bit of it – seeing it tasted a bit like pine. Diana stood up immediately once the doctor left the bedroom they had brought Tristan into to give his report.

"Is he going to be okay?" Diana questioned with anxiety and anticipation.

"A light wound on his wrist is what I found. I've bandaged it and suggested that Nirvana go in now to clean him – he's covered in blood from the trauma."

"Trauma? Is that all that it was?" Diana questioned.

"Yes," the doctor replied, "trauma. I suggest you get him some sedatives to help him rest for the remainder of the night. I'll return tomorrow to see him and do another examination, until then, that's all I can proscribe."

"Wouldn't it be smarter to get him to a hospital?" Diana suggested.

"Nothing like that would be required," the doctor remarked. "I do, however, find myself curious to know what happened to reach this predicament."

"The kids were attacked by a mysterious gunman," Svante reported. "In this country, accessing firearms is all too easy. Probably some white supremacist loon. These here kids were travelling along the roads and forced off, down the cliff when they ran to us. Apparently they had trouble with some bikers on their way here."

"Oh dear, it's a miracle that the two of you were even alive then. If you find yourself in pain later in the day, please find me in my tent so I can see you. Until then," the doctor nodded and bowed. "Good night."

"Thank you, doctor," Nirvana replied, seeing him off before closing the door. "How are you feeling, Diana?"

"I'm okay. I'm just very worried for Tristan."

"Well, I'm sure he's going to be okay," Nirvana assured her. "I'm going to go and clean him up. I'll also make him some tea."

"I should talk to Alter and see about raising security for the commune with this 'maniac' on the loose out there," Svante remarked. "We got to be careful."

"Thank you so much for all that you're doing for us," Diana said. "I really am extremely grateful."

"Nonsense, Diana. We're all brothers and sisters – medical aid is a human right. It's only fair to offer treatment when we're all family," Nirvana said in a lax tone.

"My wife is right," Svante stated with a peaceful look on his face. "Now if you'll excuse me…"

Svante left the cabin. From what Diana had heard, he was one of the leaders of the local village, or 'advisor' as they referred to them. He was a young man, possibly in his late-thirties with a thick beard, long brown hair, and circular black sunglasses. He wore a red vest over his black sweater. He also wore blue jeans and a straw hat with black boots. He spoke in a local accent while Nirvana had more an earthy accent and breathy tone. Diana had deduced that she was Amerindian.

"You and your friend are welcome to stay as long as it takes for your wounds to heal, but in return, we'd have to ask that you come and help around in the commune," Nirvana stated. "We're a small town and there aren't very many of us around. Any help is appreciated in return for the aid we're giving you."

"Yeah, of course," Diana replied. "Anything to help you, help us."

"Excellent," Nirvana replied. "River?" she shouted.

A mixed-race boy with a short nose, flat midface, and thin upper lip came down from a loft above the bedrooms. He wore a long-sleeved brown shirt and jeans. He also wore handmade boots similar to his mother. His hair was long, unkempt and dry. It was a similar shade as his mother's hair. By his appearance, he looked to be around fifteen-years old or younger. He was slim.

"What?" River questioned.

"This is Diana. She needs to be shown around the various workshops, and then taken to the barracks and cantina. Make sure you set her up with a bed with the others."

"If it's alright, I'd rather spend the night near Tristan to keep an eye on him," Diana remarked. "Please."

"Nonsense," Nirvana replied, "we'll have one of our nurses do that. Get as much rest as you can, and let your friend be our responsibility. He's in good care."

Diana didn't respond. River looked at Diana with a plain look. He then went over to a coat rack and picked up a denim jacket to put on. Diana put on her own coat and left the blanket behind. They stepped outside, and Diana looked around the supposed commune that was established in the forest. She didn't quite understand what it was that the locals were doing in the middle of nowhere, but she didn't care to find out. She simply followed River as he took her to a large pit in the middle of the village.

"This is the center of the village," River said. "We come here when the Elders have an announcement."

"Who are the Elders?" Diana questioned.

"The eldest and wisest among us," River explained. "They guide and protect us."

"Oh, so they're like a council or the government of the town..."

"We do not have a government. We are ruled only by the Elders who are immortal. Their spirit enlightens those that are chosen among us, and through these chosen, the advisors, they speak to us."

"Oh... okay," Diana replied, walking with River to another building.

River showed Diana a lumber mill, a warehouse, the cantina, an outhouse, and then a barn. The barn was large and had various fenced pens for various animals including cows, sheep, chickens, ducks, and even a goat and a horse.

"Aw, you've got farm animals," Diana said, admiring the sheep. "Do you also have a slaughterhouse somewhere?"

"Slaughterhouse?" River inquired. "We do not 'slaughter' anything in this village because that would be inhumane. All animals deserve equal respect to humans."

"You... you don't eat meat then," Diana replied. "Where do you get your protein from?"

"Only on the seventh day of the week do we sacrifice a wild animal hunted from outside to the Elders," River explained, "but even then, we do not eat the sacrifice."

"You'll kill a wild animal, but you won't eat meat?"

"Why would we want to eat our friends?" River questioned. "Cows and sheep have as much sanctity as the human life, you know. Not to mention that red meat is bad for you."

"Okay..." Diana replied, looking at the various animals. "What about milk? Eggs? Wool? I see a lot of clothing here is made with wool."

"We never take from our friends without their permission," River stated. "Thankfully, our sheep friends bless us with wool every season for us to make clothes. You ask a lot of strange questions, outsider."

"Yeah, that's me... the strange one," Diana muttered as they left the barn.

The two continued to look around the barn. Diana saw a pair of snowmobiles at the back of the barn, but didn't ask questions about them. They instead left and River showed Diana the barracks, which was a large building with various cots inside. The two went inside.

"You will sleep where everyone else sleeps," River said, showing Diana to a cot. "You will sleep in this cot."

Diana looked at the cot and then at the others.

"Jeez, how am I supposed to tell which is mine when all of these beds look the same," Diana questioned. "Where do you sleep?"

"I sleep in a cabin with my parents," River replied. "Father says that it is good that the advisors of the town sleep in their own homes."

"Okay..." Diana replied, looking back at her cot.

"I will bring you a blanket and a basket with some personal effects. When you hear the horn, you'll know that it is suppertime for you to go to the cantina."

"Thanks, "Diana replied, watching as the slim boy left her alone.

Diana sat down atop of her cot and took a deep breath. She thought to herself as she looked around the depressing living situation that these people were in. She was a minority among them – most of who had dark skin and were either Amerindian, Asian, or some sort of mixed-race. Diana did not feel comfortable around any of them, even the ones that looked white. All she could do was breathe easy knowing that Tristan was safe. Tristan was alive.

Act 5, Scene 3

Diana woke up the next morning to the darkness of the barracks and snoring of all the other colonists. The night felt like the nights she used to spend in the youth shelters on the worst nights of her life back when her father was alive. It was distinctly similar between the infighting, the public intimacy, and all the displeasing practices of which she didn't have to or want to be a witness to. A loud horn woke up the rest of the colonists as Diana uncomfortably lay in her cot. She instantly put on her boots, which were laying by her bedside, and zipped up her coat to go and have breakfast.

Last night, the colonists were fed a gruel made of barley, but this morning, it was a porridge made of oats. Diana sat down with her ration of porridge, served in a smooth wooden bowl and began to eat with the wooden spoon she had been given. She lightly tapped her meal before looking up and around to the others around her. The others either quietly ate, talked, or argued amongst each other. She couldn't help but compare the setting to a prison, but in this prison, the prisoners were here voluntarily as Diana learned as she asked some of the colonists.

"Where are the 'advisors?'" Diana asked the woman in front of her. "I don't see Svante or Nirvana around."

"The advisors are meditating in the longhouse," a woman replied.

"Yes, and bless them," a man on the right added. "The Court doesn't eat at all – they rather spend their time praying to the Elders to give us the strength and protection throughout the day as we live for the good of the colony. Isn't that wonderful of them?"

"How very noble…" Diana simply responded, "but they've got to eat, right?"

Nobody replied to Diana and instead ignored her as they finished their own meals. She looked at them and then down to her food. She then looked back to them.

"Do any of you guys like this place?" Diana asked.

"I couldn't imagine anywhere else, but here," the colonist on her right said.

"It's a harsh world and nowhere is safe like the commune," the woman ahead opined. "We are freest here."

Diana frowned at these responses and took a deep sigh. She stood up and took her bowl to clean it, and whilst she washed it, she thought to herself whilst looking at all the people around her.

"I'm in a different culture and world… one that has extended a hand to help Tristan," Diana remarked under her breath. "I am a visitor and a guest, and I will abide by their customs."

Diana left the cantina and went to the main lodge to knock and hopefully see Tristan before she went to work. Her knocks on the door revealed the doctor, Alter, who stepped forward, which forced Diana to step back. He was a man with light brown skin, slanted eyes, and yet with a Caucasoid complexion. He was older, in his late-fifties with greying hair. He looked Eurasian, or Turkish.

"How is he?" Diana questioned. "Tristan?"

"I saw him, and I am to meet with Svante in the Longhouse to discuss his condition with him," Alter stated.

"Is he okay?" Diana questioned again with more urgency and haste.

"His wrist is better, I believe. You have nothing to worry about. He's fine."

The doctor moved forward, attempting to close the door behind him.

"Wait," Diana interrupted, attempting to get by. "Can I see him?"

"No," Alter rejected. "Let him rest. You must not disturb him and cause him stress."

The doctor closed the door and then walked off. Diana looked towards the front door and stepped back as it opened again. River came out, dressed in different clothes, but in the same jacket. He wore a red headband around his head.

"Hi," Diana greeted. "Can I see Tristan?"

"It's time to work," River replied. "It's time for the first round of labor."

"Oh… okay," Diana responded in a slightly disappointed tone.

"Come with me and I'll take you to the lumber mill," River said, leading Diana there.

Diana walked alongside him.

"What's your role in the commune?" Diana questioned.

"I am with the nurses in the clinic. I like it there."

River left Diana at the lumber mill and then left to attend to the clinic. She followed the other works to grab a dull axe and walk with them into woods for a short hike. It was a heavily cold morning, but once they had reached their destination and proceeded to swing at the trees, splitting trunks into logs, and then bringing the haul back on a sled, the exercise had raised her body temperature enough to keep her warm. Diana's breakfast found her hungry quicker than she expected to be, but there was no time to eat as the second horn sounded. River showed up at the lumber mill when the labor group returned with all the wood they had collected.

"Here," River said, presenting a small basket to Diana. "It's a present for you."

Diana took the basket in hand. It contained various exotic items of what appeared to be herbs and homeopathic medicines. Before she could express her thanks, the boy had sheepishly wandered off. She took the basket and set it aside, and then returned to work where they had set on shaving the bark.

At the sound of the third horn, Diana and the others left their axes and planers behind at the mill and then made their way back to the cantina for lunch. For lunch, they ate a lame vegetable soup with a thin piece of a bitter bread. Diana sat down at a bench with the other colonists and began to take a couple of spoons of the soup into her mouth. She then looked at the others just as she did in the morning, and then at the piece of bread. She finished her soup and took the bread with her, placing it in the bowl, and leaving the cantina with it.

"Forgive me, Lord, for what I am about to do, but it is nothing more than deceit," Diana remarked under her breath.

The commune was quiet with all of the colonists, with the exception of the advisors, at the cantina in addition to the guardsmen before the longhouse. The guards wore primitive armor in the form of knee-pads, elbow-pads, and helmets. They were armed like ceremonial guards with harpoons, or spears, outside of the temple.

Diana walked over, but was blocked in her path to the front doors by the guards.

"The Longhouse is a sacred place not welcome to trespassers," one of the guards said. "What is your business?"

"I just want to talk to Svante," Diana replied, holding her bowl in her hand. "I have an offering for him."

The first guard looked at the second. They decided to allow it as they knocked on the front door for her. The door soon opened with Nirvana looking to Diana with a bit of confusion. The guards looked away from them and straight forward.

Diana smelt smoke from within the longhouse. She could also see a fire behind in the center of the room – a large bonfire with the chatter of the advisors in addition to the crackle of wood burning. However, Diana didn't only smell the distinct whiff of burning wood, but also something else… something masked. She couldn't tell what it was and she could not see what else was happening as Nirvana's large poncho blocked most of her view. Diana simply looked back at her.

"Diana, what are you doing here? Shouldn't you be having your lunch?" Nirvana questioned.

"I have an offering for Svante – my lunch, as a sign of gratitude, for his hospitality and sacrifice of fasting."

"Oh, I don't think Svante would…"

Nirvana was interrupted. Svante appeared behind her.

"What appears to the trouble?" Svante questioned. "Dana? What are you doing here?"

I have an offering for you – to show my thanks and appreciation for the fasting you and the others do in praying instead of eating."

"The Longhouse is a restricted area, especially to outsiders. You're lucky you didn't know that, because the punishment for those that do is severe. Keep your lunch to yourself…"

"I'm sorry, but I was just expressing my gratitude for the help you've done with Tristan. I heard that the doctor, Doctor… I'm not sure what his last name is, but…"

"We do not have last names in this commune, Dana," Svante corrected. "Last names are patriarchal, and in this town, we are considerate of others and only go by the names we are blessed with."

Diana didn't respond.

"Don't worry about your sibling. I spoke with Alter and he informed me that Tristan is healing. He is doing better. Why don't you come and see him after lunch?" Svante offered.

"Really?" Diana replied. "I'd love to."

"Good," Svante said. "The Elders command that you go and finish your lunch, however. You will need your strength. Please leave."

Svante closed the door as he stepped back, leaving Diana outside knowing that she would get to see her other half again soon.

Act 5, Scene 4

Diana walked to the front door of the main cabin after finishing her lunch, knocked on the door, and waited for a response. Nirvana opened the door and let her in. Diana had forgotten of the warmth of the cabin as nowhere else in the commune that she had gone was like it. Diana walked forward and looked to Nirvana as she closed the door.

"Feel free to go and see him, Diana," Nirvana said, pointing to the room where Tristan was in. "He's just there."

"Thank you," Diana expressed, walking over and opening the door.

Diana closed the door behind her as she entered the quiet bedroom where Tristan lay in a single bed carved out of wood. The bed was dressed in authentic cotton sheets and had a mattress.

"Diana," Tristan said, sitting up as he raised a smile.

"Tristan," Diana replied, walking over and hugging her. "How're you doing?"

"A little better," Tristan said in a slightly weak voice, "but I've been feeling weak. I don't think the 'medicine' they're giving me is doing me any good, but at least they set my arm…"

"Their people are doing the best they can," Diana replied. "I just hope you can feel a little better, because when you do, I'm going to take you out of here so that we can find a hospital. Okay? You just need to find some strength though… You won't make it the way you are now."

Diana jumped as she heard a knock on the door. She turned around and saw Svante enter.

"Ah, there you are," Svante said, looking at her. "You see, he's all well. The fourth horn is about to blow, Diana, and I thought it'd be welcoming to you if you came with us on a little trip out instead of returning to the mill. How about it?"

"Of course, Svante. I'd love to," Diana responded in a plain tone.

"Diana…" Tristan said in a weak, raspy voice.

"Excellent," Svante interjected. "Come on with me to the hunting lodge, and we'll set ourselves up with the right tools to go on out."

"Sure," Diana agreed, looking back to Tristan. "I'll see you later. Take it easy…"

"Diana…" Tristan protested as she left.

Diana walked with Svante from his home to the hunting lodge, which was a small shack with various items. They met with Alter there as well as River. Four backpacks were prepared, each with various supplies including a flare gun, first aid kits, bear traps, and other equipment. The main piece of equipment were two single-shot, bolt-action rifles, one given to Alter, and another held by Svante. The backpacks were given to River and Diana respectively. Svante wore a type of bandolier, or sash with bullet cartridges. Diana looked at them as they readied themselves before Svante looked to her.

"On the last day of the week, we sacrifice a wild animal to the Elders," Svante explained. "For the ritual, we require the dirtiest and most brutish of animals."

"I thought animals were considered to be friends," Diana replied.

"Not all animals deserve such mercy," Svante went on. "Some animals are of the most disgusting and foul nature, so sick that they are better dead or better off as the sacrificial offerings in this weekly ritual. Today, you will come with us and take part in the ritual tonight."

Diana didn't object and left with them. They left the lodge and then the commune, walking into the forest. Diana looked around as they walked. She appeared slightly fearful and paranoid, looking around as if she was looking for someone, or she was being looked for. The mysterious stranger was on her mind. Diana stayed close to the adults as they walked into the woods.

The forest was calm. The skies were grey. It began to snow lightly. The group travelled deep into the forest, walking for several minutes. All that there was to hear was the arctic howl of wind against the snow – the chill air. The four of them stopped and Svante looked at Alter. Diana looked around. From where they were, the trees mostly consisted of evergreen and fir trees.

"I think this be good," Svante said. "Why don't we split up from here? Alter, go on and check on that killin' and I'll stay with the kids."

Diana looked at the adults with slight confusion. Alter left and went downhill. She breathed slowly and looked over to Svante.

"Have you ever fired a rifle before?" Svante asked Diana.

"I'm familiar with them," Diana replied. "I've been taught how to fire one, but never been out like this."

"Come on then," Svante encouraged, walking up to a ridge. "River, you stay here and keep watch."

"Yes, dad."

Diana followed and came to the top. Svante came down and knelt down into a prone position. He laid the rifle in the snow, securing the bipod and holding the rifle in his hands.

"Here, take the rifle," Svante said, moving out of the way for Diana. "The scope will help you line your shot – you can see better if you close one eye and squint with the other."

Svante brought his hands onto Diana's so he could transfer his grip around the barrel and trigger to her.

"Very good," Svante remarked. "You know, the others have had nothing but praise for you. I heard from the lumber mill that you're a hard worker. They were impressed with the hustle you put in this morning, and I was taken back by your offering during lunch."

"I just wanted to repay the favor," Diana replied, looking around with the rifle as she looked down the scope.

"How would you like to stay with us forever?" Svante offered. "We could use someone like you, and your fortitude is like none other. You're an empowered woman. You and my daughter, River, could one day become wise judges."

"Daughter? I didn't realize he was a girl," Diana responded.

"She is," Svante corrected. "You can't be presumptuous of others. She may have boy parts, but she's no different than my wife. There'll be a lot you have to learn, but we'll educate you and you will learn. You and River could be the run of the town, and your litter too."

Diana frowned and gave a sigh as she said, "I'm sorry, but I'm already committed to someone else."

"To your red-headed friend, I know, and that's what you'd have to let go off because a boy like him is no good for this world," Svante explained. "His masculinity is a scourge on this world, and you deserve better. It'll only be time until he leaves you, because they always do... Boys like him are always thinking of it, and you deserve better. You see, the most foul of creatures is man."

Diana froze as she felt Svante's hand over her lower back. She lost focus in the scope.

"If River isn't your fancy, there's no reason you can't have more," Svante said. "In this township, we share and are one family, you and me."

"Even though you're white, you'd be an important asset to the commune," Svante stated. "You can leave your mark with River. Remove yourself and start anew…"

"Please don't touch me," Diana remarked, losing patience. "I'm only seventeen and Tristan isn't perfect, but he has a good heart and I love him."

"Forget about him, Dana. Alter told me the truth about him and he's dying. There's something wrong with him that extends beyond who he is. He won't last a week and he'll suffer to the end… you need to rid the beast. Look into your scope and see…"

Diana looked through her scope and looked around. In the distance, she saw Tristan being pulled by two men. He was weak and vomiting before him. Alter was nearby as they brought him over to a tree to tie him to it. Diana then tensed her body as she felt Svante come atop of her, pinning her into the ground. She attempted to struggle with him.

"Do you see him?" The suffering he is going through – the pointless suffering? You're better off without him – set him free. Stay here, and relieve yourself. Happiness awaits for you here, where you will be treated like a queen. Kill him…"

"No," Diana grunted, struggling with Svante.

Svante brought his cold fingers around Diana's waist. She broke free and hit him in the head with the butt of the rifle, firing it into the air and spooking some birds nearby to scatter.

"Oh, you little tease," Svante remarked in a perverted tone, bringing a hand to his eye.

Diana quickly stood up as Svante stood behind her. She looked at him and he lunged for her, aiming for her jeans.

Diana struggled with him again, attempting to hit him with the rifle. Diana was eventually able to push him over the ridge and below, rifle and all, allowing her to run.

River looked over to Diana as she ran down the hill. She then passed him and went into the woods and towards Tristan. He ran after her.

"Tristan!" Diana shouted.

"Diana!" Tristan yelled back. "Diana! Help!"

Diana continued to run towards Tristan until she was tackled by Alter. He was larger than Svante and heavier. He placed his weight upon her and attempted to choke her.

"Let him be free, young one!" Alter rationalized. "It is the will of the Elders!"

A shot was fired and Alter became deadweight. Diana shoved him aside and looked over to see that River had fired the shot. She looked at him briefly and then stood up to go over to Tristan. She quickly untied and removed the blindfold from his eyes.

"Diana," Tristan said, looking at her, "what's going on?"

"We need to leave," Diana replied, taking his hand. "Come on…"

The couple ran off, leaving River behind and venturing into the forest to make their escape. They ran for less than two minutes until Diana stopped to notice that Tristan couldn't keep up due to a terrible cough and shortness of breath.

"Oh damn, that's right," Diana remarked, kneeling down to help Tristan onto his feet. "Come on, we can't slow down…"

"What happened?" Tristan questioned, looking to her.

"Svante, that little pedophile, tried to grope me and get me to kill you. He tried to have me join this sick, perverted little cult," Diana explained. "I knew there was something wrong with this village, and I tried to be respectful, but…"

"Why are we running back towards it then?" Tristan questioned.

"Because I saw some snowmobiles in the barn," Diana replied. "They're our only hope now, so please keep up…"

"I'll… I'll try," Tristan replied with uncertainty.

"Come on."

Diana and Tristan continued to run forward, but a different sight ahead could be seen as they got closer. A bright, orange-red horizon lied before them that was all too familiar to Tristan. The entire commune had been set ablaze with a large buildup of smoke rising into the air as every wooden structure burned.

"What the hell?!" Diana remarked, looking around as they got to the outskirts. "Come on, we've got to find those snowmobiles!"

Diana ran with Tristan into the burning village where dozens of people were panicking, shrieking and crying out. The situation was chaotic and challenged Diana's ability to focus as she searched for the barn. Diana eventually saw it and led Tristan there.

The couple ran inside and Diana went halfway into the burning building before realizing that the snowmobiles had been taken. She stood back, stunned, and then turned around. The couple faced Svante.

"Well, well," Svante said with the rifle in hand, "still around, I see."

Svante stepped forward and cornered the kids in the barn. They stepped back.

"Stay away from us, you freak," Diana snarled, standing next to Tristan.

"I suppose I was wrong about you," Svante stated. "You're no more trash than he is – white trash that deserves to be killed off…"

Svante raised his rifle to take a shot. Diana pushed Tristan out of the way and braced herself for the shot, but instead, she opened her eyes to hear the sharp, painful shock that came out of Svante's mouth. A harpoon had inserted through Svante's chest, up through his abdomen at around the fifth or fourth rib. He leaned back with the harpoon through him, eyes and mouth open. His shirt was damp with blood that quickly poured out to stain. He then collapsed on the ground with the other end of the harpoon sticking out from his back. Svante was dead.

Diana's eyes were wide from what she had seen, but they widened further as she saw what, or who had thrown the harpoon as it was a menacing figure who stepped towards her. Diana did not step back as she was in total shock.

The Mysterious Stranger looked at Diana through the eyeholes of his gasmask. A reflection of the flames that surrounded them could be seen instead of his green eyes. Wooden beams from the ceiling fell down and separated her from Tristan behind her. The Mysterious Stranger stepped forward again and pulled the harpoon from Svante, raising his boot onto the corpse to steady it and retrieve the weapon he had stolen from the guards.

"Who are you?" Diana questioned.

Tristan saw the Mysterious Stranger face Diana, causing him to panic and look for the rifle that Svante had dropped. He saw it had fallen into one of the pens nearby. The figure raised his harpoon and threw it towards them as Tristan moved. He hit a cow instead. Diana had ducked and then straightened up as she faced the Mysterious Stranger unarmed. He hadn't replied to Diana's question and only breathed through his mask, giving the sound that gasmasks give of heavy breathing. Tristan hopped over into a pen.

The Mysterious Stranger stepped forward. Diana went towards him and attempted to tackle him. He instead grabbed Diana by the side and threw her down in a brutish manner. He then proceeded towards Tristan, which Diana took notice of and immediately recovered to grab him by the ankle, attempting to trip him. The Mysterious Stranger instead kicked her back, stopping to look at her as she covered her face.

Tristan crawled over to the rifle, grabbed it, and then sat on his bottom to fire the gun at the Mysterious Stranger. He tensed his finger over the trigger, but it didn't shoot. It wasn't loaded. Tristan looked over to Svante's corpse and saw he had plenty of cartridges to fire, so he made his way over. Meanwhile, the Mysterious Stranger walked over to Diana. She crawled away, but he eventually grabbed her by the waist. Diana mule kicked him, aiming for the mask, but hitting him in the chest instead. The Mysterious Stranger took the kick and then grabbed her regardless, throwing her into a pen. Tristan continued to crawl to Svante's corpse.

Diana landed in the pen amidst the cows and then went over to the slain cow. She brought her hands around the pole of the harpoon and attempted to dislodge it from the carcass. The mysterious figure then looked over to Tristan as he grabbed some cartridges from Svante. Tristan looked at him and attempted to get away, going towards the opposite-side of the barn from where Diana was. The Mysterious Figure went after him and vaulted over the wooden fence into the sheep pen where Tristan had crawled through. Tristan hid amidst the sheep as he loaded the rifle. The Mysterious Stranger grabbed him by the ankle. Diana dislodged the harpoon from the cow.

The Mysterious Stranger brought Tristan over and then dropped him. He then grabbed him again and brought his hands around his neck, raising him up to choke him. Tristan squirmed and dropped the rifle. With all of her force, Diana threw the harpoon and pierced the Mysterious Stranger in his right shoulder, causing him to yell out in pain and drop Tristan. Tristan quickly grabbed the rifle, pushed his body into the Mysterious Stranger, causing him to stagger back, and then hit him in the face with the butt of the rifle. Tristan then vaulted over and ran off. The Mysterious Stranger fell backwards into a wooden beam set on fire, causing it to snap and give off the weight above that came crashing down.

Tristan only barely managed to escape, but had fallen on the ground with a wooden beam at his foot. He was unconscious. Diana hopped over and went to him. She checked to see if he was dead, seeing that he was breathing, she assessed his airway and then pulled him out. Diana proceeded to help him onto his feet as she brought his arm around her neck to pull him out. Tristan regained slight consciousness to not bear too much burden on Diana.

Diana left the barn and then left the commune, going the opposite direction she had gone to hunt and returning the way she had come when she had escaped from the Mysterious Stranger yesterday afternoon. Tristan was dazed and dragging his feet as Diana pulled him with all her strength and all her resolve. Diana ran through the forest, past the underpass of the bridge, passing every little bush and trudging through every depth of snow that stuck in her path until she found herself out of breath, energy, and resistance against the harsh winds that had drawn in. She fell to her knees in a small clearing, which meant that Tristan fell next to her too.

Darkness had fallen over them as the skies were an intense grey and the sun nearly set. The snowfall had become harsher too. Diana looked around and had no idea of what to do, where to go, or where to take shelter. A flash of lightning lit the skies followed by some thunder. Diana looked at Tristan and saw that he was as pale as ever – skin fairer than Diana's to the point that it was sickly and whiter than the snow. The darkness overwhelmed her.

Tristan had fallen unconscious again and was asleep. Diana knew something was wrong with him, but there was nothing she could do at this moment to save his life. She opened her backpack, which she still had from the hunt, and rummaged through to find the flare gun. She raised it up and fired into the air, watching the red flare rise up past the trees and then detonate into a display of distress. Diana then looked back to Tristan with tearful eyes. Tristan was on the brink of death.

"God, why?!" Diana remarked, wiping her eyes. "Why?! Why again?!"

Diana went over to Tristan's body and brought herself over him by the side.

"Why?! Why?! Why am I so incompetent?! Three times! Three! Please, Tristan, wake up!"

Diana cried into Tristan's body and then straightened up to bring another hand to his forehead, feeling the coldness against his skin. Diana looked around and saw that all around her it was bright, faded, and she was breathing heavily. She looked over to Tristan once more, falling over onto her side and embracing him. She cried into him until she succumbed to her own fatigue. With one last look at Tristan from behind, Diana continued to embrace him and passed out.

Act 6, Scene 1

Tristan opened his eyes, looking around as his head spun and flashes of whiteness his him. He closed his eyes again, listening to the ambience around him of a heartbeat monitor and feeling the presence of an oximeter at his finger tip. There were two intravenous catheters in his right arm with tubes coming out. His vision was blurred and the room he was in was dark. Tristan moved around slightly in the bed.

Tristan's eyes began to finally open as he looked around himself. He sat in a bed, shirtless with various nodes on his chest. He looked at the tubes protruding from the catheters in his arms. Each had a red liquid in it, blood, each heading a different direction, but the tubes itself were hooked to the same machine that was whirling next to the heart monitor. The machine had two rotors that were spinning and processing his blood. Tristan recognized it as a hemodialysis machine.

Tristan looked away from the equipment and tried to sit up, causing a figure in the small room that was sitting at a desk to turn around and stand up as she noticed Tristan to be awake. The room they were in was small and cold. The walls were made of stone as was the floor. The room was no larger than six feet by eight feet. It barely fit a bed no less the gigantic table in the corner on the other side with all sorts of lab equipment. Tristan could recognize some of the equipment to be similar to that which Charlemagne used to have in the spare bedroom.

Tristan's eyes closed again as the woman approached him. Her face was blurred. He opened them as he tried to focus on her. The woman was dressed in a black gown, or habit. She was a nun with smooth skin that was bronze, like Tristan's. Tristan continued to look at her and into her face. Her face was round and similar to him as were her green eyes for she looked like her son.

"Mom…" Tristan exclaimed. "Is that you…?"

"Yes, Tristan," the woman replied in a calm tone. "It is me."

"I- I can't believe it's really you," Tristan remarked with a slight daze as though he was hallucinating, sitting up and stretching his arms over to hug her.

"Take it easy and lie down," the woman cautioned, going over to raise the bed for him.

Tristan lay back down and kept his eyes on her. He held a simple smile as he looked at her. His eyes began to water. She looked back at him and smiled. The woman embraced him and began to cry.

"Never in all these years did I ever believe that I'd come to see you again," the woman stated. "No less after what happened to Elisabeth."

The woman parted from Tristan and looked at her son. She brought a hand to his cheek.

"Oh, I can't believe how handsome my little boy turned out to be," the woman expressed. "So beautiful. So strong…"

"I can't believe it's really you," Tristan said. "I don't believe this is real."

"It is real, Tristan."

"How did I get here? I was outside… there was a fire, and… Diana! Where is she? Please tell me that she's okay!"

"Diana is fine," Sister Witeveen assured him. "She's resting after she donated around a liter of blood to save you. Luckily, she has a rare blood type, the same blood type as you: O negative, but I had to filter it regardless before giving it to you."

"Blood? Why do I need blood? What's wrong with me?"

"I'll explain later, but for now, please rest. Some of the sisters were in prayer when they noticed the storm, and then a distress flare that was sent out. We put together a small rescue team and went to grab you and your sister from the forest as soon as we could, and given your condition, we had to resuscitate you…"

"Where am I? Am I at the convent? I tried to come here yesterday, but they wouldn't let me in…"

"I know. I heard. Mother Doherty was intent on not having us see each other, but given the circumstances… here we are. You're in the Pacific Northwest headquarters of the Order of St. Agnus – the Convent of Our Lady's Maidens. I'll explain all about that later, but regardless of what Mother Doherty wants, you will need to come to understand…"

"What's with all the lab equipment?"

"It's my personal equipment that I use for my research. This is my cell – it's where I engineered the sperm and ovum that became you – it's where I conceived you, and it's where I gave birth to you…"

"You've only opened about a thousand more questions…" Tristan remarked, looking around.

"It's okay, my son. You'll have all the answers you hope. For now, try to heal and rest. I don't want to overburden you with too much information at once."

"Okay…" Tristan quietly replied, "but what's wrong with me? Am I sick?"

"I'm not quite sure on the specifics as I have yet to diagnose you," Sister Witeveen replied, "but I recently drew some blood and I'm still running some tests. Until then, I'm cleaning out your entire bloodstream to start anew."

"Toxins…" Tristan muttered. "I'm sore, nauseous, and confused."

"Do you have any more symptoms?" Sister Witeveen questioned.

Tristan explained his entire prognosis before watching his mother think to herself.

"Interesting, then it's worse than I thought," Sister Witeveen said.

"Why do I need to filter my blood? I haven't had a fever, so I don't think I've had any type of infection. Was I poisoned?"

"Very good, but no," Sister Witeveen stated. "You haven't been poisoned. I'm filtering your blood because your immune system has been compromised."

"So, autoimmune disease then? How?"

"No, and I'm not sure" Sister Witeveen again stated. "I'm sure it was viral, most likely a common cold or something... but it was not autoimmune"

"I'm only more confused," Tristan said.

"I'll figure it out soon enough," Sister Witeveen replied, going over to her desk. "Please, just continue to rest and give me more time."

"Sorry, I'm a bit restless."

"I can see that," Sister Witeveen remarked. "Perhaps a little intramuscular sedative is needed to calm you."

Sister Witeveen opened a cupboard over her work station and took out a small vial and a needle. She set it down on the countertop. Tristan looked at it and shook his head. Sister Witeveen looked at him.

"No," Tristan replied, "please. I think I'm okay."

Sister Witeveen smiled and put the needle away.

"I'm only joking," Sister Witeveen remarked. "I thought that'd set you off."

Tristan looked at her with a bit of stun and then smiled.

"You really are my mother, aren't you?" Tristan questioned, closing his eyes. "I really hope this isn't a dream – that, or that I died and went to Heaven, because this is too good to be true."

"Tristan..." Sister Witeveen scolded, "please don't say such things... All of this is real, and you are my pride and joy, my sweet, sweet Tristan."

• • •

Diana woke up and pivoted her legs to sit in the bed of the quiet cell she had been brought to. The door at the end of the room opened and Mother Doherty entered with two other nuns behind her. Diana looked at Mother Doherty.

Mother Doherty was the easiest of the nuns to identify other than Tristan's mother. She was the eldest, spoke in a strong and brash voice, and her habit was white instead of black. She was of fair skin and perhaps in her late-sixties. Her hair was white and face wrinkled. At rest, her face gave a strict appearance. Mother Doherty stepped forward to the right and faced Diana with her hands together at her lap.

"We have some questions for you now that the immediate crisis is over," Mother Doherty stated, "concerning Tristan's health."

"Okay," Diana replied, rubbing her eyes.

"How did you find us?"

"It wasn't hard," Diana replied.

Diana explained to her from the beginning, Tristan's dream with Maximilian Bauer, his confusion in regard to the woman in the dream, Salmar's statement about the deaths of Elisabeth and Zachariah Merrick, the events that unfolded in St. Nazaire, and the motto on the necklace.

"Does anyone else know that you are here?" the mother asked.

"Not that I know of," Diana answered. "Maybe."

"Who?"

"We only gave our directions to one person, and that was a border guard at Sweet Grass who asked for our destination, but I'm sure you would have been contacted by the police by now if they suspected that we were here."

"We've already talked to the police, yes," Mother Doherty confirmed, "and I explained to them that we did not expect any visitors. The two of you are high value targets, and every police force in the state is on high alert for your capture," she warned. "What drove Tristan's determination to come here – to evade so many layers of authority on a whim?"

Diana hesitated to answer the question.

"The last few months have been hard on Tristan," Diana stated. "Between him losing a friend, and a crisis that occurred in our town last month... all I can say for certain is that Tristan took the death of his parents, his adoptive-parents, hard. He grew obsessed to know why these people were murdered, and then he grew more obsessed to know where he had come from. I suppose there's also the consideration that he realized that he possibly wasn't an orphan as he once believed, but that there was someone out there who was of his own kindred. That as much, I can understand and empathize with... After all, people seek their own."

Mother Doherty did not reply, but instead gave a simple nod.

"What can you tell me about these 'mysterious deaths' of Mr. and Mrs. Merrick?"

"They weren't so mysterious," Diana replied. "It was a targeted assassination – whoever wanted them dead, wanted

Tristan. I'm not sure if the two individuals who attacked us in St. Nazaire had some sort of connection to the assassination, but I do know that they were the same people who later came for us at the border."

"According to government officials, the two men that attacked you at the border were in fact the same ones that came for you in St. Nazaire. However, there appears to be no record of these men anywhere, or their affiliation, or even their identities."

"I know exactly who they belong to," Diana said. "They're Huntsman of the Huntsman Legionnaires, the same people who were brought in to control the occupation of our town to find Bauer, who attacked the manor, and who we've had so many reoccurring run-ins with. All I know about them is that they're contracted by a businessman named Audric Zimmerman."

"Interesting," Doherty questioned, "and they've come for you before?"

"Yes," Diana affirmed. "The last time they were after us was for a different reason, which makes me wonder why it is they're after us now, or why they didn't pursue Tristan beforehand if they were connected to the assassination of Tristan's parents."

"Zimmerman is a dangerous man – dangerous by his mysterious nature. Our organization has kept an eye on him, and we know of his involvement in your town last month as well as the reasons behind that excursion – to capture this man, Mr. Bauer."

"You seem to know a lot," Diana remarked.

"More than you think, Ms. Cambridge," Doherty replied, looking at Diana with intent. "I believe that is all I have in terms of questions. Now, I must ask a favor from you, but your choice to accept is unconditional. Sister Witeveen spends her free-time exploring nature, the natural sciences, and performing a lot of medical research. Currently, she is researching genome patterns among the different races, and it is rare that we have outsiders visit the convent anymore. We would greatly appreciate it if you met her in our gymnasium for a physical and medical evaluation."

Diana hesitated to reply. She looked away and then nodded.

"Okay," Diana confirmed, bringing her legs out of bed. "I'd be more than happy to help."

"Thank you," Doherty replied, smiling and nodding. "Sister Magnolia will escort you to the gymnasium. We have washed your clothes and set them in the dresser, and if you wish to shower, there are some towels in the bathroom as well as some soaps."

Diana nodded. She was dressed in a gown that she had been given to sleep in. Mother Doherty left and closed the door behind her. Diana went to the dresser and looked inside. Her clothes were there, clean, pressed, and ready to wear, but Diana went to shower beforehand. Diana then dressed and left her room to join Sister Magnolia.

Sister Magnolia led Diana through the halls of the convent, which was lit in a warm orange glow against the wooden tracery paneled walls and stone floor. Norman windows were translucent and provided sunlight to pierce through and brighten some sections of the corridors. At some places, there were burgundy rugs that lay over top. The ambience of the monastery was of a light chanting of some sisters in the chapel, which echoed down the halls. The sentiment and expression on Diana's face was peaceful one, but she also appeared to be lightly skeptical and suspicious. Sister Magnolia brought Diana to a far-side of the convent where she opened a door to reveal a large room with various weight-lifting equipment, treadmills, bicycles, and other equipment.

The gym also had a small space where some mats were laid over before a wall of mirrors, and the room itself was bright due to the large windows at the back that looked out into a garden.

"I'll let Sister Witeveen know that you're ready," Sister Magnolia remarked in a shy voice, closing the door behind her.

Within the next five minutes, Tristan's mother, who Diana had already met, walked in with a clipboard in hand and measuring tape around her shoulder.

"How's Tristan?" Diana questioned her.

"He's having a nap while the hemodialysis continues," Sister Witeveen replied. "He'll be alright. Now come to this scale for me."

Diana walked over to where she led him – to an old-fashioned weight scale.

"Strip, please," Witeveen simply said, writing atop of a piece of paper on her clipboard.

"Sorry, what?" Diana questioned.

'Strip, please," Witeveen repeated. "I cannot attain an accurate measurement with your clothes on."

"Sorry, it's just… the last place I was at wasn't the most comfortable of places, and I'm still skeptical of all this."

"Diana, I am the mother of your adopted-brother. I know that we've just met, but I assure you that you can put your trust in me as much as you'd trust Tristan."

Diana looked at her and sighed. She removed her coat and then removed the black shirt underneath alongside her jeans. Diana stripped entirely and then stepped forward onto the platform of the scale. There was a moderate chill in the gym and it didn't help that Sister Witeveen took her time in adjusting the scale to get her measurement. Diana simply stood there with dignity.

"Good," Sister Witeveen said, writing on her sheet. "You can step off now," she added, taking her measuring tape into her hand and setting the clipboard on a table.

Sister Witeveen proceeded to measure Diana from head to toes. She measured her chest, shoulders, upper arms, lower arms, and hands. She also measured her waist, hips, thighs, and lower legs. Afterwards, she took a skin caliper and began to measure Diana's body fat, and then she took a cranial caliper and began to measure Diana's skull. She wrote all her data into her clipboard as well as some observations of Diana's skin. Once Sister Witeveen was done, she had Diana change into a pair of shorts and a tank top.

Diana was brought to a treadmill where Sister Witeveen attached some electrode nodes onto Diana's torso and a blood pressure cuff at her arm. An initial, or control was taken before the start, and a machine next to the treadmill produced a graphed sheet with a curved line that peaked into a triangle and then declined into a curved line. Sister Witeveen ripped the sheet off and kept it. Diana gave a nod to the nun once she was ready, and the test then began with Diana running at a low speed, moderate speed, and then an extremely fast speed. Sister Witeveen wrote her observations and the machine printed out more sheets while also measuring her blood pressure and heart rate. At the end of the exam, Diana was given a moment to breath and walk on the treadmill until it started again, but at a steady pace of around six-miles per hour for half an hour. Afterwards, there was a break, and then it began again at seven-and-a-half miles per hour for fifteen minutes, and then nine-miles per hour for twelve minutes. Diana held her own.

Once the two were done with the treadmill, Diana was given a moment to rest and rehydrate. She was then taken from the gym, to a room with a table and a device overtop, pointing down. Diana was brought onto the platform and laid down. Sister Witeveen then moved the device around and began to take an x-ray of Diana's limbs. Afterwards, they moved to another room where Diana was asked to remove her tank top so that she could have an ultrasound of her heart, gastrointestinal tract, and uterus. From there, the two went to another room where Diana was tasked to blow air into a small tubular device with a cable attached to a machine. Sister Witeveen placed a clip on Diana's nose. The two then moved on to another room where Diana had some blood taken from her for some serology.

"Right, I believe that will be all," Sister Witeveen said, placing the vials of blood into a container and the leaving a small plastic jar atop of the counter. "All I need from you is a urine sample, and after that you can go to your room and rest. For now, we would prefer if you didn't wander the convent until Tristan woke up – there's lots I need to explain to him, and I'd prefer if you were there to support him."

"Okay," Diana replied, taking the small jar.

"You can take that into the washroom across the hall and then I'll take you to your room. Thank you."

"No problem."

Act 6, Scene 2

Later in the day, Diana was brought to Sister Witeveen's cell by Sister Magnolia. The sister knocked on the wooden door that led into her room, and the door opened with Tristan's mother on the other side.

"You're just in time," Sister Witeveen remarked, allowing Diana to enter.

Diana smiled as she saw Tristan on the bed immediately before her. His skin displayed a healthier glow as his color had returned. Diana went straight to him.

"Hey," Diana greeted, looking to him and bringing a hand to his cheek.

"Hey," Tristan replied in a weak voice, looking back at her. "How've you been?"

"I should be asking you that," Diana replied, stroking his cheek.

Tristan removed Diana's hand from his cheek as Sister Witeveen turned around.

"I'm the same – sore, tired, mostly confused…"

"Well, that'll be about to change," Sister Witeveen said, taking a large syringe with blood and going to Tristan's intravenous needle in his left arm. "I'm about to start your treatment."

"So, what's wrong with him?" Diana asked, sitting down next to the bed.

"Well, where do I begin?" Sister Witeveen replied, injecting Tristan with the blood in the syringe. "Tristan, have you ever wondered why it is that you've never fallen ill like other children, or had any sort of sickness?"

"Never," Tristan replied. "I thought all the sports I did just made me a healthy guy."

"Well, while good health makes good health, the reality is that you have no immune system."

"What do you mean?" Tristan asked.

"To be more specific, you have no white blood cells, no leukocytes, and no phagocytes, mast cells, plasma cells – nothing of the sort that Diana and I have to defend our bodies against foreign pathogens. You were genetically engineered, Tristan, because I had prepared you to be something better. Inside you is a prototype nanomachine that has worked quite well as of yet, and is more intelligent, knowledgeable, and efficient than any natural cell of one's immune system, and you've had them since birth. I called them 'leukobots' and they've given you a super-immune system."

"Really? Why am I sick now then? Are the bots shutting down?"

"I'm not entirely sure, but from what I've managed to see, these nanomachines have short-fused for some unknown reason. I don't know how, but it's possible that because of their age, they've simply died out..."

"What about an EMP?" Tristan questioned. "We had an EMP blast over our region on Halloween. Could that have caused them to die?"

"Yes," Sister Witeveen replied, "but the point is that they've died and left you vulnerable to foreign agents. If the onset of all of this was last Halloween, then I'm surprised you haven't collapsed due to a bacterial or viral infection earlier. I'm not quite sure what viral infection plagues you at the moment, but I'm sure it is viral... I collected some of your spinal fluid and will have a look to see if I can isolate the pathogen."

"Wait, but why was I left without an immune system? Why couldn't I have had both?"

"Your super-immune system came at a compromise," Sister Witeveen rationalized. "In my preliminary experiments with rats, the leukocytes attacked the leukobots, and vice-versa. So, it had to be one or the other, and I altered your genotype so that the cells that you do produce for immune system purposes are defunct. Your mesenchymal and hematopoietic cells continue to produce T-cells and B-cells, but they don't do anything and don't fight. They become food for the nanomachines to flourish in addition to the other debris, such as dead blood cells, that they also pickup. At any rate, this is what you were made to be – the first of an entire next-generation of superhumans as the Order desired."

"I'm a lab rat?" Tristan stated. "A test subject?"

"Heavens, no," Sister Witeveen rejected, "you're a new Adam, Tristan. Your existence is not because of some science experiment, but because I wanted you to be greater than great – to give you the quality of life that no other human could have – so that could and your descendants could be the next-generation and next-step in human evolution."

"So, I'm not human then?" Tristan asked, looking at Diana.

"What is human, humanity, and the designation of humanhood? All of these have been so far bastardized by modern thinktanks that they've fallen from truth. From a genetic standpoint, you continue to be human because your genotype is hardly affected by these mutations."

"Mutations? What else did you do to me?" Tristan asked with slight horror.

"Do not speak like that, Tristan," Sister Witeveen scolded. "Do not speak like you were made out to be something other than what you are. You are, in all your existence, what you are and nothing more. Your characteristics are amplified to exhibit the best handpicked genes from both me and your father."

"Who?" Tristan questioned. "Who's my father?"

Sister Witeveen hesitated to answer.

"Maximilian Bauer," Sister Witeveen stated. "You met him last month from what I've heard from Mother Doherty."

Tristan didn't respond.

"I'm sorry," Sister Witeveen said, "but in truth, I had no idea he was alive until I learned of what happened in Allabrese. He is your biological father, Tristan, and when I made you, I took his genes with mine to give you the best the both of us could offer. As a result, you were born…"

"Why?"

"What do you mean?"

"Why was I born? For what purpose?"

"No purpose, Tristan," Sister Witeveen remarked, "other than that which God asks and gives of all His Children. All of this is the mandate of the Order, to preserve humanity and ensure our survival, which can only be done in this manner. You see, my work at this monastery was discovered by a man named Tristan Williamson, a member of our brother organization, the Order of St. Athanasius. He was intrigued in my work and had ambitions that tied into this mandate. He trusted me to see it through and financed my experiments, providing me with a specimen of your father's gametes at my request, but before you were born, there was a terrible accident. Bishop Williamson had been killed in an assassination plot and in the crossfire, your father was assumed to have died, but I held on to hope. I prayed for him as I prayed for you all these years. A few weeks later, I received a journal – Bishop Williamson's journal, which contained all sorts of important and valuable information with a set of instructions on the last page to dispose of the diary. I didn't. I couldn't. And then they started to attack us, because they knew of what had been sent here – our enemy."

"Who?" Tristan questioned.

"I cannot say who they are, but only that their existence is permeated throughout the system of the world – they are a foreign enemy, a small rootless international clique," Sister Witeveen explained. "One day, when returning from Mass, I had found my room to have been ransacked, but thankfully, the journal was safe. Mother Doherty instructed me to destroy the journal, but I couldn't because of the knowledge, the truth that was within that needed to be preserved... which is when I decided to take a risk. All of this occurred before you were born, but when I was pregnant with you. During this immediate time, I translated all of the data from the journal, encrypted it, and transferred it into a second-class of nanomachines called 'leukobytes' and I injected them within you after you were born in addition to the leukobots."

"Why?" Tristan asked.

"What safer place to hide such secrets?" Sister Witeveen asked. "Of course, then came the need to hide you. I couldn't keep you in the convent, but had to send you out – and this became truer after a fateful night, whilst at a meeting of all North American branches, when an enemy agent attempted to assassinate me – but the shot, poetically, pierced my uterus and made me unable to bear any more children... I lived, but it forced me to send you off..."

"I knew it," Tristan said with a smile. "I knew that was a memory and not a dream. I knew that I had seen it sometime before... I just didn't realize it was so early of a memory or how on Earth I was able to recall sometime from so long ago, but it makes sense... it makes sense why I was so small, or why I wasn't able to talk or do anything. I was, what? A month? Two-months old?"

"You were little over a month old," Sister Witeveen replied. "I'm awestruck that you were able to recall such a memory…"

"Bauer…" Tristan replied. "I mean, my dad… He was there, implanted in the memory telling me to pray because God has something to tell me. I know what it was that He wanted to tell me… it was all of this."

Sister Witeveen was slightly confused by this response. Tristan explained into depth his father, his powers, and the psionic experiments that Zimmerman Corporation conducted on him.

"Interesting," Sister Witeveen responded. "I'll have to inform Mother Doherty of this, but at the heart of it all, I suppose your father's determination for you to know the truth drove you here."

"What happened next?" Tristan questioned.

"Mother Doherty visited me in hospital and told me that you weren't safe with us and that the convent was no place to raise a child. In truth, she was right. A child needs his father as much as he needs his mother, and neither was possible, together or apart, so I had to make a hard decision. According to a contact in St. Nazaire, tasked with keeping in touch with my sister, he had told me that she was infertile, so it was logical of all places to send you to her – that I at least send you to someone who was of your own blood, your aunt. I thought it'd be safe enough where we would have distance, you'd be able to grow and have a normal life, and Bishop Williamson's secrets would be safe in you until the time was right – if there ever was a time. Over the years, I envisioned our reunion just as I had envisioned my reunion with Maxim before his death. My aspiration – our aspiration, was to be together with you…"

Tristan looked at his mother. She was saddened by the thought.

"Anyways," Sister Witeveen said, wiping her eyes, "after Elisabeth and Zachariah died, we were all stunned. Mother Doherty permitted me to attend the funeral and it was there that I learned that you had been placed into the care of some lawyer, Salmar Cabernet. I didn't trust him, but the Order was powerless to manipulate anything. I simply hoped he was nothing like his brother, the man you are with now, and then when he was incarcerated, my anxiety heightened."

"Charles' been good to us – both of us," Tristan reasoned. "I prefer being with Charles and Diana than I ever did with Salmar. Under Charlemagne, Diana and I have learned so much, been through so much, and had what he calls a 'human experience' that others don't often have. I'm happy where I am."

"I'm happy to hear," Sister Witeveen remarked, "but it was irresponsible of you to leave the safety of Charlemagne in this hot pursuit for me. What were you thinking? You're under-aged, you've broken so many laws, and you have no idea of the work it's going to take for the Order to reverse this damage…"

"I wanted to meet you," Tristan simply replied with a single tear falling from his eye. "What will the 'Order' do to 'reverse' the damages?"

"A lot of work," Sister Witeveen simply stated, "because the power of the Order isn't what it used to be. The Order is weak and dying, and it'll be a miracle if we can even get you home safely. The pair of you are going straight back to Canada as soon as I'm done with you."

"What about you?" Tristan asked. "Will we be able to talk? Why don't you come with us if you're concerned about your safety? You'll be safe in Allabrese, and I feel like you and Charles would get along really well – you're both brilliant and passionate scientists. If you were to put your powers together, I doubt there'd be any mystery that you both can't solve."

"I appreciate that you'd like to incorporate me back into your life, but my place is here with the Order and my sisters. I can't abandon my post, the others, or risk putting myself and your new family in danger. You have Diana and Charlemagne now, Tristan. I'm happy that we had a chance to see each other again, but we probably won't be able to see each other ever again."

"Why not?" Tristan questioned with a whine.

"You know the answer to that," Sister Witeveen stated, taking a deep breath as she stood up and looked to her son. "In nature, there comes a time when a mother must see her child off so that he can continue his natural mission. We are no different, Tristan. You are my blood, my pride, and my joy, and it is time for you to move forward with your life with Diana. Your life is just beginning, and it is a life you will never be able to live if you have me in it to keep you in the past. Don't be fooled though – I do love you, and I would love nothing more than to watch my baby boy as continued to become the man he will become, but I can't. My sister has done her part in raising you, and now it is time for you to do yours with the people in your life."

The hemodialysis machine began to beep. Sister Witeveen walked over to the machine and took the canister out. She then turned off the machine and the tubes flowing in and out of Tristan's cardiovascular system stopped transporting blood.

The machine was pushed aside so that Sister Witeveen could look at the intravenous catheters.

"Ah…" Tristan remarked as his mother pulled them out.

"Oh, quit being such a baby," Sister Witeveen remarked, putting the needles away and then patching up Tristan's arm. "Take it easy for the rest of the day. I've filtered your blood, given you new nanomachines, but there'll still be some old ones lingering in your system – leukobots and leukobytes. I still have to diagnose you for what was causing your symptoms, but it isn't much of a priority at the moment since the nanomachines will root out the problem with ease."

"Thank you," Tristan replied in a quiet voice.

Sister Witeveen kissed her son on the forehead. She then walked over to her desk to place the canister. She then walked back over to look to Diana.

"You can stay here with Tristan if you'd like," Sister Witeveen said. "I have chores and will be back before supper. Keep Tristan company, and if there's an emergency, please pull the string at the door or the fire alarm underneath."

"Okay," Diana replied, watching Sister Witeveen go to the door.

"I'll be back," Tristan's mother said, opening the door and leaving.

The door closed behind her, leaving Diana and Tristan alone for them to look at each other. Diana put his hand on Tristan's warm forearm and smiled at him. She then rested her head onto Tristan's shoulder who also rested his head on hers to enjoy a moment of peace after all that had happened thus far.

Act 6, Scene 3

Sophia and Tristan walked through the forest behind the monastery on the next day. The day was beautiful. The sky was cloudless and light blue. The sun brought down an unexpected warmth and kept the highlands bright and cheerful. There was neither wind nor fog to interrupt them. Mother and son simply walked together, smiling as they bantered on as if they had never separated and knew each other for the length of Tristan's life.

Sister Witeveen was dressed in a thick cloak while Tristan wore his blue jacket. They both walked peacefully through the forest, venturing in search of the pickup truck. Tristan appeared to not only be happier, but healthier than he was earlier in the week. Sister Witeveen was also happy with a calm smile on her face.

"Perhaps I was wrong to doubt Charlemagne as a guardian for you, Tristan," Sophia remarked. "I find it important that you've learned so much through experience in the field rather than to have your mind polluted, indoctrinated, and brainwashed as so many other children have through the public system. You are not a child of the state. You know, your aunt and I were also homeschooled by your grandparents. We learned all that we needed to jumpstart from them, and then whatever more we learned from ourselves. Of course, your aunt, being the older sister, did pass on quite a lot onto me, and I was grateful for that..."

"I could never do what you're doing," Tristan admitted.

"I don't expect you to because even though we are of one kindred, you retain your individuality and are your own person. If anything, I expected you to become like your father... but that isn't set in stone, because you should become whatever God requires you to become…"

"I want to become a doctor," Tristan stated, "since I was a little boy I've wanted to become one."

"The vocation of a physician is not an easy one, but it is an important one. Physicians are defenders of the people, and to cure as Jesus cured is an honorable path as long as one remembers that they cannot save us all like Christ can, and that you seek through your work to glorify the Lord in your action, and life."

"How did you become a nun?" Tristan questioned, looking at his mother. "I mean, between you and my dad, you're both devout Christians. Why?"

"The Order of St. Agnus is an old organization that used to have influence throughout the Western world because it used to have ties with the Church… but ever since the last century, that's changed, and it's mostly hidden itself in the shadows. I found myself in this path when I was sixteen. Your grandparents, as you may already know, were Dutch immigrants – *Boers*, who had left the Netherlands to come to the United States when they were young. We were protestants, Calvinists. I was baptized as such, but I was a defiant teenager, influenced through the teachings of Bishop Tristan Williamson to embrace the one true Church; the New Israel, the new nation and community of believers, because I had placed value on truth that the Catholic Church was that people who believed together since those who believed with St. Peter. Bishop Williamson was a minor figure, hated by the Holy See because of his emphasis on the value of truth, and hated by mainstream society to be honest. His teachings are hard to locate, but I had found them when I was fourteen, in the local library of our small town, which is where I borrowed them to listen and learn about Christ. He spoke of Church theology, routine dogma such as the Trinity, morality, and other hot topics, but also of philosophy, of Aristotle, and Saint Thomas Aquinas, and Saint Augustine, and it really there that I saw an entire worldview form. A worldview in which God holds transcendental value in the skies and the trees, because God is goodness, he is beauty, and he is truth. Wherever it is that you see that is good, you see a reflection of God, and only because God exists do we see what we see, for without God, we'd see the antithesis if we could even see at all. The opposite of goodness, of beauty, and of truth – of unity and love, are negations or absences of such values, because just as darkness is the absence of light, evil is the absence of good, indifference the absence of love, and lies the absence of truth. A world without God, is evil, indifferent, and full of lies and deceit. From these core principles, I had my faith and it was a trying faith because my parents did not approve. I constantly fought with them. I even contemplated running away, but I held through. In these difficult times, I was never alone. I was with Christ and through all the hard times I've struggled through, God has always been there with me and He had never needed to intervene because God had blessed me, as he has blessed you, with all that we need to overcome. At the age of fifteen, a tornado struck the town and I became bereaved because I had lost loved ones. I was emotionless. I was depressed. I only had God. I only wanted to be with God, so I decided to join a convent at the first instance I could – I personally sought out this convent because of its relation to Bishop Williamson, and when I turned eighteen, I joined.

Your father was raised in a Roman Catholic household. I believe his parents originated from Bavaria, which is a Roman Catholic region of Germany. I must admit that I've influenced him in regard to his own beliefs because when we first met, I had told him that I was in love with Christ. He took it personally and became religious for the wrong reasons – because he wanted to be closer to me through God. Nonetheless, while I may have influenced him, I know his faith was strengthened by external forces and that his faith was never as shallow as I may have made it sound. There was depth towards it, and I recall us sharing in this passion for beauty and truth as we strolled through Saint Peter's Basilica together, admiring the artwork that evoked the beauty of God in its fine details. For your father, however, his passion was more towards life and family – typical German that he was. He wanted to have children, raise a family, and such, all admirable and divine aspects because God asks us to be fruitful, but I wasn't confident and wanted to wait. I told him to wait… He waited. I wish I could say that we waited too long, but to be honest, we were only twenty-one when you were born and it was still too late. To answer your question, Tristan, your father and I came together because of our faith, and through that faith you were born and given the life you have. I wish we could have shared in our religiosity with you…"

"What's the deal with this Order?" Tristan questioned. "When I was in Egypt last year, we were saved by some nuns at a similar convent in the Sinai region. How many more are there? What's the point of them?"

"The Order of St. Agnus is a worldwide order divided into regions," Sister Witeveen responded. "The point of them is the preservation and care of women in preparation for motherhood – to safeguard their sanctity and innocence for their vocation. You see, civilizations rise and fall, but the Church is said that it will always stand – we are a part of that pillar, and through the community of true believers, such as us, the Church will never die out. Sadly, the Vatican is under occupation of our terrible enemy, so we are the worst of times, but we continue to sit in the shadows, biding our time so that we can push the Church up from its ashes to rise. In these shadows, we continue with our mandate, which includes our womanly duty as caregivers to ensure the health and fruition of our children, the preservation of our descendants akin to our ancestors, and triumph of life. You see, the central unit of society is the family, and the mother is the guardian of the family – our role is pivotal in the upkeep of society itself, but no less nor greater than the role of a man, but complimentary as man is complimentary to woman. Young girls come and go from the convent where we prepare them for what God asks of them, whether that be motherhood or not, they are prepared and when that crisis comes, our centers will safeguard the many different peoples of the world…"

"So, these places are like conservation centers then," Tristan replied.

"If that's a metaphor that helps you understand, then yes," Sister Witeveen responded. "For God created the Earth and set us in charge to conserve, and the same rules shall apply to humans to conserve all that God has created, including ourselves in all our diversity. Us, humans, animals, the surrounding landscape – all that is physical in this universe from here to Mars and beyond, the physical realm is good because God said that it was good when he created it, and to the people he created, very good. To us in the Order, our lives are dictated by these natural laws, the rules of nature, and to preserve and create rather than destroy. When destruction strikes, the Order is there to ensure creation is maintained."

"What if it shouldn't be maintained," Tristan pondered aloud. "What if it should be replaced? A new humankind entirely, not just like you've done with me, but revolutionary so that men can become gods? Humans are only different from our orangutan relatives, or any other mammal for that matter, in that we're domesticated and intelligent. Other than that, we still have the same animalistic drives to breed, eat, and be comfortable. What if we can alleviate all that? What if we could create a human that superseded these primitive characteristics that chain us?"

"What you're suggesting is a separation of man from his original sin," Sister Witeveen stated. "What separates us from animals? You say, 'domestication,' but is a dog not domesticated but it continues to perform obscene acts? What separates man from animal is his morality in pursuit of God, and that endeavor and path cannot and never should be replaced. Man abstains from indulgences. He hones his strengths. He learns from his weaknesses. He overcomes his animalistic tendencies and attempts to perfect himself to become a man-god. There existed only one man, as you proposed, and his name was Jesus Christ who walked among us, and there should always be an expectation that you cannot become perfect like Him, but in the least can attempt to become better than you are. The human that you propose cannot be created because you cannot separate man from his original sin."

"What if it is possible," Tristan went on. "What if I've seen such creatures that have separated themselves from their primitive self?"

• • •

Diana looked around the chapel of the convent, examining the various religious imagery whilst listening to the chant of nuns from nearby. She was on her own as Tristan and his mother had left, so she wandered and came here. Diana made the sign of the cross underneath the door frame into the chapel. She then stepped forward, down the aisle, and towards the altar where she then knelt down to remake the sign of the cross. Diana then stood up with a lone frown across her face.

"Your strength is admirable," Mother Doherty said from the entrance into the chapel.

Diana's ears poked up and she turned around.

"For a seventeen-year old girl to have been through so much, there's something peculiar about you that we haven't seen in many women."

"What's that supposed to mean?" Diana questioned with a saddened face.

"What happened to your parents, Diana?" Mother Doherty asked, walking down the aisle with her hands together at her lap.

"One was shot, and the other overdosed on heroin," Diana answered.

"What was their background?"

"I'm not too sure about my dad's side, but I'm pretty sure it's English on both ends."

"Ah, Anglo-Saxon," Mother Doherty replied, passing Diana to go to some candelabras at the front of the chapel. "A remarkable, determinate people with a stiff upper lip."

"Why did Tristan's mother test me? What's really going on here?"

"It was a simple examination of your fitness. Sister Witeveen is intrigued by the ideal, and she saw in you, powerful expressions. For example, how you were able to carry Tristan through the forest. Had you stopped anywhere before where you did, we'd have never seen the flare. Sister Witeveen is interested in your genetics because she's a woman interested in the best of all people, which for you, is a lot. She created Tristan to carry the most advantageous genes of herself and Mr. Bauer, so it is only logical that she'd have approached you because she's interested in you. We're interested in you…"

"I believe in God," Diana replied, "and I believe in Christ, but I don't believe in any of this nonsense… Isn't this eugenics…?"

"What if it is?" Mother Doherty replied. "Is it sinful to desire our offspring; future generations, to be healthy or to inherit the best of what is available, and to conserve separate peoples? We are all of rational spirits, but physically we are separate by God's command. We don't force anything on anyone either, my dear, for that would be sinful; coercion, and we do not have that authority from God to coerce people. In this house, we value the word of Christ, we value suffering, but we also seek to project beauty into the world as is the wish of Our Lord. None of our desires are forceful, and nobody comes to this convent but out of their own free will."

"It all seems too much for me – even the idea of dedicating my entire life to God. I don't understand how any woman could want any of this…"

"Understandable, because it is a lot," Mother Doherty replied, "but we do not train women, but maidens, young girls, to prepare them for motherhood, because women are made when they become mothers."

"By your logic, are you not a woman?" Diana questioned.

"No, because I am not a maiden," Mother Doherty answered. "I am a mother to four children and was once upon a time, married, but now widowed. My children are all grown up, and through my maternal skills, I joined this convent and eventually became the Prioress Provincial of this region. All of the sisters of the convent are unmarried, but their membership is not for a lifetime unless they so choose. Here, they enjoy solace and take a vow to chastity. In the words of St. Paisios of Mount Athos, it is important for young people to live spirituality and preserve their chastity, because this secures their physical and spiritual health. The health of a people is paramount to their survival and the Order wishes to bring good, healthy people into the world. The minimum age to join us is eighteen, and it isn't until these women are in their mid-twenties that they are encouraged to leave and marry, given that they believe they are ready, but their exists exceptions where some instead remain to devote their entire lives to Christ and thus take a vow of consecration. Both are serious decisions that require a great deal of self-reflection and evaluation to come to. We are a safe-place for them, especially now in a world of sexual degeneracy and deceit – malice."

"What's the purpose? You want better mothers, but whether we like it or not, there will always be bad mothers, mothers who abandoned their children or neglect them. You can't change society and purge the sinful nature of the world."

"Our mandate doesn't seek to purge sin from the world, because that would be a heretical mandate. There will come a time in which the decadence of society will cause society to collapse in on itself – and in that time, the Church and Christianity will survive so long as there are those, like us, who hold at heart the true principles of God and Jesus Christ."

"Mothers have come and gone for thousands of years, and it's a natural instinct to mother a child," Diana argued. "I don't think a convent like this is necessary to educate people of something they already know."

"And yet, your own mother died of her own self-interest," Mother Doherty countered. "Our Western world tears mothers from their homes and places them in the workplace to become slaves to the Beast. You do not understand, because you have not experienced the hardline battle that is to raise a child, the challenges, the adversity... it is all foreign to you for now, but when you do experience it, you will come to understand. The role of the mother is what makes societies, and in taking women from their natural roles, we are opening the collapse of society. Why do you think there is so much for decadence than there has ever been? The emancipation of women by our enemies has seen to this and never before, in the last thousand years, has there been so much poor health and stability in our children. You may believe that you are an exception, and perhaps you are, but not all are as lucky as you.

The feminine power is of the emotion. Our skills are of no use in the larger world, where men are domain, and where physical and mental strength takes priority, but come to apply to the larger world because us, mothers, are the ones that see boys into men. Our emotional skills drive us to care and love for our children, to hand to them the care and affection that they need to survive on their own when it comes time for them to leave. What is wrong with children of poor health is that they weren't loved enough and in this cursed life, they come to seek from others what can only be given from a mother and in this, they never progress and are likely to remain children forever. A boy needs a mother until he becomes a man, after which, he can rely on his friends, and if he is called to marriage, his wife. A girl needs her mother until she has learned all that she can learn so that she can herself blossom and become a woman. A wife plays an important role to a man, because she cares for him like a mother. What our convent offers to those that come to us is a lesson in sacrifice, the highest form of love, because mothers that sacrifice and condition in their children to know that sacrifice is of the noblest act, create the purest children that will be able to love as Christ loved. However, it is our talents in connection with the talents of the father, where the healthiest children are made as woman is man's counterpart, and men instruct their children with skills that directly apply in the outer world from the home – both parents are needed."

"I didn't have a father..." Diana remarked. "Tristan was lucky to have both."

"You, Diana, are an example of the perfect physique of a woman from what has been seen, but you are still naïve and ignorant. You have a lot to learn, most of which could be taught to you here... Do you not think your life could have been different had your parents been loved properly?"

Diana didn't respond and instead looked to the ground.

• • •

Tristan finished explaining to his mother his extraterrestrial adventure last year. He explained to her about the aliens he had met, and how they were a species of creatures that had deviated themselves from their primitive origins to become purely rational, immortal, and wise creatures. Once Tristan was finished, he looked to his mother as she thought for a moment.

"Hm..." Sophia said aloud, "it appears to me that these creatures have burdened themselves in an effort to become emotionless, because emotions are not a curse, Tristan. What a painful world we would live in if there were no emotions, no happiness, and no sadness, no fear, and no confidence. You cannot have one without the other, because it is a matter of composites."

"I don't want to suffer," Tristan remarked. "Wouldn't the world be better if we couldn't suffer?"

"If we couldn't suffer, man would become too arrogant and proud," Sophia answered. "Suffering reminds us that we are imperfect creatures and subordinate to God. If we weren't to suffer and become emotionless like these aliens, we'd hold no empathy to care for each other. We'd become a desolate society no better than insects. Our emotion, our empathy, and our emotional control are what set us apart. Our suffering leads us to Christ, and through our sufferings we come to relate with Him, care for one another, and become strong. Your ideas, Tristan, are noble from where they come from, but dangerous and of Satan because their consequences, of which you don't know of, would be disastrous."

"Charlemagne said that psionic powers are attained through suffering," Tristan said. "Why is that?"

"I'm not sure, but if I'd have to hazard a guess, I'd say that the powers of the mind are attained through strong minds, and strong minds are made through suffering."

Sophia stopped and took her son's hands.

"You are in pain, my son," Sophia remarked, embracing him. "Your sufferings are unfortunate, but you must endure... I know that you can and will endure them because you are strong – my child."

Sophia moved away from her son and placed a hand on her cheek.

"Come," Sophia then said, taking her son's hand and walking him to a clearing. "Come to your knees, and I will teach you to pray."

Sophia got down on her knees with Tristan. She brought the palms of her hands together and bowed her head. She then brought them apart and raised one hand to make the sign of the cross. Tristan looked at how her hand was positioned, with her pinky and index finger bent over her palm and under the thumb, and the thumb brought with the other two fingers, pointed forward. Sophia looked to Tristan so that he could follow.

"*In nomine Patris et Filii et Spiritus Sancti, Amen.*"

Tristan looked at his mother as she brought her hands together again and closed her eyes. He then moved his gaze from her and looked forward. He closed his own eyes, tilted his head, and brought his hands together to pray with her.

Act 7, Scene 1

The next day, Diana and Tristan entered his mother's cell with understanding that she wanted to see them both. Sister Witeveen was at her desk, writing furiously into a notebook before dropping her pen down. She then looked to the children with a strict face.

"Ah, there you are," Sophia remarked, standing up and offering them a chance to sit down. "I've finished analyzing your blood and spinal fluid, and found the pesky pathogen that caused you to have aseptic meningitis, Tristan. Curiously, it was a human immunodeficiency virus that caused your symptoms. Specifically, HIV-1."

"What? I thought I didn't have an immune system," Tristan responded. "How did it replicate?"

"You don't have an immune system, but you have macrophages and microglial cells. My hypothesis is that the virus went to these cells and became attracted to the brain to cause meningitis. From the time that your nanomachines became ineffective, you must have caught the pathogen in the last couple of weeks, but needless to say it is surely gone now."

"Wait," Diana suddenly remarked with alarm, "how did you get HIV? I thought you could only catch it by having sex with an infected person…"

Tristan felt the weight of suspicion from Diana fall upon him. He became pale and held a look of shock and embarrassment. He quickly looked to Diana.

"I haven't slept with anyone, Diana," Tristan remarked. "Honestly, I swear!"

"Okay, but how did you get it?" Diana asked, highly suspicious of Tristan. "I'm not infected, although I might be now thanks to you…"

Tristan blushed and his heart sank. He looked over to his mother who looked at the two of them. Diana looked at Tristan with his own guilt as he realized what she had just said.

"I'm sure there's a rational explanation that we're missing here," Tristan remarked. "Right? You can only get the disease from having sex, and we haven't done that..."

"Tristan, just tell her..." Diana replied in a mild hush, slightly annoyed at him.

Tristan looked at her with absolute fear. Diana looked back at him with disbelief. Her face reddened as Tristan remained silent, but not out of embarrassment, but anger. Tristan shook his head at her. Diana clenched her fists and looked at him with betrayal and sadness. She stood up and left the room.

"Wait, Diana," Tristan remarked, going to her.

"Don't touch me!" Diana shouted, pushing him back before growling. "You're pathetic!"

Diana stormed off, forcing Tristan to attempt to go after her, but he stopped as his mother called his name.

"I- I haven't slept with anyone," Tristan assured his mother, looking at her with anxiety. "I have no idea how I could have become infected with HIV, seriously. I haven't had sex with anyone..."

"Do not lie to me, Tristan," his mother intensely scolded. "If there is one thing I want for you to take from seeing me, it is that you do not lie to the women you love, whether that is myself or your girlfriend."

"She's- wait... You know?" Tristan questioned.

"Of course I know," Sophia responded to him. "Tristan, I've known about your relationship with Diana since I heard from our sisters in Sinai about one of them seeing you two intimate with each other. My heart wonders why on Earth would you keep such a detail secret? What possible shame do you have to admit that your 'legal' sister is the woman you love?"

"I- I didn't want people to think negatively of us," Tristan admitted. "I know we're not related, and that it's not incest, but people wouldn't make such an easy connection. You have no idea of how hard that's been on me, to balance being with her and not being intimate in public, even at home, out of fear..."

Tristan's mother looked at him. She let out a sigh.

"Sit down," Sophia remarked, sitting down at her desk.

Tristan sat down at the bed.

"There is no shame in the fact that the woman you love is your adopted-sister, because she is not related to you. Whatever anyone has to think of that, is their own problem, but from a moral perspective, there's nothing wrong... and you know that. You have a problem with accepting that commitment, and it's understandable to me, because I had a similar problem with your father when we met... I didn't want to be in that position, but it's not that we have a problem with the commitment... but that we take such commitments so seriously, that we're hesitant to be locked in such contracts. You have doubts."

Tristan didn't respond.

"You have anxiety. You're afraid that something might go wrong and that others will see that failure, because if nobody knows, then there is no backlash, but if everybody knows, then it is an officiation and you are bound to their thoughts and ideas."

"Diana hates that I don't want to tell anyone," Tristan said. "Between this, and the fact that I had HIV, it's why she ran out like that just now. I just... I like the secrecy, even if it's a pain in the ass to be intimate at home, but if I tell others, then it's suddenly a public deal, and everybody knows and what do I care about what other people think? It's just annoying…! My friends thought that I was gay when I ran out on a girl so that I could be with Diana… I don't care what people think – I just want to be left alone with her. I'm not scared about the seriousness of our relationship. I love Diana. I just… maybe I am scared of the commitment. We've been together for almost two years, and ever since I returned from England, I've felt a shift in our relationship. She told me earlier this week about how we're a team, and that our emotions are interconnected, and… I'm not sure I'm ready for that. For the course of this trip, she's done nothing but make sacrifices for me, to care for me, make sure I'm alright, and what have I done? I ran from the authorities and nearly got myself gunned down. I kidnapped her and took her to my hometown… I'm an awful boyfriend… If I tell Charlemagne about us, I won't be able to sleep with her anymore and we'll be forced apart at night. If the town knows, Diana will expect us to be intimate in public, hold hands, and kiss, and people will look at us and think, 'There are the Cabernet kids…' And what if we break up?"

Sophia sighed.

"If you love her, you will make this small sacrifice… Is it not worth it for her, because the alternative is an end to what was, and I don't think you're ready for that or that it's fair for her," Sophia explained. "I wish your father was here to mentor you in this, but he's not. At the bottom line, Tristan, you have to choose and be courageous with your choice. Aside from that which I disapprove, specifically, your pre-marital sex and cohabitation, I speak to you purely… as if I were speaking to your father in relation to me. You are in a serious relationship, and such are not treaded so lightly, and Diana does not deserve to be kept hidden because she's a woman, your woman, she deserves some respect from the man that she loves."

Tristan sighed and replied, "Yeah…"

Sophia looked at him as he looked to the side, out the door. He was silent and then stood up from the bed.

"I should go and find Diana," Tristan said. "I need to apologize and talk to her."

"Let her have a moment to herself," Sophia encouraged.

Tristan nodded and then looked to his mother.

"Wait," Tristan remarked, looking at her, "what about the HIV? Did I really have it, and if so, how? I'm confused as to how I could have come into contact with the disease, because Diana is the only person I've ever been sexual with, ever. Is there any other I could have caught the disease?"

"Have you come into contact with contaminated blood in the last month?" Sophia questioned. "Come into contact with a used needle?"

"No," Tristan denied.

"Do you have any idea of anything that's happened in the last month that could have transmitted the virus to you?"

Tristan shrugged. Sophia sighed.

"There is a possibility that Diana is infected and that she gave it to you instead," Sophia explained, "and although I doubt this hypothesis, it is the most likely. I examined her and she appears to be in peak health, but HIV-1 is an unpredictable virus with a latency of up to ten years. I'll have a look at her blood and see what I can find…"

"I- I don't think Diana's had other partners…" Tristan remarked. "I'm fairly certain I'm the only one that's ever been with her. She said that when we had sex for the first time, and I know she wouldn't cheat on me."

Sophia looked at her son with discomfort.

"Again, aside from the uncomfortable fact that the two of you are engaging in premarital sex…" Sophia remarked in a strict tone, "I'll have a chat with her when she returns. If she had HIV, then it is a serious problem because it is more immediately life-threatening to her than it is to you."

"Can you cure her?" Tristan questioned. "Can you give her some nanomachines and make her like me?"

"Calm down," Sophia insisted. "Nanomachines can only be given to people with suppressed immune systems, so I suppose, if she is in a critical state of auto-immune deficiency syndrome, it could be a possible treatment, but regardless of that fact, she will be okay. In the meantime, I think it'd be best if you both stayed until I was certain."

"Okay…" Tristan replied.

Act 7, Scene 2

Tristan sat in a lone wooden chair, looking out of the glass of his room and to the clock tower of the convent with strained eyes. He then looked out to the forest beyond as the sun set. Several hours had passed since Diana had run off and he had been alone in that time. Diana had yet to return. The clock tower struck top of the hour and the bells echoed throughout the convent. Tristan stood up, left his room, and went to Diana's room to see that she was still not back, so he went to his mother's cell, stopping outside as he heard voices from within.

"They look nothing alike," Sister Witeveen said, "but they…"

The rest of what Sister Witeveen had said was inaudible.

"Don't be absurd, Sophia," Mother Doherty replied. "How could it be…?"

"I don't know," Sister Witeveen instantly remarked back. "Perhaps it's him… I'm not sure. She said her father was a criminal with ties to a widespread gang… the Harlech Syndicate."

"From what she told me, they had met him not only here, but also in France where he attempted to assassinate their guardian, Charlemagne. For what reason?"

"I'm not sure," Sister Witeveen responded. "I just find there to be so much that is interesting with the pair of them. It's… concerning. Diana is a remarkable specimen. Her physical capabilities are outstanding for her age, her brain function is optimum, and my recent tests have revealed that she is immune to HIV-1 for reasons that I'm not certain of yet… I wouldn't be surprised if she possessed 'the gift' at this point too."

"The pair of them in love is almost too ideal," Mother Doherty said. "A child between them would result in an even more superior human being for sure."

"The only problem, from what Tristan's said to me, is that he's afraid. He has doubts about his relationship and I believe it might not come to last... no less because of the sin between them. They're too young, and the strains Tristan has had – strains that are necessary for his growth, are having an adverse effect on their relationship. Diana is devoted to him – not many people can run two-kilometers, tugging one-hundred and seventy pounds through a blizzard, collapse, and then wake up soon after and donate half a liter of blood... Meanwhile, Tristan is not sure if he wishes to dedicate himself to her."

"It's out of our hands..." Mother Doherty confessed. "Whatever it is that they wish, will be what God wills."

"I want to keep them around for a little bit longer," Sophia stated. "I want to study her genome and investigate this paradox a little further..."

"Very well," Mother Doherty permitted. "However, tonight I will be contacting their guardian to let him know of their location. The final decision will be in his hands..."

Tristan frowned and knocked on the door. The two nuns grew silent before the door opened.

"Oh, Tristan," Sophia said, looking at her son.

Tristan held a grim expression on his face as he looked at his mom and then over to Mother Doherty.

"Have you found Diana?" Sophia questioned.

"Not yet," Tristan replied. "Have you?"

"I'm afraid not," Sophia answered as Mother Doherty brushed past them.

"Apologies, but I'll be in my cell," Mother Doherty remarked to Tristan and then Sophia. "I'll leave the two of you have a chat."

"I'm sure she will return soon," Sister Witeveen responded, walking into her cell and sitting down. "Please be patient."

"I am patient," Tristan replied, walking in and sitting down. "What were you talking about just now? About Diana and me?"

Sister Witeveen froze at her desk and looked at her son. She took a deep breath.

"One of the components of the Order of St. Agnus is the future of the human species. We're in a delicate period of history, and must be prepared. In addition to conserving people through these monasteries, we are also invested in the improvement of the genetic quality of all distinctions of peoples."

"Oh my God," Tristan replied, "that's eugenics."

"It's genetic engineering – we're not sterilizing anyone, or interfering in the natural law. We are making advantageous adjustments as God has allowed us. Unlike your proposal, we are not dehumanizing humanity, but improving it by choosing to select the better genes of two people, like how you were created. We are not removing people from their original sin, if anything, we are creating a people who necessarily crave for the Lord to overcome our human burden and who will more likely confront suffering than avoid it, and thus approach the Lord. The Order of St. Agnus wishes to bring to the world a healthier and stronger people for the Church. The status-quo holds that two people of the opposite-sex come together and leave the fate of their children to chance, and as a result, some children are born with inferior genetics, while others with superior genetics, and often time, a mix of the two. Our interest in Diana is her continuation with you, because we're interested in seeing that the two of you have a healthy and strong child. Wouldn't you want that?"

"I mean, yeah... I suppose," Tristan remarked, "but I'm only seventeen. I can't think of having kids right now. I need another... ten years in the least."

Sophia rolled her eyes.

"Regardless, Diana has some interesting genes that I want to look at closely, especially in terms of her resistance to HIV-1. I've managed to determine that a significant number of white blood cells were infected by the retrovirus, but at around fifty copies per milliliter of blood with above average CD4+ cells in her bloodstream. In other words, I've found the virus to not be latent, but unable to infect her properly. I'm not sure what, or how this is possible, but it is likely that she is either a long-term progressor, or simply has innate resistance to the disease. It's... extremely interesting..."

"So, she's a carrier," Tristan replied.

"Yes, although I'm curious as to how or when she was infected. She's been with you for the past two years, but when she was initially infected could be anywhere in the last ten years, if not earlier. Her mother could have been infected at birth, but I doubt that unless both of her parents were infected and her father later became infected, so that leaves sexual transmission or accidental exposure."

"Diana grew up in the city, and she didn't live in the best of conditions. She told me that she grew up in one of the 'worst slums of North America,' and her father... a pathetic drunk, forced her to spend the occasional night on the streets. It wouldn't surprise me if Diana got infected in such a trivial manner, such as a discarded needle, or anything that might cut and penetrate her bloodstream. I know for certain though that Diana didn't cheat on me."

"We can only speculate until we ask her, but what we can know right now is that the virus is effectively harmless to her as much as it is to you. She'll be fine, but I'll pass-on to Charlemagne to monitor and look into this... I will attempt to screen her for potential genetic mutations that are known, but if that does not turn in anything, then all I can do is suggest that she is monitored for the next ten years."

"Can't we clean her blood like we cleaned mine?"

"No," Sophia rejected, "because the virus has inserted itself throughout her entire body and it would take more than to flush it out when it's already burrowed within. I'd simply reduce the numbers and create room for a genetic drift to occur amidst the viral population. What I will say to you, Tristan, is that Diana is a permanent biohazard and her blood is a lethal weapon."

"I'll keep that in mind... all of it," Tristan replied.

Sister Witeveen walked over to the opposite-side of her desk and opened a gray metallic compartment underneath. She took out two cylindrical compartments and set them on the desk.

"I have these for you to take home," Sophia said. "These are samples of your leukobots stored in lead-containers that are dormant, floating in a small sample of your blood at a high volume. There are further instructions inside each of them in the unfortunate event that you come under another EMP blast."

"Can I ask you a question?" Tristan said, looking at the containers. "What if I were to have kids one day, with Diana for example... Is it possible that our son or daughter to inherit my crappy immune system?"

"No," Sister Witeveen stated, because the genetic mutations I made are regressive and you are the only human being with them. "I had already thought about that when I engineered you."

"Good," Tristan replied, smiling. "Diana and I will have the best kids…"

"I could envision it, and all I can hope is that you two stay together, because you're good together. Take care of her."

Tristan frowned.

"I hope she returns home soon…"

"Are you sure she hasn't returned already? She could be in her room, or in the chapel…"

"I stayed in my room, looking out to the forest to see if she'd return, but she hasn't. A part of me thinks that she might have left for good to return home, but her stuff is in her room – the stuff that we recovered from the crash that is."

"She might be on her way back then," Sister Witeveen replied, looking out her window blinds and seeing that it was dark.

"I'm worried it's worse…" Tristan stated. "She didn't even come for lunch and it's almost dinnertime."

Sister Witeveen looked at her son and went to grab her winter cloak. She put it on and then looked over to Tristan.

"I'm going to go look for her," Sophia explained. "I'll be back. Go and have supper. If I'm not back before dinnertime ends, tell Mother Doherty and she'll know what to do."

"Let me come," Tristan pleaded. "I should be out there looking for her. It's my fault!"

"You're the one that upset her and you're recovering still," Sophia replied. "Besides, I'm worried about that hunter you encountered in the commune. If he's out there, you're of more value to him than I am."

"Please let me come," Tristan continued to plead. "If it's that risky, I don't want you to place yourself into danger like this... not again!"

"Tristan, I've faced more danger than you think. I'll be fine. Wait here and expect our return. Do not leave the convent," Sophia stated, looking at him with a stern face. "I'll be back soon."

Tristan nodded and watched his mother close the door behind her. He looked at the door with worry, simply sat on the bed, and waited.

Act 7, Scene 3

Tristan waited on his own as he sat at his mother's desk, staring at the clock on the wall and waiting for the hour to complete. Neither Diana nor his mother had returned, which meant that it was time for him to talk to Mother Doherty. Tristan stood up and walked over to the cell door, leaving to go and find her.

The convent was quiet and eerie. The howling of the wind outside could be heard, and it was turning to be dark outside. Tristan walked to the other side of the convent, knocked on Mother Doherty's cell door, but no answer came. He looked around the corridor, freezing for a moment as he heard some chanting from outside. Tristan walked over and looked outside into a courtyard, but he couldn't see anyone. A lone statue of the Virgin Mary stood in the center of the courtyard, embracing her child in her arms as snow fell around them.

Tristan left the corridor and arrived at the main foyer of the convent. It was a medium-sized room that led to the chapel directly forward from the main doors and past the stairs on the remaining sides. From where Tristan was, there were a set of double doors that went to a balcony where the choir sang from. Tristan stepped close to this door and listened, but the singing was not coming from here, but still close. He looked around the foyer. Tristan went down the stairs and to the left, through a large set of doors that led into the main dining hall. The dining hall was a large, long room that stretched for almost fifty feet. It had four long rows of polished and old wooden tables.

At the end of the hall, the nuns were at the steps of a fireplace. Mother Doherty was lighting one of the three purple candles, which in between the second two was a pink candle, on the fireplace mantle, and then after the last purple one a white one. A large evergreen tree was propped next to the fireplace and decorated with ornaments and ribbon. At the top of the tree was an angel figurine. The nuns were quietly chanting a Christmas hymn with the convent mother. Tristan watched and caught the attention of Mother Doherty who broke from the group and went to him.

"You, Diana, and your mother missed dinner. Where is Sister Witeveen?"

"She went looking for Diana," Tristan replied. "She left about an hour ago, and neither of them have returned. She told me to tell you if she hadn't returned by now."

"Oh dear," Mother Doherty remarked, looking over to the other nuns. "We must assemble a search party immediately."

Mother Doherty walked over to a double-door entrance and passed it to put her hands around a string and ring a bell. She pulled the string and caused a high-pitched bell to ring and cut the singing of the other sisters who all looked to her.

"Your attention, please," Mother Doherty addressed in a loud voice. "Sister Witeveen and Ms. Cambridge had disappeared. All search and rescue party members, please meet me in the armory!"

"Armory?" Tristan questioned as the nuns scrambled.

"Follow me," Mother Doherty said, walking out of the foyer and going into the corridor past the stairs, before the chapel, but going left.

Mother Doherty led Tristan to a set of double doors that brought them to a stone corridor around the courtyard. They went around and re-entered inside to reach a set of double doors. Mother Doherty pushed her hands against the doors and stepped into a large room with garage shutter doors at the opposite end and eight jeeps parked in two groups of four across the length of the room. Behind the vehicles were various supplies, munitions, and a cache of weapons and ammo alongside some lockers and benches.

The other nuns poured into the room, going towards the locker and changing from their habits into a one-piece white jumpsuit with a thermal ballistic vest, utility belt, and other important equipment for them to venture into the cold. Atop of their jumpsuits they wore white camouflaged ponchos. Some nuns had arrived with slim, eloquent German Shepherds that were on leashes.

Tristan stood around, looking at all the maidens as they had transformed from pious monks into a professional search and rescue team in a quick minute. Once they were ready, they met with Mother Doherty in the middle-rear of the room where she was waiting with two other elderly nuns. They surrounded a table with a map of the nearby region. Tristan stepped over and looked at the map.

The map included their immediate location as well as the surrounding gorge with the location of the commune and freeway. It also included some components that Tristan was not familiar with in regard to the wider forest.

"Alright, we all know the drill for a missing member, so let's not waste time," Mother Doherty stated. "Matthew and Bartholomew Team have the north regions. Francis and George Team are in the south. Sebastian and Thomas Team are in the west, and Anthony and Nicholas Team are in the east. Let's move out!"

Tristan watched as each group of four or six nuns, each with one or two dogs, got into a jeep. The large garage doors opened. Some of the nuns were armed with assault rifles, while others carried thermal goggles and stun rods. Their professional appearance was reminiscent of the Protection Squad or the Huntsman Legionnaires. Tristan watched them for another moment before looking to Mother Doherty who was looking at him.

"Tristan, you're coming with us to the command center in the clock tower. We're putting the grounds on lockdown and the remaining nuns will hold the convent. I'm required to ensure your safety in case we come under attack."

"Let me go with them," Tristan requested. "I want to join the search party."

"It's too dangerous. We can't afford to lose you too."

"It's my fault they're both missing. Let me redeem myself, please," Tristan begged.

Mother Doherty looked at Tristan before looking over to the last jeep as its engines started.

"Sister Gemma," Mother Doherty shouted.

"Yes, mother?" Sister Gemma replied.

"You're supervising Mr. Merrick who will be joining you. Do not let him out of your sights."

"Yes, mother."

"Thank you," Tristan said to Mother Doherty.

"Wait," Mother Doherty said, going to the cache of supplies and returning with a thermal ballistic vest and poncho. "Wear this."

"You got it," Tristan replied, taking the vest and poncho, and putting them on.

After Tristan had put on the vest, he ran to the jeep and was brought aboard. The jeep pulled out of the garage and drove straight forward before turning left as it came into the forest. The snowy landscape was difficult to navigate, but thankfully, the chained tries were able to push through the woods for about two kilometers until they stopped at a clearing.

"Alright, everybody to a partner!" Sister Gemma shouted as the sisters spread out. "Fan out, but stick together! We'll go two kilometers from this position and on until we find them!"

"Affirmative," a nun replied.

"Mr. Merrick, you're with me," Gemma said as she jumped out.

Sister Gemma helped Tristan out of the jeep and onto the ground. Tristan stayed with her as they went into the forest. She paused fifty meters from the jeep and handed Tristan a flashlight and a knife.

"Be careful and stay in my line of sight. If you see anything, you shout and run to either me or Sister Veronica, okay?"

"Yes, ma'am," Tristan replied, taking the tools into his hands.

Both Sister Gemma and Sister Veronica had assault rifles with flashlights that lit up their field of vision. They split up in a fanned-shape, leaving the center for Tristan to sweep. The air was colder than usual, but the thermal vest he was given kept his torso warm, especially as he lightly jogged. His hair was naked to the snow, and his cheeks reddened from the wind. Tristan could hear the sisters' voices nearby by the chatter of the radio as well as the light projecting from their rifles. At about a kilometer, the hopelessness began to set in as all that was around them was snow, snow, some trees, and more snow.

The sudden snap of a branch nearby caught Tristan's attention, causing him to turn and wave his flashlight around to search for the source of the noise. He looked up and around, seeing nothing as he lightly panted and listened to the dead-cold ambience.

"We're turning!" a voice shouted.

"Turn around!" Gemma yelled from not too far away.

Tristan looked over to the silhouette of who he thought to be Sister Gemma, and he began to run back the way he came. He swept the surrounding area with his flashlight and reconvened with the two nuns at the jeep before the others arrived.

"We're travelling another two kilometers deeper," Sister Veronica said as she drove. "No reports from the other search groups so far."

"Understood, let's move out then," Sister Gemma replied. "Are you doing okay, Tristan?"

"Yeah, I'm good," Tristan replied, frowning as they failed to find them.

"Have a drink," a sister said, passing a canteen to him.

Tristan took the metal bottle and drank some electrolytic fluid from it. He then returned the bottle and the jeep continued to travel another two kilometers until the sisters poured out again.

"We're going to find your mother," Sister Gemma said to Tristan as the others left.

Tristan nodded and then sighed. He looked at Sister Gemma.

"Can I stay in the car?" Tristan asked. "Please?"

"Of course," Sister Gemma replied. "We'll be back in ten minutes. If you see anything, there's a radio at the dashboard."

"Thanks," Tristan replied, watching her go off to join Sister Veronica into the forest.

Tristan sat back and looked around him into the forest, keeping an eye out for the sisters until they got too far for him to see. He was suddenly alone, sitting in the rear of the jeep with the engine humming and lights shining forward. He listened to the chatter of the sisters from the radio on the dashboard, but physically, he was alone. Tristan held a depressive look on his face. He began to shiver as he looked around. He looked over to the dashboard as he heard the sisters talking, but his eyes wandered as he saw a bit of light ahead, past the headlights. Tristan squinted to get a better look, and then he stood up to look over. He then hopped out of the vehicle and went around. He walked in front of the jeep and turned on his flashlight, shining it ahead as he saw a red light. Tristan proceeded forward, walking slowly and cautiously before picking up speed and dropping down as he got close enough to realize it was an emergency red flare that had been dropped in the snow. He looked at it for a moment and then passed it as he saw another one further ahead.

The flare behind him continued to burn. Tristan looked at it as he looked back to the jeep further ahead and hesitated to go on. He then turned back around and continued into the forest, alone. Tristan went onwards as he hurried to find either his mother, Diana, or both. The next flare led him to spot another two more, and when Tristan got close to the next, he began to see a structure in the distance.

Tristan ran over, shining his light forward to guide him as he came to the next flare, and then the next until he finally reached the stone structure in the midst of the forest in a clearing. He passed his light around the foundations of the building and examined the rest of the structure. There was a circular stone window above a set of wooden double doors at the base, and based on the architecture, it had a church-like appearance, but it had been abandoned and left to nature. Ivy had grown overtop the exterior walls and the windows on the side had been shattered. Around the structure there were some tombstones. Tristan briefly examined the structure and then returned to the front where he saw a bit of light through the front doors. He turned off his flashlight and then turned it back on to confirm the source of light from within. Tristan then went up the steps and pushed against the rusted doors.

The interior of the mausoleum was lit by several dozen candles around. Sarcophagi were lined up, some were broken, but they all faced a large one at the end where before it, lay Sister Witeveen and Diana.

"Mom! Diana!" Tristan shouted as he saw them.

Diana was passed out on the ground, while his mother was also lying on her side, but with her hands and feet tied. Her mouth was covered in a rope. Tristan ran to the both of them, spotting stains of blood on the stone ground as he got close.

"What happened?" Tristan questioned, shining his light around as he observed the scene.

Tristan immediately turned around as he heard the front doors shut behind him. A menacing and familiar figure stood in front of the doors, looking onwards to Tristan with empty hands and nothing but intimidation. Tristan took a step back as the figure started to make his approach. He held his flashlight in one hand and the knife in the other. He raised both arms before him and rested his right wrist atop his left wrist as he shined the light and pointed the knife forward like a commando in preparation to defend himself.

The Mysterious Stranger looked similar to how he did at the commune, but without his coat. Instead, he simply wore a ballistic torso-piece with a tactical vest overtop. The gas mask was still over his face, but one of the eyeholes was cracked. He faced Tristan from the other side of the aisle and simply breathed menacingly. The two looked at each other for another moment until he proceeded to step forward. Tristan braced himself, looking at the Mysterious Stranger with determination that drew him to go forward and attempt to swipe at him. The

Mysterious Stranger backed out of the way at Tristan's swipes, evading him and then grabbing Tristan's wrist.

Tristan dropped the knife and then felt the other hand of the Mysterious Stranger grab him by the neck. He was thrown back and onto the ground. The Mysterious Stranger stepped forward and picked him up by the neck again, chocking him relentlessly as he walked towards a pillar and pushed Tristan back into it. Tristan was forced into the pillar while the figure took something from his belt and jabbed it into Tristan's neck to extract his blood. Tristan cried out in pain as the Mysterious Stranger siphoned him for his blood and continued to be choked. He tried to kick back, but it was of no use. Tristan grew pale and his eyes tired.

When he was done, the Mysterious Stranger dropped him onto the ground and then put the large vial of blood away into a pouch. He then walked over and picked up a device that had been set atop of the altar. He pressed some buttons and then left the device to walk down the aisle, calmly leaving the church and Tristan to his demise. Tristan watched as he left, holding a hand to his neck as blood ran down and looking over his enemy escaped before he could do anything. He was too weak. The Mysterious Stranger was gone.

Tristan opened his eyes after losing focus for a split minute. He started to stand up and walked over to his mother and Diana. He knelt down and looked at the ties around his mother's ankles and wrists and then looked over to Diana. Tristan then looked at the black device with cables sticking out from within and connecting to white packets on the pillars of the mausoleum. The device was a bomb and it had a timer set to fifteen minutes. Tristan proceeded to attempt to wake his mother.

Sister Witeveen squirmed and woke up.

"I'll get you out, mom," Tristan said, standing up and going to find his knife.

Tristan found his knife near a sarcophagus and went over to cut the ties from his mother's wrists with the weak strength that he had.

"I'll get you out..." Tristan said again, feeling his vision fade.

Tristan shook his head and tried to refocus. He cut her ties and then fell over. Sophia took over and picked up the knife to remove the rope from her ankles and mouth. She then went to Tristan.

"Easy there," Sophia said to him, checking on him.

"Th-there's a bomb," Tristan murmured.

"Don't worry about that right now," Sophia replied, helping him up and examining the wound on his neck.

Sister Witeveen took off her head-piece and exposed her dark strawberry-blonde hair similar to Tristan's, but long. She ripped some of the fabric and tied it around her son's neck to stop the bleeding.

"We... need to get out of here," Tristan said, sitting down as he looked at his mother.

"I know, sweetie," Sophia replied. "My ankle is broken though. I can't stand properly."

Sister Witeveen went over to Diana, examined her and found that she was breathing. She then went over to the bomb and attempted to stand up at the central tomb, supporting her weight. Tristan helped her stand. She looked at the bomb. The timer had twelve minutes left.

"Okay..." Sister Witeveen said, looking to Tristan. "I need you to do me a favor. I need you to muster up all the strength you have left, and get Diana and yourself out of here."

"What about you?" Tristan questioned.

"I'm going to disarm the bomb. It's the only way I'll be able to get out of here alive."

"Do you know how to disarm a bomb?"

"I understand the mechanics, but I want you and Diana to get out of here in case I fail," Sophia replied, removing the cover at the back.

"You won't fail though, right?" Tristan questioned. "You know what you're doing?"

"Now is not the time to argue, Tristan," Sophia remarked. "Get Diana and yourself out of the blast radius before it's too late!"

"I don't want to leave you here!" Tristan responded, leaning against the altar as he struggled to stand. "I can help you!"

Sister Witeveen took a deep breath and looked over to Tristan. She gave a light smile and put a hand on his shoulder. She looked at him with intent.

"I know what I'm doing, sweetie. I'm going to be okay and I'm going to make it. Don't feel like you need to repay us for all this, because it is not your fault. It's never been your fault. I created you and brought you into this world. I nursed you. I made the decision of keeping you out of my life for the better of yours, and you've become such a beautiful, intelligent, and kind-hearted young man that any mother could have asked for. You've made me proud up to now, and extremely joyful to see you again, but let me tell you that this is not the end for us. I love you, Tristan, and it's your time now. Time to do your duty as it is time for me to do mine; protect Diana and get out of here, now!"

Tristan looked back at his mother and he slowly nodded before going over to Diana. He picked her up, grabbing her and bringing her across his shoulders in a fireman's carry just as he had carried Finn last summer. Once Diana was set across his shoulders, he turned around and looked at his mother. He gave one last look at her and then walked down the aisle to leave with his girlfriend, placing all his strength and energy into carrying her through the deep snow and dark forest.

The flares that had been set to bait Tristan had died out, but the direction to the jeep was fresh in Tristan's mind for him to follow as he began to see the headlights in the distance.

"W-what's happening?" Diana questioned, waking up. "What's going on?"

"I'm getting you back to the jeep," Tristan replied.

"Where am I? Where's the Mysterious Stranger?"

Tristan arrived at the jeep and saw that it was abandoned. He lowered Diana at the side of the car and then went inside to grab the radio microphone on the dashboard.

"I'm... I'm so sorry, Tristan. I couldn't hold back. I- I told him about the blood, and I'm sorry..."

"It's okay, just take it easy..." Tristan replied, pressing down on the microphone to talk. "Hello? Is anybody listening? This is Tristan calling all units. I've found Sister Witeveen and Diana, over. I'm at the jeep near the cemetery, please hurry!"

Tristan let go of the mic.

"Copy that," Sister Gemma replied. "We're returning to your location. My team, let's move, double-time. All other teams, proceeded to our coordinates."

"Roger that, Nicholas Team," Mother Doherty remarked.

Tristan let go of the microphone and left the keep to kneel down in front of Diana. Diana looked at him with apology. Tristan smiled to her.

"You're going to be okay, Diana," Tristan said. "Everything is going to be okay."

A loud boom was heard from nearby, causing them to both look away from each other and into the forest. Tristan stood up and looked ahead as horror struck. The boom got louder and was accompanied with the bright lights of an explosion ahead at where the abandoned mausoleum was. The entire forest was lit by the massive explosion and a fireball erupted upwards and dissipated into the air above.

"N-no," Tristan said, stepping forward.

"What was that?" a nun on the radio questioned.

"No!" Tristan shouted, running forward before tripping and falling into the snow.

Diana quickly stood up and kept Tristan down as she noticed debris rain down from the sky, pelleting the jeep. Tristan looked back up and sobbed as Diana restrained him from going forward to his certain death.

"Don't," Diana said, holding him back. "Please, don't."

"No…." Tristan cried, crying into the snow.

Tristan stood up and fell to his knees as he looked forward. The entirety of the mausoleum had been decimated, leaving fire around the surrounding perimeter or blast zone, and the impossibility that anyone, no less his mother at the epicenter of the blast, could have survived. Tristan's entire body shook as he stared ahead and his heart plummeted.

Diana wrapped her arms around him, looking to the disaster with him and embracing him. Tristan didn't react. He simply stared ahead with tearful eyes. Diana continued to hold him, comforting him as he faced another tragedy in his life, because he was orphaned once more, and she was all that he had.

Epilogue

Diana sat with Tristan at the hood of a jeep the next day with their backpacks and Tristan with his gym bag. Two sisters from the convent armed with assault rifles, dressed in a white combat gear similar to the one they had worn last night, guarded them. It was midday without a cloud in the sky. They had been driven far from the convent and to an open snowy field with an exposed tarmac stretching a fair takeoff distance.

Tristan had his eyes dropped to the ground as he kept quiet, much as he had been since last evening, while Diana felt a strong resentment and pity for him whilst looking around and noticing the incoming private jet from afar.

The landing gear of the familiar plane opened up, and it made its touchdown onto the salted asphalt of the tarmac before coming towards the opposite-end where the couple waited. Diana stood up, looking at Tristan before looking over to the plane as it stopped. The nuns made their way over to the doors of the private jet as the stairs opened to reveal Charlemagne at the top of the stairs.

Charlemagne looked down at the kids with an unhappy face. He stepped down and came onto the surface of the tarmac to meet with the nuns.

"It's time to go," Diana softly said to Tristan.

Tristan looked over to Diana and nodded, standing up and joining her as they walked over to the plane. The two stopped behind the nuns. Diana felt anxious to reel the punishment that awaited them and knew she'd have to do the talking with Charlemagne seeing that Tristan was in no mood to talk or grumble.

"Thank you," Charlemagne said to the nuns. "Thank you for keeping them safe."

"No need to thank us, Mr. Cabernet," a nun replied. "Our people have given you a clearance to leave the United States and return to your home in the next hour. You shouldn't have any trouble with the authorities."

"It's greatly appreciated," Charlemagne replied, looking over to the kids and giving a pitiful frown as he noticed the gloomy expression on Tristan's face.

The nuns bowed to Charlemagne and then left to return to their jeep, leaving the couple to face their guardian together. Charlemagne's eyes went to Diana, who appeared to be timid and with a sad smile.

"Children..." Charlemagne said, greeting them for the first time since last week.

"I'm sorry about leaving you in the dark and running away... in my case, for the second time..." Diana remarked. "You know what's happened though, right?"

"Mother Doherty told me the gist of what happened last night," Charlemagne simply said, looking to Tristan with a sigh.

Tristan looked at Charlemagne and his eyes began to water. He tightened a fist in his right hand and frowned.

"Diana and I are in a romantic relationship," Tristan stated to him in a choked voice. "We've been like this for almost two years, and all these times I've been asking you hypotheticals about my attraction to her, it was to test what you'd think of us."

Diana's cheeks flushed. Tristan looked to the side and crossed his arms. Charlemagne was stunned and didn't immediately respond.

"Well," Charlemagne replied, "thank you for letting me know, but you're still in trouble for disobeying me."

"I know…" Tristan coldly replied, sighing. "I just wanted to get that out in the open. I'll take my punishment, including Diana's as this was all my fault. I'm sorry for doing it. I regret my approach and decisions, but I don't regret the grand scheme of it all. I just… I just want to go home now, please."

"Understood," Charlemagne responded, stepping out of the way for them to board the plane. "Let's go home then."

Tristan walked forward, climbed up, and boarded the plane. Diana looked to Charlemagne with slight embarrassment and went up behind Tristan. Charlemagne then joined them at the top to see that Tristan was already seated inside, looking out a window. Charlemagne placed a hand atop of Diana's shoulder.

"How's he been?" Charlemagne asked.

"We haven't really talked," Diana replied, walking forward and going into the main cabin.

Charlemagne watched as Diana approached Tristan and gave a deep sigh. He then went into the cockpit to leave them alone. Diana sat down next to Tristan. Tristan simply looked out the window.

The plane began to move and make its departure when Diana brought a hand to Tristan's hand. Tristan felt Diana's eyes looking at him, which forced him to look at her.

"I'm sorry about what I did yesterday – I'm sorry I didn't tell her," Tristan said. "I don't want to hide it anymore. If people know, it's not a problem."

"Okay…" Diana replied, nodding. "Don't worry about it though…"

"I'm going to be okay," Tristan said. "I'm going to be okay. She's dead, but I'm not. I'm her son. If I live, she lives too. After all, we know what happens when people die. We've seen ghosts… She's still out there… I know it."

Tristan looked away and out of the window. He had an unsure look on his face. Diana looked at him uncertainly.

"Don't forget," Diana said with a sigh, "you have me. I'm here, Tristan, and I love you."

Diana held Tristan's hand. He looked at her and smiled.

"You'll always have me," Diana assured him. "Always."

Tristan nodded. The two turned their heads away from each other as the jet took off from the surface. Diana's eyes wandered to a muted TV displaying some news. Charlemagne returned from the cockpit and joined the couple. He picked up a remote and unmuted the TV.

"Zimmerman Corporation has announced a new discovery in what could be a breakthrough in cancer treatment," the TV announcer said. "The multi-billion-dollar tech company made the announcement earlier and has called for a special press conference from their headquarters in Kyoto..."

"Absolute rubbish," Charlemagne scolded, turning off the TV. "Sorry about that... I had it on from earlier."

"It's okay..." Tristan replied in a coarse voice.

Charlemagne looked to them and sat the remote down. He then left them alone again and went to the cockpit. Tristan leaned his head against the window and crossed his arms. Diana looked at him with pity and held on to his crossed arms from the side as she leaned on him. The two stayed this way for the most of their journey home, each with mixed-emotions at the end of their own adventure.

"Likewise, older women are to be reverent in behavior, not slanderers or slaves to much wine. They are to teach what is good, and so train young women to love their husbands and children, to be self-controlled, pure, working at home, kind and submissive to their own husbands, that the word of God may not be reviled."

– Titus 2:3-5